## "Has Max told you about me and your uncle?"

"No, Papa hasn't told me much, but everybody knows that you and my uncle—" Tatiana lowered her voice and leaned toward Lianne "—that you were lovers."

Lianne had to smile. "That's true. But now that Max and I are . . . seeing a lot of each other, there's something else you should know about your family history. Your uncle and I had a child."

The girl's eyes widened. "Really?"

Lianne nodded. "But I was very young, too young to take care of a child, and the baby was put up for adoption."

The girl's eyes grew even rounder. "For adoption? But do you know where the child is now?"

"No, I don't. I haven't seen her for fifteen years, not since the day she was born."

"Oh, Lianne, how terrible for you!" Suddenly Tatiana blushed deeply, feeling panic-stricken. Last night she'd phoned her uncle and told him to come home. She'd wanted to make trouble between her father and Lianne. Now she realized things were far more complicated than she'd known.

## Books by Janice Kaiser

HARLEQUIN SUPERROMANCE

187–HARMONY
209–LOTUS MOON
224–MEANT TO BE
242–LOVE CHILD
256–CHANCES
287–STOLEN MOMENTS
403–BODY AND SOUL

# The Big
# Secret

## JANICE KAISER

# Harlequin Books

TORONTO • NEW YORK • LONDON
AMSTERDAM • PARIS • SYDNEY • HAMBURG
STOCKHOLM • ATHENS • TOKYO • MILAN
MADRID • WARSAW • BUDAPEST • AUCKLAND

Published April 1992

ISBN 0-373-70494-1

THE BIG SECRET

For Sybil Genevieve Kaiser,
with love

# *PROLOGUE*

LIANNE HALLIDAY could hardly contain herself. She was certain today would mark one of the most important and wonderful events of her life. Yet she had to keep to her bed, pretending to be mortally ill. It had been torture listening to Nanna putter about the house, getting ready to leave. It was all Lianne could do to keep from screaming, "Go, Nanna! Please go!"

It seemed forever, but finally Marguerite Gevers went out the front door and descended the steps of the town house to her waiting car. When Lianne heard the chauffeur slam the doors of the ancient Bentley shut, she hopped out of bed and sneaked to the window. Pulling the lace curtains open a crack, she was able to see her grandmother's car disappear up the rue Beauregard.

It was all Lianne could do to keep from bouncing with joy. Alex would arrive in only a few minutes. She turned from the window, pulling her nightgown over her head. She felt only the briefest pang of guilt over her miraculous recovery, but her time alone with Alex was much too precious to let anything mar it.

She climbed into the jeans that hugged her rump and thighs so enticingly. Alex had told her once that seeing her in them drove him to distraction. And that, more than anything, was exactly what she wanted to do. Next she got the skimpiest bra she owned and slipped into it. Then she put on a white silk blouse, leaving it unbuttoned as far down as she dared. She felt very mature, tantalizingly wicked.

From birth Lianne Halliday had been appreciated for her beauty. She had thick ash-blond hair, gray eyes and incredibly long legs that gave her a look of elegance and maturity beyond her years. Back home in Connecticut the boys flocked around her. The only true disappointment she had faced in her young life was growing too tall to ever be a professional ballerina.

But Lianne wasn't the type to brood. Literature, her second love, had become the passion that replaced dancing. But, of course, that was before she'd come to Geneva for the summer to visit Nanna. And it was before she'd met Alex Julen. In the course of a few weeks Lianne had fallen in love. Now nothing seemed to matter much beside Alex.

She was having a final look at herself in the full-length mirror when she heard the chugging throb of Alex's old Citroën Deux Chevaux outside the house. She dashed down the stairs, taking them two at a time. Alex hadn't reached the door yet, so Lianne darted into the kitchen.

It was Mrs. Weber's day off, and the room was empty, devoid of all sound but the ticking of the cuckoo clock and the hum of the antique refrigerator. Lianne quickly wrapped up some of the wonderful cookies the housekeeper had made. Then she grabbed an apple and a pear from the large ceramic bowl on the counter.

As she finished gathering her booty, there were two impatient rings of the doorbell. Lianne hurried to the entry hall, where she put the food down on a side table.

The bell rang again, and she could see Alex's silhouette through the curtains. Her heart began to race as she threw open the door.

Alex Julen stood there with a half smile on his handsome face. He was a lean young man with chocolate-brown eyes, a straight, narrow nose and a mouth that always seemed poised on the verge of an ironic grin. His dark brown hair was combed straight back in the European fashion. He wore an Italian-style knit shirt with the sleeves pushed up to the middle of his forearms. Though he had on jeans, he didn't look boyish in the least. He was different than the other men she'd met in Geneva. Alex seemed comfortable with casualness, as though he knew something the others didn't.

His eyes were resting on her. He hadn't moved. Then he let his delight show with a broadening smile. "How's my little cabbage today?"

They both laughed. It was their private joke—the idiom translated literally. Lianne reached out and pulled him in the door, throwing her arms around his neck. Alex gave her that wry, sexy, manly look that always made her feel weak inside. His arms tightened around her, and his pungent European cologne filled her nostrils, spoiling forever the English Leather that every boy back home seemed to favor. After Alex, Lianne was sure there could never be a boy in her life again.

Her heart was pounding as he leaned forward and teased her lower lip, enticing her before he kissed her deeply. No one had ever kissed her the way Alex did. Lianne wanted to be in his arms forever.

When his head pulled back, she was slow to open her eyes, slow to give up her dream. Her breasts seemed to swell, and she knew then what it felt like to be a woman. Alex kissed the end of her nose, smiling.

*"Je t'adore,"* he whispered, and she was so happy that she felt like crying. "Maybe we should stand here all day," he said in English, "and I'll adore you all day."

"What about our picnic?"

"With you in my arms, how can I think of food?"

She blushed. Alex's teasing always embarrassed her. "I've been looking forward to our picnic for days," she lamented, though she knew he wasn't serious. "I couldn't get to sleep last night, thinking about it."

Alex pushed the door closed with his foot and kissed her once more. This time his hand touched the side of her breast, and she felt a warming glow. She pressed her face into his neck.

"I love you, Alex," she whispered.

He took her face in his hands, smiling as he peered into her eyes. "Come, my little one. I want to take you to my mountain."

Lianne got her things and they descended the steps to where Alex's Deux Chevaux was parked. He'd inherited the car in total disrepair from his older brother, Max. The engine had a sound to it somewhere between a lawn mower and a sewing machine, and it frequently backfired, giving it a personality and life all its own. It was the car of the French working class, but Lianne felt at home in it, knowing it was Alex's, knowing he'd personally nursed it back to health with the help of an obliging mechanic and the few francs his father gave him as a stipend.

But Alex always associated the car with his brother. He had told Lianne how he was just a boy when Max took him for his first ride in it. Even now he referred to the car as his "Maxmobile." Lianne had never met Max Julen, but judging by the awe with which Alex spoke of him, she decided he must be a remarkable man. He was in his late twenties, six years Alex's senior. He had married the year before and was living in Paris where he ran one of the many companies their father, Alberte, had acquired over the years. The family was involved in everything, it seemed, from electronics to heavy industry, from merchandising to insurance.

"Max is like my father," Alex had told her. "One day he will run the entire family business."

"What about you?" she'd asked.

"Business is not important to me. I want my own life. I want to be free to roam the world."

That had been when they first met, at the beginning of the summer, before they'd fallen in love. Alex hadn't talked much about his future plans since then, but he'd made his fondness for Lianne clear. It was her first important romance, the first time she'd truly been in love.

After putting the sack of cookies and fruit in the back of the Deux Chevaux, they took off through the streets of Geneva. As the Maxmobile chugged along, its tattered cloth top fluttered here and there in the breeze. Lianne reached over and caressed Alex's cheek. He took her fingers and kissed them.

They were soon at the lakeshore and went along the south edge of it, following the Quai Gustave Ador. They went past the Jet d'eau, a fountain that shot a hundred yards into the air before its waters rained back into the lake like a waterfall spouting from an empty sky. Downwind the air was filled with microscopic droplets that often blew all the way to the shore, dampening the skin of passersby and coating windowpanes.

As they passed the posher lakefront apartment blocks and restaurants farther up the quay, Alex took her hand, massaging it gently with his thumb. She looked at him, seeing wisps of his dark hair blowing in the wind that swirled through the gaps and holes and missing window glass of the car.

Alex was so handsome. And he loved her—perhaps as much as she loved him. How incredibly lucky she was, and she not yet eighteen. He was four years older, but he treated her with all the respect due a woman. How glorious, how incredibly wonderful their love was!

The city had barely turned to suburb when they came to the French border at Hermance. In the space of only a few yards, from one side of the border to the other, the earth took on another color, wore a different set of clothes.

They drove along the lakeshore through the village of Yvoire and then on the narrow ribbon of road to Thonon where they turned inland. From there they followed first the Dranse River valley, then the Brevon up into the mountains toward the Col de Jambaz.

They didn't talk much during the drive. It was enough that they were together. Still, the atmosphere was pregnant with expectation. Lianne knew it was the day she would give herself to Alex, the day he would make her a woman.

Though her mother and grandmother were forever reminding her how young and inexperienced she was, Lianne knew that what she felt for Alex Julen was uncommon. Of course, she could see how a young girl could be misled by her feelings and desires. But this was different. Nanna didn't understand that.

They soon left the mountainous road and went along a hedgerow for a way, deep into the bosom of a collateral valley. The track they followed dwindled to faint ruts that led eventually to a group of farm buildings hidden in some trees at the base of the mountain.

The house was barely a cottage, its facade tattered, its shutters cocked and hanging askew. Green and yellow strips of plastic hung over the doorway. In front there was a faded wooden table and a couple of chairs under the largest tree. On the table was a liter of cheap wine, three-quarters empty, its clamp top open, flies hovering around its mouth. There were several dishes with scraps of cheese rind, bread crust and fruit.

Alex turned off the engine, which gave a final flatulent cough. Lianne turned to him apprehensively. "Is this it?" she asked.

"No, you silly cabbage. It is the home of the lord of the manor, my friend Gonnet. He grants me the use of his estate for the amazingly modest price of a bottle of brandy." Alex reached under the seat and took a small package wrapped in paper. "I'll only be a minute," he said with a wink.

As he got out, a little man stepped through the plastic strips of the doorway. His gray hair was thinning and the lower half of his face was dusted white with several days' growth of beard. He wore faded blue work pants and a sleeveless undershirt. A large gray cat appeared, arching against the grimy, bunched cuffs of the man's pant leg.

The two men spoke for a moment or two, the package changed hands and Alex returned to the car. "The estate is ours for the day," he announced, trying to sound diabolical.

Alex started the car, and they drove through the barnyard, scattering several chickens and ducks as they went. Then they followed another track that ran along a stone wall for a hundred yards or more. When they came to a gate, Alex stopped.

"This is as far as we can drive. The rest of the way we must walk."

Lianne opened the flimsy car door and stepped into lush grass speckled with tiny wildflowers. At some distance was a white goat tethered to a stake. The animal was erect, looking in their direction, its short, thick horns curved back over its head, the whiskers on its chin swinging with each mechanical sweep of its jaw.

Lianne went to the back of the car where Alex leaned into the truck, unpacking the picnic basket and blankets. Standing close to him, she caught a whiff of his cologne and was drawn again into intimate awareness of him. She lightly stroked his back, needing to touch him.

When they gathered their things, Alex took her hand and they began following the path up the side of the mountain. The trail rose gradually through woods and open meadows. As they went, they heard the hollow clang of cowbells on the slopes above. From time to time a bird soared into the open expanse of valley that spread out below them. The sky was mostly clear above the Alps, though to the south and west a gray band of thunderclouds was piling up on the horizon.

"It's so beautiful and peaceful up here," Lianne said. "I feel like I'm a million miles from everywhere."

Alex laughed softly. "We're only a few dozen kilometers from Geneva. The lake is behind this mountain. From the top you can see Lac Léman, from Geneva all the way to Lausanne."

"Are we going to the top?"

"No, just to a special place on the side of the mountain. You'll see."

There was a lilt in his voice that made her wonder. There had been other girls, she knew, perhaps lots of them. If Lianne thought about it, she got jealous. But she tried hard not to let it bother her. All that mattered, she told herself, was that Alex loved her more than the rest.

They climbed the slope for half an hour before they came to a rough-hewn little hut built into the flank of the mountain. It was lodged under the protective boughs of some trees. Alex told her he had found it years ago when hiking with friends.

Although the cabin was primitive, it was tidy. They didn't go inside. Instead they sat in front on the carpet of lush mountain grass that came right to the doorway. Alex unpacked the lunch and uncorked a chilled bottle of May wine.

Now that she was seventeen Nanna allowed her half a glass of wine with dinner, so the taste was no stranger to her. But she'd never had enough to become truly tipsy. She watched Alex pour the wine into the tumblers he'd brought. Her heart began to race with excitement at the thought of sharing a whole bottle with him. Their eyes met, and Lianne felt deliciously wicked. He handed her the glass.

"To the most beautiful woman I know," he said. "Perhaps the most beautiful woman alive."

Lianne blushed again. Alex loved to flatter, but there was sincerity in his manner. She had been able to talk to him more than with anyone she'd ever known. Though he didn't know a lot about English literature, he would listen as she told him about the poets she loved so.

When they sat alone in Nanna's parlor, Alex would listen attentively as she read aloud her favorite poems. Sometimes, as she read, he would play with wisps of her hair or draw a finger along her jaw or down the side of her neck. But when she finished, he always had something insightful to say. Once or twice he'd brought along books of poetry himself, which he read to her in French.

Naturally those celebrated moments were always under the watchful eye of Marguerite Gevers. Now, for the first time, they were truly and completely alone!

They sat for a time in silence, staring out at the magnificent vista, sipping their wine, their fingers entwined.

Between sips Alex fed her bites of the food he had brought. Lianne didn't know if it was possible to be any more in love than she was just then.

The wine was having a curious effect on her, making her desire all the more potent. She held out her glass and he filled it. She drank quickly, savoring the sensation. They each had a third glass.

After a while Alex leaned his head back against the log wall of the hut, his face a bit flushed. He was staring off into the void between the mountains. It seemed, by the look in his eye, that he was somewhere else.

"*Où es-tu?*" she whispered.

"Here. Just here."

Lianne heard something in his tone, a wistfulness that was unmistakable. She hadn't questioned him in detail about this place, but there was little doubt his attachment to it involved other women. Jealousy surged through her. "You're remembering someone else," she said, letting her hurt show.

"Yes," he admitted, "but it was the mood, my state of mind I was recalling, not the person."

"Can they be separated?"

"It was an innocent train of thought, Lianne, believe me. I was remembering my first time. It was a long time ago."

"Was it here?"

"Yes."

She closed her eyes and saw naked bodies—Alex's and some faceless girl's. The place suddenly took on a different cast, suggested a different meaning. She pulled her hand free. "Why did you want to bring me here?"

He took her chin in his hand and made her look at him. "To share it. To relive it with you."

"That's not flattering," she said, pulling back a bit.

"But if we were to make love, and if it were to be beautiful, and there were to be someone else someday, wouldn't you think of sharing all this with them?"

"No. Never. It would be your place, Alex. No one else would belong here." A sudden gloom fell over her. "I shouldn't have come."

"Lianne, I don't mean it in that way." He stroked her cheek, but she turned from him.

"No woman wants to be a substitute."

"That isn't what I was saying. The other person doesn't matter. Not now."

Her chin quivered, but she tried to sound resolute. "You're trying to relive the other experience, and you're using me to do it."

"No..."

She got to her feet, staggering a bit from the wine. She moved a few steps away and looked toward the Alps, letting the warm, humid wind that had begun blowing down the valley caress her. Thunder rumbled in the distance.

Alex got up, too. But Lianne wanted to be alone, so she turned from him and waded though the thigh-high grass to get away. She half expected to hear him call after her, but he didn't, so she continued to walk, her pride driving her on.

She had gone perhaps fifty yards before realizing she had no destination in mind, no objective except escape. She stopped and looked back. Alex was ambling after her, his face sullen and flushed. He wasn't really pursuing her; he was simply preventing her from leaving him.

She started to move on, but changed her mind. There was no point in being childish. Besides, the wine had given her courage, and the exercise had doubled its numbing effect.

Alex came silently up beside her. Lianne felt woozy, enough that she had to sit down. The grass was taller than she, and the world, save the nest around her, was cut off from view. She wrapped her arms around her knees and stared straight ahead.

He moved close enough to touch her hair lightly. She glanced up at him, still feeling indignant and hurt.

"I'm sorry," he murmured, toying with her ear. "It was insensitive of me."

In the face of his contrition Lianne felt badly, like a spoiled brat. "I'm sorry, too," she murmured.

He dropped down beside her in the grass. The bottle of wine was in his hand. "Does that mean we can drink together again?"

He put his hand on her shoulder, the effect of the gesture more intimate perhaps than he had intended. When she lowered her eyes, he ran his hand over the fiery skin of her cheek. Then he drew his finger down her neck to the opening of her blouse. Just that quickly, Lianne forgot her anger. Alex was touching her, turning her flesh to jelly. His nearness sent a warm throb through her.

She took the bottle from him, wanting to proceed with what they had started. She took a long swallow of wine to show him she was up to anything he was. If she was going to be a woman, she'd be one now.

Alex drank after her, then set the bottle down. He leaned over and kissed her neck, drawing his tongue along her soft skin. Lianne moaned. Nobody had ever done that to her before.

She fell back into the grass, her body hollowing out her shape, reminding her of the snow angels she'd made as a child back home in Connecticut. She looked up at Alex, seeing a young god.

"Do people always want to make love when they drink this much?" she asked.

Alex traced the opening of her blouse with his finger. "Is that what you want to do?" he asked in French, adding weight to the question.

"I love you, Alex."

He lay on his elbow beside her. Then, leaning over, he kissed the exposed skin of her chest and touched her hip with his hand. "I want to make love with you."

She stared deep into his soft brown eyes, seeing a resolve that hadn't been there even moments earlier. Lianne trembled, knowing it was fear—the first she had ever felt in his presence. Alex seemed to understand. He kissed her lips softly, giving her time to adjust.

Thunder rumbled on up the valley again, sounding closer now than before. Though the sun was still shining, it seemed likely there would be a shower before long. The air didn't yet smell of rain, but she felt it coming.

Alex was patiently watching her, the slightest hint of a smile at the corners of his mouth. He seemed to know exactly what he was doing, what was needed. He didn't pressure her. He was content to let her set the pace. Lianne touched his cheek.

"Tell me you love me," she whispered.

*"Je t'adore."*

She pulled him down on top of her so that his chest pressed against her breasts. They kissed for a long time, his tongue teasing her lips before slipping more deeply into her mouth.

After a few minutes, she was very excited. The place between her legs had grown moist, yet her desire frightened her. She told him she was afraid, and he calmed her with his quiet affection.

Alex was giving her every opportunity to refuse him. It was as though she were on a riverbank on a searing hot day with the water below inviting her into its cool embrace. She didn't know how exquisite, how harsh, how perfect or shocking the experience would be. She only knew she must be a part of it—plunge her body into its depths. Alex was the pool, the river, the sky, the sun. All she had to do was dive in.

"Alex," she whispered, "I *do* want to make love with you."

He gave her a reassuring kiss, knowing her fear. Then he slowly unbuttoned her blouse down to her jeans, his face a shade more intense, his fingers a little more anxious. He touched the flesh swelling from her bra before unhooking it. Lianne tensed. Only one boy had ever touched her so intimately, and that was in the dark.

He lifted the cups of her bra, first one side, then the other. He stared at her breasts, his expression making her heart beat anxiously. Everything he saw was reflected on his face. She felt her nipples pucker under the wash of his breath. He kissed first one and then the other.

"You see how good it feels?" he whispered, and ran his tongue around the bumpy surface of her areola. "I want it to feel nice. Very nice."

Lianne cradled his head in her arms, moaning at the rising throb deep within. She had never felt such excitement before, not with such immediacy. When he ran his hand over her jeans, lightly grazing her mound, she gasped.

*"Ma petite,"* he murmured, then kissed her again.

"Oh, Alex, I want you, but . . ."

"You are protected, aren't you? The pill or something?"

She had only thought of that in passing, because she would never make love with anyone whose child she wouldn't have. This wasn't a commitment of the moment. For her it couldn't be. It was a commitment forever and ever.

"Yes," she replied, afraid the truth might stop him.

He kissed her again, then sat up and pulled off his shirt. Thunder rolled down the valley as the sun slipped behind a cloud.

Lianne had never seen his bare chest before. It was manly, covered with a dark mat of hair. Though she was shy, she couldn't help staring. Alex smiled.

"Touch me if you like. Here." He took her wrist and dragged her palm over his chest and stomach.

She kept her eyes on his, seeing his sexuality in the way he used them to look at her. Instinctively she squeezed the muscles between her legs, craving his touch.

"Do you like that?"

She nodded.

Alex unfastened her jeans, then peeled them back. Without cue she lifted her pelvis, and he pulled off her pants. She felt more vulnerable than she ever had in her life, and yet her fear abated when he eased down beside her. He ran his hand lightly over her breast and stomach, venturing lower again, this time letting his hand rest on her pubis.

"You feel so soft and sweet. It's making me hard," he said into her ear. "Can you feel it?"

She shook her head nervously, afraid he'd ask her to touch him there. But her craving was growing more intense. She *did* want him. She kissed him, forcing his mouth hard against her lips.

By the time the kiss had ended, she was panting. Her whole body seemed on the verge of convulsions. Her desire seemed so much stronger than her fear.

"Please, Alex," she murmured, not knowing with certainty what she was asking. "Please."

He stripped off the rest of her clothes and, though the air was warm, she shivered. Alex looked at her naked body. Her muscles grew taut under his eyes. Again he caressed her, and this time his fingers entered her soft, downy hair.

Lianne clutched him to her body, trying any way she could to master the powerful sensations, the dread, the desire. Just when she thought she wouldn't be able to stand it any longer, Alex rolled away from her and undressed himself. Then he moved back beside her. For a long time they clung naked to each other.

Staring at the sky, now filled with boiling nimbus, Lianne felt her eyes bubble. Her heart ached and she wanted to cry, but she didn't know why. The damp smell of rain was in the air. It all seemed so monumental.

Alex's hands roamed her more aggressively, his kisses growing harder and more eager. His excitement compounded hers. His erection was hard against her leg, but she tried not to think about it, choosing, like the diver, to close her eyes to the reality of the plunge.

When his breathing grew labored, he slid his body over her, his knees wedging her legs apart. She tensed again, confused by her conflicting desires. Lightning flashed somewhere in the graying sky, and thunder rolled down the valley. Alex pressed himself between her legs, opening them. Her heart clawed at her chest. She was that diver again, afraid, but poised and waiting.

He forced himself against her opening, and she gasped as he entered her. He didn't move until she seemed comfortable with the sensation. Lianne relaxed a little then and concentrated on her love for him.

Around them the grass leaned and swayed in the wind. She felt the kiss of the breeze on her wet skin and the sting of desire between her legs. Beneath her was the hard earth, above her Alex's eager body, slowly beginning its erotic dance. And as she closed her eyes and concentrated on the sensation of him in her, she knew her life would be changed for all time. Lianne Halliday had become a woman.

# CHAPTER ONE

FIFTEEN YEARS WAS a long time to be away from the city that had once meant so much. And yet, under the circumstances, Lianne had dreaded her return to Geneva—the inevitable moment when she would finally have to face the past, to confront the living as well as the dead.

She stared out the window of the limousine, watching the suburban apartment blocks drift by—the cafés and shops, the gas stations, taxis, buses and motorbikes. Ahead, against a sky filled with towering clouds, the profile of the Cathedral Saint Pierre rose from the shoulders of the old town, sparking remembrance, like a photograph or drawing in a childhood book.

The route they followed was nearly the reverse of the one she had taken when she left Geneva all those years ago, though she had little recollection of anything but her heartache at the time. It had been a painful chapter in her life, one she had tried to avoid when possible.

The chauffeur Monsieur Pronier had sent glanced in the rearview mirror as the limousine entered the Place Neuve and passed the Grand Theatre. Lianne saw the look and knew he was awaiting instructions, but she wasn't sure herself just where she wanted to stop.

*"Ici, madame?"* he asked when no comment was forthcoming.

"No, farther on," she replied.

The limousine mounted the hill, passing the gray stolid buildings that were as unobtrusive as they were obdurate, just like the *genevois* themselves. Seeing the town again, Lianne thought of her grandmother. Poor Nanna. Marguerite Gevers had accomplished in death what she couldn't in life—she had gotten Lianne back to Geneva.

It had all been so unexpected, so sudden. The transatlantic calls, the incongruity of Monsieur Pronier's French amid the warm, noisy air of Manhattan drifting through her open window. She recalled the sound of a Sunday football game in the apartment across the hall as the porter came to take her hastily packed bags to the waiting cab. Then there had been the flight from one lifetime to an earlier, more tragic one.

Scooting forward, Lianne saw a familiar profile of trees coming up on the left. The leaves had already begun changing color, looking much as they had that day years earlier when she left. She tapped on the back of the chauffeur's seat.

"Just there," she said. "Stop here, please."

The limousine pulled up to the curb and Lianne got out, telling the chauffeur she wouldn't be long. Then she turned and went into the Jardin des Bastions, swinging her aubergine jacket over her shoulder.

The park was much as it had been the day she'd left, a beautiful warm Indian summer day, though in Europe they didn't call it that. There was a pungent, earthy smell in the air that brought forth a cascade of memories.

It didn't take long to find the green lacquered bench where they'd had their last conversation. A schoolgirl of fourteen or fifteen was sitting there now. She was leaning over, her elbows resting on her knees, her book bag between her feet. She looked sad, perhaps upset over some boy, a broken relationship or other disappointment.

Lianne sat down at the other end of the bench. During the flight from New York, she had decided that the first thing she would do in Geneva would be to come to the park. She needed to make her peace with Alex, and she would do it in the place of their parting.

For a long time after her return to the States she had continued to love Alex Julen. And, in a way, she would always love the memory of that poignant summer.

She knew in her heart that Alex wasn't entirely responsible for all that had happened. He had been willing to marry her. But even at seventeen Lianne had sensed the difference between a desire of the heart and duty.

The decision about the baby had been made on a transatlantic call at the beginning of September. Lianne and Nanna had talked with her mother in Connecticut, each of them in a separate room of Nanna's town house. Lianne had clung to the extension in the sitting room, hearing Nanna's clocks ticking throughout the house as the old woman had told her daughter of the tragedy.

There was a stunned silence. "Pregnant?" Eloise barely managed. Lianne heard the dismay in her mother's voice from across the Atlantic. "Pregnant?"

*"Oui, chérie,"* Nanna said. "It's my fault. I take full responsibility for not supervising her properly."

"Are you sure she is?"

"Yes," Nanna said somberly. "I've taken her to the clinic."

"But who is he? What boy? Mother, I hope to God it was a boy, not a man."

"A boy, a young man," Nanna said, her voice quavering. "He is a Julen...Alex, their youngest. You know the family."

In the silence that followed Lianne whimpered, feeling shame at hearing the two most important people in her life talking about her as though she were the family maid. And to hurt her widowed mother, knowing she was suffering the first stages of a cancer that would ultimately kill her, was almost too much to bear.

"Lianne," Eloise said, "I don't know how you could have done this." It was the only critical remark either she or Nanna uttered. Neither of them chastised her after that, treating her instead more as an errant child than an adult, though unquestionably with her best interests at heart. The tactic forced her to acquiesce, and the decision became Lianne's as though it had been her own.

"The father's family is hardly a matter of concern at this point," her mother said. "At seventeen marriage is out of the question."

"I know she's young...but they are fond of each other, Eloise. I'm of a different generation, it's true, but I wonder if marriage shouldn't be explored."

"Absolutely not."

At the time Lianne didn't understand why it was so obvious that she was too young, because she was convinced she knew her heart. But in the end they gave her no choice.

"And what does the boy say?" Eloise asked. "Is he aware?"

"No, Lianne hasn't told him."

"Should she, Mother?"

Lianne was clinging to the phone, tears streaming down her cheeks. There had been a lump in her throat the size of a grapefruit, but she couldn't keep from speaking. The baby might belong to her mother and Nanna, but Alex didn't. He was the one thing she did have. "No,

Mama! You can't tell me what to do about Alex. He should know. I want to tell him.''

After a brief pause that was more powerful than a direct rebuke, Eloise addressed her mother again. "It's not a matter of finances. The Julens' money isn't necessary for the birth. I'll bear those expenses."

"I guess it depends on what we'll do with the baby," Nanna said matter-of-factly.

"She'll have to have it." Eloise's voice shook. "Abortion's unthinkable."

"Of course, of course."

"She'll come home, and we'll see that it's placed for adoption here. Let me know when she'll be arriving. I'll see to matters."

Lianne had mumbled her goodbyes through her tears, but all she had thought about was Alex—what he would say when she told him, and what he would think of her.

The call had lasted no more than ten or fifteen minutes, but it had been monumental. And it had set the tone for the rest of the ordeal. Lianne had gone to the park that day fifteen years before. Alex had been waiting, sitting virtually where the schoolgirl was sitting now.

Remembering the conversation, Lianne's eyes filled. She looked at the sky overhead through the rusty leaves. The air was warm and languid, its musky perfume pervasive.

It had been cooler on that earlier day. There had been a breeze that Lianne had felt blow right through her. She had felt so empty, so vulnerable, so stripped of her worth as a human being. And the love in Alex's eyes couldn't stop the feeling, couldn't heal her.

She ran her fingers over the lacquered surface of the bench, wondering if Alex had ever returned to think of her nostalgically. She had never seen or heard from him since that day, although she'd later learned he had tried to contact her.

The girl at the other end of the bench rose and looked at Lianne for the first time, nodding in the respectful way the youth of the country were taught. *"Au revoir, madame,"* she said, then turned and headed up the pathway.

For a moment Lianne looked after her, knowing her own daughter—whom she always thought of as Alexandra—was similarly approaching womanhood. But her child was learning to face a grown-up world without her, oblivious to her existence, though hopefully in the bosom of some decent family.

She sighed deeply, knowing she had never completely accepted what had happened. The past—her child—was always with her, clinging to her determinedly. Alexandra and her father would never go away, not completely.

Lianne looked at her watch. She had already taken longer than she had intended. She got to her feet, glanced around, then retreated back up the walk. When she arrived at the boulevard, the chauffeur held the door and she climbed into the back seat. She took a deep breath and told herself that Alexandra and Alex were in the past. There was nothing to be done about them now.

MONSIEUR PRONIER, a smallish man in his sixties with wire-rimmed glasses that pressed deeply into the flesh of his temples, greeted Lianne formally. She wasn't surprised. Nanna would only have retained someone who was correct in every detail.

"I am terribly sorry about the passing of your grandmother," he said in English, though he was aware she spoke fluent French. "Madame Gevers, I valued not only as a client but as a friend. If I may say so, *mademoiselle,* I, too, feel the loss profoundly."

"Thank you, Monsieur Pronier. It's a difficult time for me. Nanna was all the family I've had for a number of years."

Her grandmother's passing had been a blow, though not an unexpected one. Lianne had cried when she received the news, but her mourning seemed somehow removed, like a role she was walking through on stage. Perhaps she had exhausted all her grief at the death of her mother a few years before. Perhaps there was no pain left.

Pronier bowed his head, a further expression of his condolence. "I know you are expecting the interment to be tomorrow, but there has been a small conflict. The mortuary has asked if it might be held this afternoon. Apart from yourself there will only be a handful of *madame*'s closest friends in attendance. They have been alerted and will go to the chapel—" he looked at his watch "—in just a few hours from now, if you have no objection, *mademoiselle.*"

"In a few hours?"

"I know it is short notice, but *madame*'s instructions were that there be no elaborate service, and that only certain designated persons be at the interment. If you will permit it."

"Certainly, Monsieur Pronier." Lianne thought for a moment before she spoke. "The Julen family. Will they be at the funeral today? I know my grandmother was close to them."

"Alberte Julen was very close to Madame Gevers, but he has been dead for several years now. He was quite elderly, you know."

"What about the rest of the family?"

"As a courtesy to them, Max, the elder brother, was on *madame*'s list."

Max Julen. It had been years since Lianne had thought of him—the only Julen she'd never met. Still, because of all the stories she'd heard, Max had once been very real to her.

Lianne's thoughts drifted back to Alex. She pictured his vaguely haunting image. "And what about the other son, Monsieur Pronier? Will he be there, too?"

"I think not, *mademoiselle*. The younger Monsieur Julen is abroad. To my knowledge he hasn't been in Geneva in months. As I understand it, when he comes, it is only briefly."

Lianne felt relief, but also a vague sense of disappointment. "I see." She was embarrassed for having asked, though there was no way Pronier could have known the reason. "I...was just curious," she explained.

The lawyer said he would arrange things so that she could go to her hotel to rest and freshen up before the funeral. Before she left she asked if settling her grandmother's affairs would take long.

"These things are not simple, *mademoiselle*. Perhaps months. Of course, you needn't stay in Geneva the entire time. A week or two to effect the necessary documentation would be helpful, however, especially if you plan to sell the town house."

"I haven't decided what I'll do. But staying a while is no problem. I'm working on my dissertation at the moment. All my class work has been completed, so I brought everything I need with me. I plan to write while I'm here in Switzerland."

"Then we can count on you staying?"

"Yes, for two or three weeks at least. Perhaps more."

"*Très bien.* There's no reason to detain you any longer this morning, Mademoiselle Halliday. I'll have my driver take you to your hotel."

ON THE DRIVE to the Intercontinental, Lianne realized that her return was proving to be every bit as emotional as she had feared. The town had rekindled her feelings for her child, the baby she'd never seen after that brief glimpse in the delivery room. But even more than her little girl, Alex had come tripping back into her consciousness.

Once Lianne had returned to Connecticut, his name had barely been mentioned for fifteen years. He had been taboo in her mother's mind, and it wasn't until Eloise Halliday had lain ill in a hospital bed that more than the briefest reference to him had been made, and then only as the result of a dying woman's wish to purge her soul.

Eloise had taken Lianne's hand and confessed that she had hidden several letters that had come from Alex years earlier. "I didn't throw them away, though maybe I should have. I thought that someday when you were older you ought to see them—or at least have the choice."

She had looked up at Lianne, pleading in a quiet way for forgiveness. "They're at the bottom of that little hope chest I keep in my bedroom, darling. Find them and read them if you want. Or throw them away. The decision is yours. I just had to tell you they were there."

Lianne had taken her mother's hands and pressed them against her cheeks. "Don't worry, Mama. It doesn't matter. None of that matters now."

Several weeks after her mother died, Lianne had finally gone through the chest, found the letters and read them. There were four. Three had been sent before the baby was born, the last shortly afterward.

They were exactly what one might have expected. Alex had expressed his love, his desire to see her, his willingness to do whatever was necessary. But more than anything else there was a profession of remorse, and guilt. "I know you never want to see me again," he said in the last letter, "because you haven't answered. I understand that, and I accept it. My only regret is that you don't just tell me so. It would be far easier for me to take."

What it really amounted to, Lianne had realized, was that Alex had wanted to be forgiven. By hiding the letters, Eloise had spared her daughter the anguish of her loss, but she had also denied Alex the forgiveness he had wanted.

Lianne had wanted to close that final chapter with dignity, so she had written to him at the only address she had—his parents' home. Not too surprisingly, she had never gotten a response. She hadn't really invited one, though. Her sole motive had been to give him the peace he had been denied.

But now, driving through the streets of Geneva, Lianne was remembering him—his light chocolate-brown eyes that seemed perpetually whimsical, even irreverent, his dark hair and narrow, rather handsome face. Lianne remembered his nose was a bit pointed and his bone structure rather too angular to be perfect. In recent years she had imagined him having a touch of gray at the temples, though it was hard, even in her mind, to add the lines and maturity the years had surely brought.

Alex Julen, her grandmother had told her in a letter once, had decided on a life abroad, traveling to the distant corners of the world as an official with the International Red Cross. He had neither a family nor a home. It was a life well suited to his temperament.

Lianne now realized that her grandmother had been preparing her for this day. Everything Marguerite Gevers owned in the world, which amounted to a great deal, was now hers. Nanna had wanted to make it as easy for her as possible to return to Geneva and claim it.

The limousine arrived at the Intercontinental Hotel, and the doorman helped Lianne out. As her bags were being tended to, she walked to the entrance, feeling terribly weary from her long trip. Just as she passed through the door she nearly collided with a handsome dark-headed man. For an instant she thought it was Alex.

*"Verzeihung!"* he said in German, and slipped past her. It wasn't Alex. It was only a man vaguely resembling him. Lianne gathered herself and went to the registration desk, her cheeks lightly tinged with color.

AN HOUR LATER Lianne was on her way to the chapel where the service was to be held. Jet lag had set in, but in a way she was glad for the change in schedule. It would be good to get the funeral behind her.

The mourners were gathered, awaiting her arrival. Monsieur Pronier received her with the solemnity befitting the occasion. There were about eight or nine people in the tiny chapel, but Lianne's attention was drawn to the casket. Seeing it brought home the awful reality. She felt a terrible weight descend on her.

Steadying herself by grasping the stone pier beside her, she stared at Nanna's coffin. She was aware of Monsieur Pronier beside her, his controlled breathing, but his presence was hardly more noticeable than the statuary, the stained glass windows or tapestries.

After a moment, she began moving slowly toward Nanna, the lawyer with her, a deferential half step behind. She stopped midway between the entry and the bier.

Her breathing was heavy, labored. A feeling of light-headedness washed over her, and she felt faint. As she stared woodenly ahead, the candles at either end of Nanna's casket began to shimmer.

Unexpectedly Lianne felt her knees buckling, and she reached out. Monsieur Pronier immediately took her elbow. She touched her face and was surprised at how alien her clammy flesh felt.

She tried to steady herself, tried to think of her grandmother, but it didn't help. Everything—the jet lag, the emotion, the memories—caught up with her. Suddenly she felt helpless.

"Oh, my," she murmured, her eyes fixed on the quivering images before her. "Oh, my..." And, despite Monsieur Pronier's tightening grip, Lianne fell to the floor.

The next thing she knew she was lying on some sort of couch. She heard the voices of several people. They were all speaking French.

"Is she all right?"

"Perhaps a doctor should be called, *madame.*"

"I don't believe she's ill."

"No, probably just emotion."

"She flew in from New York this morning. She may be fatigued."

"Here, Monsieur Pronier, let me put a damp cloth on her head."

Lianne opened her eyes in the midst of the patter.

"There! She's coming to."

Lianne looked into the unfamiliar face of a middle-aged woman hovering over her. She blinked. "What happened?"

"You fainted, *madame.*"

Then another voice. "Are you all right, *mademoiselle?*" It was Pronier.

"Yes," she mumbled. Lianne saw that she was in a small room filled with a muted yellowish light from a nearby lamp. Two stained glass lancet windows were on the wall behind the faces. "Where am I?"

"In a reception room adjacent to the chapel," the lawyer replied in a low tone.

"Oh. I'm so sorry." She started to get up, but the woman gently restrained her.

"Rest for a moment, *madame.*"

Lianne let her head fall back on the coat that had been rolled up to make a pillow, then looked around. Apart from the woman attending her and Monsieur Pronier, there were two women of her grandmother's generation, watching wearily and speaking in a low tone.

The woman at her side, whom she gathered was an employee of the mortuary, patted the back of her hands with the damp cloth. The room was in focus now, and Lianne was embarrassed. "I don't know what happened. I've never fainted before."

"It's morning now in New York," the lawyer replied solicitously. "You should be waking, and you haven't yet been to bed. It was unwise to move the schedule ahead. I take full responsibility."

Then another man appeared, coming to the couch. He stood over her, smiling slightly, though the expression in his eyes was sober. The face was vaguely familiar, reminiscent of someone, though she knew she didn't know him.

"What we have done is most unfair," he said with perfect though slightly accented English. "We owe you an apology, *mademoiselle,* for rushing this."

It wasn't the voice, the accent or even the man's mature good looks. Perhaps it was the eyes. They were so similar to those that had been burned into her consciousness fifteen years before. The man peering down at her had to be Alex's brother, Max Julen.

"Miss Halliday, I believe we should take you back to your hotel and reschedule for tomorrow, as originally planned." His voice was commanding, yet he had a gracious manner.

Max Julen wasn't as stiff as many of the Swiss Lianne had known, but he did have that reserved, well used formality about him. His black suit was a conservative European cut, one that was worn on such occasions. He managed to look correct and benevolent at the same time.

"No, *monsieur*. I'm sure I'll be all right in a few minutes."

His blue eyes indicated little more than a strong sense of propriety. "We have not met, *mademoiselle*. I am Maximilian Julen. My father was a dear friend of Madame Gevers." He bowed respectfully. "The decision is yours, of course. But no one could blame you for putting off the service a day." He spoke in French, his speech clipped and formal.

As he spoke she kept seeing flashes of Alex, which was a bit unnerving. Surely Max knew all about her and his brother. And yet, if there was any awareness on his part, he didn't betray it.

She had grown embarrassed by all the attention and lifted herself to her elbows, gesturing for Madame Graf to permit her to sit up. She swung her long legs off the couch, feeling the color rising in her cheeks almost immediately. She looked up at Alex's brother.

"I would prefer to go through with the funeral today," she said. "I'll be fine." She glanced at Madame Graf. "If I could just have some water, please."

The woman nodded, then withdrew.

"And maybe something to eat," Max called after her in French. "Biscuits or something, if you have them, *madame.*"

"*Oui, monsieur.*"

Max, who had been towering over Lianne, sat on the couch beside her. "I am very sorry about this," he said, speaking English again. "We haven't welcomed you back to Geneva very well, have we?"

The soft lilt in his accent pleased her. She didn't remember Alex's manner of speech precisely, except that her French had been better than his English, and she had teased him a lot. She recalled only the way they would make a game of catching each other in a misused idiom.

"Please don't worry about me, Monsieur Julen."

In the background Pronier and the two matrons spoke in muted tones, then began making their way to the door. Max glanced at them as they left the room. "It's unfortunate that we meet under such circumstances," he said. "I would have preferred a happier occasion."

"Me, too," she replied. "Of course, I once knew your family quite well. So it's not like we're total strangers, is it?"

"You're referring to Alex."

Lianne felt sudden relief at the mention of his name. Max would say nothing to embarrass her, she was quite sure, so it was just as well to get the subject in the open. "Yes, Alex." But then she was at a loss what to say next. "I understand he's abroad."

"In West Africa at the moment." He looked into her light gray eyes, making Lianne uncomfortable. There were obvious similarities between Max and his brother, though there was a directness about the elder Julen that was distinctive.

"Is Alex well?"

"Yes, he's fine. I don't see him often, of course. He's rarely home."

Lianne could see there would be no easy way to get any information—not without being blatant. And it hardly seemed the time or place, anyway. Mercifully Madame Graf returned, pushing a small cart with a tray containing a tea service, a glass of water and several wafers.

"*Voilà!*" Max said. "Tea is an excellent idea."

It did sound good. And seeing the biscuits brought a sudden appetite. Lianne reached over and snatched one from the plate as Madame Graf poured. Then she picked up the plate and offered Max a cookie, but he declined. "You don't have a fainting problem, I take it," she said wryly.

"No, *mademoiselle*," he said with a grin. "I don't."

The woman handed Lianne a cup and saucer, then left the room, her heels clicking on the stone floor. Lianne sipped the tea, liking the warmth of it.

They were alone again. Max contemplated her. "If you would like a few minutes to yourself," he said, "I can withdraw with the others."

"Oh, no. Please stay." Lianne sipped her tea again, worrying that she might have sounded a bit overeager.

Max leaned back and crossed his legs in the European manner, his bearing a bit more relaxed, though still precise.

Lianne munched on another biscuit. "I was sorry to hear about your father's death," she said, affecting the characteristic Swiss lilt to her French.

"That was several years ago, but thank you."

"How is your wife, Mr. Julen? And do you have a family? As I recall, you were newly married when I was last here."

"My wife has unfortunately passed away," he replied. "My only family is my daughter, Tatiana...and, of course, Alex."

"Oh, I hadn't heard about your wife. I'm very sorry."

"Look at us," he said, shaking his head. He had switched back to English. "We're off on dreary subjects. It must be the surroundings."

"Your daughter!" she said brightly, eager to accommodate him. "Tell me about her."

Max hesitated. "She's a lovely child, of course. But you'd expect me to say that. I'm her father."

She nodded. "That's the way fathers are supposed to be."

When he didn't comment, Lianne wondered about him. The man had been very kind, he'd humored her, but she was holding people up and she knew it. Enough pampering, she thought. No need to be inconsiderate.

Her thoughts returned to Nanna. She pictured the old woman's beloved face. It was time for Lianne to do her duty. "The tea has been very nice, Mr. Julen. I feel well now. Perhaps we should go so that the business we came for can be done."

"Of course." Max got to his feet. He waited for Lianne to rise, offering her his arm. She looked into his eyes and saw more than a simple gesture of courtesy. Nothing was said, but it was apparent he had sensed what she needed at the moment. Maximilian Julen, Lianne decided, was a gentleman.

# CHAPTER TWO

LIANNE SAT at the window, listening to the sound of an occasional vehicle passing along the rue Beauregard. Spread out before her were her research files, her papers from graduate school, some course notes and a partial draft of her dissertation on Shelley. But she hadn't really looked at them. She was listening and thinking instead.

It was her second day in Nanna's town house. After meeting with Monsieur Pronier, Lianne had concluded it was just as well to check out of the hotel. There was no point in letting the house sit unused.

Around her Nanna's many clocks were ticking discordantly. They were perched shoulder to shoulder on the mantel, on tables, on the walls, in other rooms. She listened to them, each with a distinctive voice. The sound, the smell of Nanna's house, took Lianne back to her childhood.

Over the throbbing and ticking in the sitting room, she heard the soft clatter of dishes in the kitchen. Ida Weber was doubtless preparing tea. The housekeeper was older even than Nanna had been, but she had survived her mistress, as both women had known she would.

The phone rang just then, giving Lianne a start. Her first impulse was to answer it, but then she remembered it was Ida's responsibility to take calls—a task not to be appropriated lightly. The housekeeper was a crusty, often cantankerous woman with a strong sense of duty.

Lianne sensed she didn't approve of her, frequently hearing what sounded like reproof in the harsh edges of Ida's Swiss-German accent.

But the woman had been loyal to Marguerite Gevers, who had provided generously for her in her will, instructing that the housekeeper would have a salary as long as she was able to work and a pension thereafter. Ida had told Lianne she wanted to continue on as long as the house remained in the family.

Lianne had made no final decision on keeping either the house or the housekeeper. For several years she had lived alone—first in Storrs, while she was teaching at the University of Connecticut, and for the past year and a half in New York, where she had been working on her doctorate—and the idea of live-in help was alien to her.

The telephone seemed to ring on incessantly before the staccato noise finally stopped. Then Lianne heard Ida's muffled voice in the kitchen. A moment later the housekeeper appeared at the doorway and shuffled slowly across the room on swollen, vein-streaked legs.

"It's a gentleman," Ida said. "Monsieur Julen asks for you. Are you in, *mademoiselle?*"

Lianne immediately assumed it was Alex. *He's returned to Geneva!* she thought. Then, just as quickly, she realized Ida hadn't said *Alex* Julen. Perhaps it was Max. "Which Mr. Julen?" she asked.

"Why, Monsieur Maximilian Julen, *mademoiselle.*" Ida hadn't added "of course," but Lianne heard it nonetheless.

She went to the extension in the sitting room, realizing it would be the first time she had held the instrument since she had spoken with her mother that autumn day long ago.

*"Oui, allô?"*

"Good afternoon, Miss Halliday," Max said. He spoke in English, his tone friendly and engaging. "I hope I'm not disturbing your repose."

Lianne smiled at the stilted turn of phrase. "Not at all, Mr. Julen." Lianne watched Ida return to the kitchen.

"If I may say so," Max said, "I've worried about you there in Madame Gevers's house amid all the clocks and thought perhaps you could use an excuse to get out. If I'm not yet too late, could I take you to tea?"

Lianne gave a little laugh.

"Did I say something funny?"

"The clocks," she said. "I'm glad to hear I'm not the only one..."

"Heavens, Madame Gevers's clocks were her persona."

She was pleased with the shared observation. "Yes, they were, weren't they?" She glanced toward the kitchen. "Thank you for the invitation. It would be nice to escape for a while."

"And a pleasure for me. When may I come?"

Lianne had thought some about Max Julen in the two days since they'd met. He'd been a surprise—attractive, mature, kind. She hadn't quite known what to make of him. But she was very pleased that he had called. She'd liked him. "If I could have half an hour..."

HALF AN HOUR LATER Lianne waited for Max to arrive. The prospect of seeing him pleased her more than she would have thought. He had been kind to her the day of Nanna's funeral, and very gentlemanly. He had held her arm during the service, been there for her to lean on.

She wondered about the warm feeling he'd given her. Was it his connection to Alex? she wondered. Probably. Though Max was quite different from her memory of the young man she'd known years before, he *was* Alex's brother.

She was at the window when his silver Mercedes pulled in front of the town house. As he got out, he glanced up and saw her. Lianne waved. Max smiled and waved back.

He was in a tailored camel topcoat, his dark hair combed back. His strides were purposeful, his manner direct. She watched as he mounted the stairs. She got to the door before he rang, not wanting to bring Ida from the kitchen unnecessarily.

"Good afternoon, Miss Halliday!" he said, catching his breath from the climb. He smiled, looking pleased at the sight of her.

Briefly his eyes skimmed her. She was in a shell pink silk blouse and gray wool skirt, nothing particularly alluring, but he made her feel attractive. She extended her hand. "It's Lianne."

"Very well then, I'm Max."

She invited him in. He closed the door, shutting out the crisp autumn air, which had cooled considerably since the day of the funeral.

"You look much more rested," he said.

"I am feeling better now, thank you. That day I arrived was a very difficult one."

"I worried about you."

She lowered her eyes. "You were very thoughtful."

He took her in again with a sweeping look and smiled. "Lovely," he said in English. "Most charming."

He seemed sincere. Lianne was flattered, though a bit embarrassed. The awareness between them was strong. Somehow she hadn't expected that. "I'll just get my coat."

He waited for her to return from the closet. Taking the garment from her, he helped her slip it on.

Lianne turned to face him. With a touch of gray in his dark hair Max looked distinguished. She had a strong sense of his quiet strength. Strangely, though, she still saw him through Alex's eyes. Max—the elder brother, their father's favorite, the object of Alex's adoration. And perhaps jealousy.

"I'll tell Ida I'm going," she said, and went to the kitchen.

When she returned, they went down to the car. There was a strong smell of fall in the air. He helped her in. Lianne watched him walk around to the driver's side and climb in beside her.

"There's a tearoom at the Parc Mon Repos that's pleasant," he said. "We can walk in the *jardin* for a bit if that suits you."

"That would be nice."

During the drive across town, they chatted about little things. Lianne discerned a friendliness on Max's part that was more than mere social courtesy. She wasn't quite sure of the basis of it, unless it was out of a sense of obligation because of Alex and what had happened.

Max stopped on the rue de Lausanne next to the park. They got out and made their way through the garden to the promenade along the lake. Lianne looked out across the water. The air was brisk and clear, but there was also the promise of rain as clouds had begun piling up on the horizon to the east.

They walked in silence for a while. Max had slipped his hands into the pockets of his topcoat and seemed to be in thought. Ahead on the walk, before it twisted behind a thicket of trees, there were perhaps a dozen people strolling along, some in pairs, some alone, some in the company of a companionable dog. There were a number of elderly people sitting on benches, looking out at the gray water and sky.

"How long will you stay in Geneva, Lianne?" he asked.

"I haven't decided. I brought my dissertation with me. That will keep me busy for a while."

"So you are a professor of English."

"I hope to be a full professor one day. That's why I took a leave of absence from teaching to get my Ph.D. In academia it's essential."

"What is it you write about?"

"Shelley."

Max smiled. "You certainly have come to the right place. Mont Blanc is over there in the mists, you know."

"Yes, I recall." Lianne looked across the lake at the opaque sky. There, hidden in the clouds, was not only Mont Blanc, but the Col de Jambaz, where she had gone with Alex. She turned away, not wanting to linger on that particular memory.

Ahead, coming toward them, was a young couple with a large blue perambulator. Though years had passed, it still bothered her to see a mother with her child. As the pram passed, she looked out at Lac Léman.

"Nothing has changed, and yet it seems so strange to be here again," she said. They were speaking in French and, though she hadn't spoken the language regularly since her mother had passed away, the patterns of speech were beginning to come more easily to her.

"This is the first time back, then," Max said, "since..."

"Yes," she replied.

"It must have been difficult, considering how close you were to Madame Gevers."

"Oh, I didn't stay away because of a lack of feeling for my grandmother. She met me in Paris or London quite regularly. We managed to see each other in spite of my...sensitivities about Geneva."

"*Alors,* Alex remains a problem for you."

Lianne looked at him and shrugged. "I suppose, in a way, he does."

Max seemed to search for the right thing to say, but in the end fell silent. Neither of them spoke for a while. They walked and the gulls cried overhead. Then he said, "I shouldn't have brought him up."

"No, don't apologize. There's no reason I shouldn't be able to discuss your brother. Or...our baby." She noticed his repentant expression. "Please don't feel badly."

"It's not my business."

"Maybe it's just as well I talk about it. Maybe it's exactly what I need."

Max looked embarrassed.

"Unless of course you would prefer not to," she said.

"It's up to you. Of course."

She thought for a moment. "It's been years since I've discussed it with anyone. My mother and grandmother never wanted to talk about it, so I simply pretended it hadn't happened. But deep down I knew someday I would have to come back here and face it, if only in my mind."

Max said nothing.

"I keep referring to her as the baby," she went on after a minute or two of silence. "Do you know she's practically a young woman now, Max? And I've never seen her. Not since the day she was born."

Lianne knew she was sounding maudlin, but she couldn't help herself. Once the floodgates had opened, it was hard to hold back. "Sometimes I think that when she's eighteen I might try to find her. But then I don't know if that would be fair. It might upset her life." She glanced at him. "What do you think? What's right?"

His eyes were lowered. He looked solemn. "I don't know."

"It would probably be selfish. I've given up my rights. Even so, a part of me refuses to let go of her." Lianne tried to smile, but tears started flowing, anyway.

Max glanced at her, looking upset. She realized she was being unfair to him, putting burdens on him that belonged to Alex, if anyone.

"I shouldn't be saying this to you," she said.

"No," he assured her, "I don't mind."

"You're too kind, Max."

"I'm sincere," he said.

Lianne faced the wind, letting it dry the tears from her eyes.

"I get the feeling it's Alex you'd like to say all this to, not me," he said.

"You're probably right," she said with a laugh. "If you'd said that a week ago, I'd have denied it. But the past few days I've thought about things I hadn't considered in years. When you get into a habit of denying something, you start believing it yourself after a while."

"What have you denied?"

She looked at him for a moment before answering and saw that he genuinely wanted to know. "My personal life, my needs. I've devoted myself to my teaching, all the while pretending that was enough to fill my life."

"You're saying you're still in love with Alex."

Lianne stopped. The comment shocked by its directness. She started walking again. "No, not really. After all, it was only a summer romance. I was seventeen. I'm thirty-two now. Could I still be in love with that boy? No."

"You seem sure."

"I recognize the problem for what it is. The matter was never properly resolved, that's all. And then there's Alexandra...."

"Alexandra?"

"That's what I call her," Lianne said with embarrassment. "I have no idea what her adoptive parents named her." She flushed. "I don't know why I'm telling you this."

"Because Alex is not here and I am," he said cheerfully.

Lianne smiled and took his arm. It was a very European thing to do, a gesture of friendship that wouldn't be misconstrued. They walked a bit farther. "How is Alex, anyway?" she asked.

"He's well, I believe. We rarely see each other. He came more regularly when our father was alive. Now there is only me and Tatiana."

"Your daughter?"

"Yes."

Lianne thought of the irony of her meaningless avoidance of Geneva. It seemed Alex, too, was in exile. They both had run from the place. "And why do you suppose he has stayed away?"

"Because my brother was always a dreamer. Alex could never be content here. He's got to keep moving. The contours of the land, the face of the towns and the people must change."

They came to an observation point that jutted out over the lake. Lianne walked over to the railing and stood there, watching the choppy water lapping at the rocks. "Is there anyone in his life?" she asked.

"There have been women," Max replied, "if that's what you're asking. But as far as I know, no one special. He's never married or even come close."

"Poor Alex."

"Why do you say that?"

"His life seems sad to me."

"Less than yours. Perhaps my brother denies things, as well."

Lianne looked at him. "Because of our child?"

"I don't know."

He studied her, watching the wind toss her hair. Lianne pulled the black wool coat tight at her neck. She stared blankly at the cloudy vista, then turned to him, her eyes glistening.

They looked at each other for a long time. Then Max reached out and took her into his arms. She put her head on his shoulder and tried hard not to sob. His body was warm and protective. She hadn't been comforted by a man in a very long time. Finally she stepped back, taking a handkerchief from her purse. "I'm sorry."

Max touched her cheek with his gloved hand. "There's no need to say anything."

Lianne tried to return his smile.

"*Viens, chérie.* Let's have us a warm cup of tea."

THEY HAD BEEN SITTING quietly for a long time, their teacups half empty, the view of the lake their excuse for not talking. Lianne was still embarrassed about her display of emotion, though Max's response had been touching.

Max Julen was a surprising man in so many ways. Lianne had trouble thinking of him as a widower. She wondered why he hadn't remarried, or if there was someone he felt strongly about. Yet, for some reason, she was sure there wasn't. She sensed an affection on his part that went beyond simple kindness.

Lianne decided what was needed was small talk, anything to fill the void. But nothing came to mind. She glanced at Max. He wasn't helping. He seemed deep in thought, unconsciously sipping his tea as he stared across the lake.

"I hope I haven't put you into a mood," she said.

Max shook his head. "*Pas de tout.* I was just thinking."

"Should I ask what about?"

"I was wondering if perhaps you would like to meet Tatiana."

Lianne put down her cup. There was a seriousness in his tone that was at odds with the suggestion.

"I thought perhaps a youthful face would cheer you," he said.

She could see he intended kindness, but the idea made her vaguely uncomfortable. "It's nice of you to think of me, but I wouldn't want to interfere."

"Interfere? You're Madame Gevers's granddaughter. Almost family."

They sat in the little tearoom, amid the tattoo of voices, looking into each other's eyes. Lianne saw something in his expression, something more than kindness. A long moment passed. Thunder faintly rumbled across the lake. He stared into her light gray eyes, then looked at his watch.

"Before long I must pick Tatiana up at her dancing lesson." A happy expression filled his face at some inner thought.

"There's no need for me to go along simply because we happen to be having tea. You can drop me at Nanna's."

"No, it will be a surprise for her. I do a little something different from time to time. A book or a box of chocolates. For us it's a game." He hesitated, searching for the right explanation. "Because her mother is gone we're a bit closer than a father and daughter might otherwise be."

Lianne heard the emotion in his voice. She'd never really had the chance to know her own father, since she'd been quite young when he died, but she had seen enough of Max Julen to know he was just the kind of parent a young girl should have.

"All right," she said. "I'd like to meet Tatiana."

THE GENEVA ACADEMY of Dance was situated in an old classical building on the boulevard Helvetique, not far from the Ecole des Beaux Arts. The ornate facade of the structure hinted at something far more grandiose than a school of dance. The building was constructed in the middle of the nineteenth century, Max told her, though it had been dedicated to the education of the city's young only since the war. Just looking at it gave Lianne a sense of rich tradition, although she had no idea whether the actual instruction was worthy or not.

As Max parked the car in a defiantly small space, Lianne recalled her own days at Mrs. Barton's School of Dance on the edge of Westport. The school had been in the instructor's home, a large old farmhouse with a downstairs that had been virtually given up to the requirements of Mrs. Barton's students.

There, in what had once been the dining room, Lianne had labored at the bar for nine years until she'd lost all hope of ever becoming a professional. Eloise Halliday had finally acceded to the inevitable, realizing that Lianne had grown much too tall ever to be a ballerina.

When Lianne and Max got out of the car, the first students were rushing through the heavy wooden doors that swung open under an ornately sculpted tympanum. The youthful faces, flushed cheeks and mounting voices were in contrast to the solemnity of the building itself. Girls were still coming out as Lianne and Max squeezed in the door. A number of youngsters were still inside, their voices echoing in the chamber. A few were in dance costume, but most had changed back into their school uniforms or street clothes.

At the rear of the large vaulted room behind an enormous dimly burning chandelier was a spiral staircase. Girls were streaming down it, obviously anxious to find their friends and be on their way. Max and Lianne stood to the side, watching.

"I usually wait here," he said.

She looked at the faces of the girls, some of whom were glancing curiously at them. The children were of various ages, though most were adolescents, some about the age Alexandra would be. Lianne hadn't considered that.

"How old is Tatiana?" she asked, realizing Max had never mentioned her age.

His eyes briefly met hers. "She'll be fifteen in April."

Lianne felt her heart skip a beat. "So will my child. What day?"

"The seventeenth."

"Ah, my daughter's is April 10. They're just a week apart!" And then she realized what she was saying. She was about to see a girl whose age was within a few days of her own child.

A moment later Max pointed out Tatiana at the top of the stairs. "There she is," he said. "In the blue jacket."

Lianne stared up to see a lovely girl with long, thin legs in white tights protruding from a ski parka. She gave Max a self-conscious wave as she continued down the steps.

Lianne watched her descend, a hand gliding along the massive wood railing, her movement graceful and lady-like. She had long light brown hair that hung down her back in a single loose braid, a white bow tied to it. Lianne studied her face with curiosity.

Tatiana's cheeks were rosy, the rich cream of her skin vibrant and pure, innocent. Hints of maturity were beginning to show. She had the Julen bone structure, Lianne could see that. But the coltish elegance must have come from her mother's side.

Tatiana bid the girl she was with goodbye and came over to them, her eyes shifting from her father to Lianne. There was questioning and mistrust on her face.

"*Hé, Papa,*" she said as they briefly embraced, kissing her father first on one cheek then the other. She looked at Lianne.

"*Ma chère,* I'd like you to meet an old friend of the family. This is Mademoiselle Halliday from America. Madame Gevers's granddaughter."

"*Bonjour, mademoiselle.*"

Lianne took the girl's thin hand.

"Hello, Tatiana. I'm very happy to meet you."

The child gave the slightest curtsy, showing respect. There was shyness and diffidence in her manner. She looked at her father for further explanation.

"Mademoiselle Halliday and I were out for tea and I thought she'd enjoy meeting you, my dear," Max said, slipping his arm around her shoulders. The three of them began to move through the milling dancers.

"Did you know my mother then, *mademoiselle?*" Tatiana asked.

Lianne shook her head. "No, unfortunately I didn't."

"Mademoiselle Halliday's mainly a friend of Uncle Alex," Max explained.

Tatiana grinned back at them as she led the way outside. "Uncle Alex is super! My very best uncle."

"Your only uncle," Max corrected.

"Then you can't say he isn't the best, Papa!" She bounced down the steps ahead of them, tugging on the braid of a friend before pirouetting up the sidewalk toward Max's Mercedes.

"She's adorable," Lianne said, speaking English. "Is that Catrina's spirit in her?"

Max shook his head. "I think not."

Lianne glanced at him, wondering. They made their way toward the car. There was more thunder. It was nearer now, and the clouds overhead were quite dark.

"Hurry, Papa!" Tatiana called, "before it rains!"

Lianne wanted to ask him more, but they were almost to the car. Tatiana assumed a dignified air.

"You mustn't be so impatient," Max said in English as he unlocked the car door.

"Must we speak English?" she asked with stiff, though otherwise perfect, pronunciation.

"I think that would be an excellent idea," Max said as he opened both the front and back door. "It's not Saturday, but a wonderful opportunity for you."

Tatiana groaned, then slithered into the back seat with catlike grace. Lianne got in the front. Max went around to the driver's side.

"We speak in English on Saturdays," he explained as he got into the car. "Even if it's only the two of us."

"And sometimes it's very boring," the girl said from the back seat.

"Tatiana!"

"I was only teasing," she protested.

Max started the engine and pulled into the boulevard. He hadn't mentioned where they might go, but Lianne hoped he would be taking her back to Nanna's. She looked out the window, feeling in one way more at ease with Tatiana present, and in another more uncomfortable.

"Have you known Uncle Alex for a long time?" the girl asked in carefully measured English.

"Yes, for a long time," Lianne replied. "For fifteen years."

There was a brief silence in the back seat. "Did you and Uncle Alex have an affair, miss?"

"Tatiana!" Max looked back at her furiously.

"I spoke in English," she protested. "What's the matter?"

"It's no excuse for being impolite."

"What did I say, Papa?"

Lianne laughed. "It's okay. I don't mind the question. Let's say your Uncle Alex and I were good friends." She glanced at Max, whose neck had turned red. "No harm done," Lianne said, touching his arm to reassure him.

"It's not exactly what I had in mind for an English lesson."

"Forgive me for saying so, but you asked for it," Lianne said.

"What did I say?" Tatiana implored.

"You asked if we were lovers," Lianne told her and, over Tatiana's gasp, she chuckled again. "Everything sounds harmless in a foreign language."

They drove for a while and no one spoke. Lianne thought about the irony of the situation. Only days ago she was in New York, moving through her life like a drugged sleepwalker, and here she was suddenly in Geneva with Alex's brother and his niece. And what was she to them? Just the woman Uncle Alex had had an affair with once, long ago.

Only a minute earlier he had been the source of a lighthearted moment, but the more she let herself think about Alex, the more her mood changed. Thinking about him did her no good whatsoever.

"Do you do recitals, Tatiana?" she asked, wanting a subject that would interest the girl. "I should like to see you dance sometime."

"I think my dancing career is about over, miss," she replied. "I mostly come to the dance class because it pleases Papa."

"That's not so," Max protested. "You like to dance. Have I made you go?"

"Not precisely, Papa . . ."

Lianne gave Tatiana a wink. "I was a dancer once myself, but then I got too tall and had to give it up."

"Yes! It's the same with me," the girl replied. "Madame Sterne says I am already much too tall."

"Oh?" Max said. "This is new to me."

"I've told you before, Papa. You didn't want to hear."

Lianne and Tatiana exchanged smiles.

"Don't you agree, Miss Halliday, that a person should give up dancing when they're not the right size?"

"It was necessary in my case, I must admit."

"You see, Papa!"

"Tatiana," Max said, "I believe you have an ally."

The girl grinned happily. "Thank you, Miss Halliday."

Lianne reached back and grasped Tatiana's hand. "You'll soon be a woman," she said, "and one of the things to learn is that we women occasionally must stick together."

The girl nodded.

"That's American propaganda," Max teased. "We Swiss are not so quick to experiment."

"Maybe we should be," Tatiana shot back without hesitation.

Lianne laughed and looked at Max, who didn't seem entirely amused. The Mercedes turned onto the rue Beauregard and soon stopped in front of Nanna's house. Max started to get out, but Lianne stopped him.

"Don't bother. American women are used to making their own way." She offered him her hand. "Thank you for the tea, and for my little escape from the clocks."

He watched her, holding her hand a moment longer than he should. "We should have dinner some evening. The three of us."

"Yes, that would be nice." She looked back at Tatiana, who sat silently, innocently. Lianne saw something of herself in the girl, perhaps sparked by her recollections of Mrs. Barton's School of Dance. But she also saw the Julen blood, running true and proud in the child. "I'm very happy to have met you, Tatiana. Perhaps someday you can call on me, or we can go out for a ladies' lunch and shop, if that would please you."

"Thank you very much, Miss Halliday. It would."

"Call me Lianne. Please. Hasn't your father told you Americans don't have last names?"

Tatiana giggled. Lianne winked, sealing their bond more firmly.

"I'm sorry about Uncle Alex," the girl said softly.

Lianne nodded as if to say it was all right. "It was nothing. Don't give it another thought." Then she got out of the car and watched them pull away. As she stood there, scattered raindrops began falling. The girl waved through the back window, and Lianne waved back.

She stayed at the curb until they disappeared up the street. When they were gone, she still looked after them. It was strange to think that for the first time in fourteen years she had exchanged more than a few words with a child. And it was even stranger that the girl was the same age as her daughter. Suddenly the urge to see Alexandra was stronger than it had been in a very, very long time.

# CHAPTER THREE

MAX JULEN GAZED out on to the avenue Dumas at the pelting rain. The trees, the vehicles, even the street lamps and the buildings seemed to bow under the pounding downpour. A pedestrian moved under the fragile protection of a huge black umbrella. He pitied him, knowing how soaked the poor fellow would be by the time he reached his destination.

Since seeing to it that Tatiana was diligently immersed in her studies, Max had sat quietly in the fading light of the salon, thinking about Lianne Halliday. But no matter how much he tried he couldn't brush aside the fact that he was attracted to her. And that was a problem, because he suspected that she was still in love with his brother.

Even worse, by having introduced her to Tatiana, he had created still another problem for himself. It had been a foolish thing to do, getting them together. He wasn't sure why he had done it, unless it was compassion, an impulse of the heart.

One thing was quite certain, though. He wouldn't play with Tatiana's happiness. Nor could he afford to permit anything to happen by accident that might jeopardize his child. Max turned from the window and paced across the room. Finally he went to the telephone and dialed the international operator.

It took three calls to Lagos, but he managed to get a number where Alex was supposedly staying. The woman answering sounded British. She briefly explained that Alex was out, but she would have him call. Judging by her tone of voice, she wasn't merely a casual friend. Max thanked her and placed the receiver in the cradle.

"What are you doing, Papa?"

He spun around at the sound of Tatiana's voice. "Oh, hello, darling. You startled me. I thought you were in your room studying."

"I was, but on my way to the kitchen I thought I heard you talking."

"It was nothing. I was on the phone, that's all."

"In the dark, Papa?"

Tatiana was standing in the doorway. The light from the hall revealed her dim silhouette through her gown, though her face was deep in shadow. Max stared at the golden highlights in his daughter's hair, illuminated by the glow behind her, and he thought again of Lianne.

"Papa?"

"It's all right, darling. I ... simply haven't turned on the lamps yet. I've been sitting here, listening to the storm."

"Why?"

He gave a little laugh. "Why not? Nature can be most soothing."

She moved gracefully through the room to a table across from him. She switched on the lamp, filling the chamber with a soft, mellow light. Before she turned back to him Max saw that her large braid had loosened, freeing errant strands of hair. It wasn't a conscious thing, but there was a sexuality about hair like that, the sexuality of a woman preparing for bed.

"Are you sad?" Tatiana asked. She went to the chair nearest him and plopped down heavily, more like a child than a woman.

"No. Listening to the rain doesn't mean I'm sad."

"Were you thinking about Mummy?"

He smiled at the directness of his daughter's thinking. "Perhaps a little, yes."

"I was, too. In the middle of my math studies."

"That's not an unusual time for such daydreaming, is it?"

"It had nothing to do with math," she replied, not seeing his joke. "It was your friend, Mademoiselle Halliday."

"*My* friend?"

"Yes, Papa. I've decided she's not Uncle Alex's friend. She's yours."

Max looked at his daughter. "What do you mean?"

"I mean, she may have been Uncle Alex's girlfriend once, but he's in Africa and you're here. So it must be you she likes."

"A very interesting theory, Tatiana. But the fact of the matter is I've only known Mademoiselle Halliday for a few days."

She looked skeptical. "This afternoon you called her Lianne."

"And so did you."

"Because she told me to."

"The same for me."

Tatiana gave a little frown.

"What's the matter? Don't you like her?"

"Yes," the girl replied. "I like her very much. I mean . . . she's quite nice. Different, of course, but that's only because she's American."

"And this is what you've been thinking about during your math studies?"

"That's not all. I was thinking about Mummy, too."

"Your mother and Lianne. Why those two?"

She contemplated her father. "Papa, you don't understand women very well, do you?"

He struggled to keep a sober expression. "Are you referring to your mother, Miss Halliday or yourself?"

"Me, of course. You think I'm jealous of Lianne for Mummy's sake. But it's not true."

"Then what is the truth?"

Tatiana was looking at her nails, more as a woman would than a child. She spoke, but still avoided his eyes. "Will you marry Miss Halliday?"

Max was shocked by the question. "Marry her? Of course not, Tatiana. I hardly know the woman."

"Then you won't?"

"No."

"Good."

He couldn't help the smile. "I take it you were concerned that I was in danger of marrying the lady?"

"I like Miss Halliday. I like her very much. But I think we should all be friends and nothing more."

"We are friends with her, Tatiana. You and I both."

There was a pause before she spoke again. Then she said, "It's not that I care, Papa. But I know how much you loved Mummy."

"I understand, darling. You needn't explain."

Tatiana got to her feet, sticking out her lip. "Since Maria's off, would you like me to make you some supper?"

"Do you want to eat?"

Tatiana put her hand against her abdomen. "I'm not feeling too well. I had a few biscuits and some milk earlier but I don't think I can eat a whole dinner."

"Then why don't you go on to bed. I can fix a bowl of soup or something later. Maria said the kitchen was well stocked."

"Yes," the girl replied ironically, "there's plenty of beans and flan and rice." She gave her father a tight little smile and headed for her room.

As she left, Max noticed again the incipient womanliness of her body. His little girl was growing up.

Outside lightning flashed, illuminating the buildings and gray-green trees across the street. The gold and ebony reflection of the lighted room contained his own image—Max sitting quietly in his chair, Max in thought, Max alone. He listened to the thunder rumbling, rattling Catrina's crystal in the large antique case against the wall.

He stared at his image and thought of Tatiana's question about Lianne. Why had she worried about the possibility that he might marry? Was it simply a daughter's jealousy and perhaps a protectiveness toward Catrina? He didn't know. And he wasn't sure if the question was prompted by something Tatiana saw in him or in herself.

For half an hour he tried to read his paper, but his thoughts kept drifting back to Lianne. He pictured her tear-streaked face as they'd stood on the lakeshore, and recalled his impulse to hold her. She had taken it as compassion, and that was the way he had intended it. But he'd known, even if she hadn't, that there was more—more than compassion, more even than the guilt he felt. Lianne Halliday evoked something in him that he didn't yet fully understand.

The phone rang then, breaking the stillness of the house. Checking to see that Tatiana's door was closed,

Max took the receiver and sank into the tall wing chair by the table.

*"Max, est-ce toi?"* It was Alex.

"Hello, Alex. Thank you for calling back. I hope I didn't disturb you."

"It's not an emergency then? When I heard you'd called, naturally I thought—"

"Not an emergency, no. I probably should have said something to the woman who answered, but I wasn't quite sure who I was speaking to."

"Her name's Marsha, a friend of mine. My place is being painted, so I moved in with her for a few days. But this isn't why you called. What's up, Max?"

"Marguerite Gevers died last week. The funeral was a couple of days ago."

"Sorry to hear that. But that can't be why you called, either."

"No, it's not. Lianne Halliday is here in Geneva, Alex. She came back for the funeral."

There was a silence on the line.

Max waited. Finally he said, "I know that may not be monumental news, but it raised problems. And I wanted to discuss them with you."

"What sort of problems?"

"It looks as though she might stay for a while." Max drew a long breath, slowly letting it out. "I feel uncomfortable living our lie with her, Alex."

"What do you mean? Has she inquired?"

"No, she has no idea. I'm sure."

"Then what's the problem?"

"The problem is I have to deal with her. Not to mention Tatiana. They met today, this afternoon. There was an affinity between them. A natural affinity. I watched them carefully. I saw what they couldn't see. The resemblance is very strong, Alex."

His brother didn't reply.

"I know we were hoping she'd never return, but she has, and I have doubts now that the pretense can be maintained forever. I'm not sure it's right to keep the truth from her."

"What do you want from me, Max? Permission to tell her?"

"You have as great a stake in this as I do."

"I thought you and Catrina never wanted to tell Tatiana the truth."

"Catrina's gone now, Alex," he said quietly.

"So you think Tatiana should know?"

"I always thought not, that is, until today. I'm not suggesting it's necessary, but simply that now that Lianne is back on the scene, it must be considered. Tatiana *is* her child."

"She's been Lianne's child all along. I never heard you wanting to dash off a telegram to her before now."

"Catrina and I had doubts about the secrecy business from the beginning," Max said. "I suppose what made it necessary was Mrs. Halliday's insistence. And Father's, of course. But they're both gone now, Alex. It's up to you and me."

"Whatever we do, we shouldn't be rash."

"Perhaps I'm jumping the gun a bit," Max said, wondering if it had been a mistake to call. "But I thought you ought at least to be aware. If nothing else, you deserved the option of seeing Lianne, if that's what you choose to do."

Alex hesitated. "Did she ask to see me?"

"I can't say she was eager. But if you want my guess, she considers it may be healing. For both of you."

Again there was a long pause.

"Alex?"

"You can't imagine what a shock this is, coming out of the blue."

"Yes, I can. But I didn't want the responsibility of keeping you in the dark. The point is, I've informed you. What you do with it is up to you."

"Naturally I'm not eager to jump into the boiling soup," Alex said.

"I understand that."

"The problem with telling Lianne is she may not be content just having the knowledge. And there's no way of knowing the effect it will have on Tatiana."

"That's my main consideration—Tatiana's happiness and well-being."

"It's ironic that you called about this. As a matter of fact, I have to come to Geneva. Sometime in the next month or so. There are no dates set. It might have been awkward if I showed up in the middle of things."

"Well, then it's good you're forewarned." He hesitated. "What will you do when you get here?"

"I don't know. I'll have to think about this."

"Well, we mustn't think only of ourselves. Tatiana and Lianne must come first."

"Yes," Alex replied, his voice fading.

"Call me if you need to."

Alex agreed and said goodbye. Max slipped the receiver back into the cradle.

Outside the wind gusted, blowing the rain hard against the windows. He went over to where the water was pounding against the pane and stood peering down at the street below. It was deserted now. No one was fighting the deluge.

A WEEK LATER a chilly wind blew down the rue Beauregard, sending an odd piece of paper skittering along the pavement and kicking up a pocket of dried leaves from the gutter. Three girls of about ten years of age were walking past the delivery truck out front, the collars of their coats pulled over their ears against the wind.

Lianne watched from the window, her eyes fixed on the men who were unloading her things onto a hand truck. The airfreight shipment from New York had arrived.

Ida Weber had stationed herself at the door as the men carried each load up the steps, then deposited the cartons in the middle of the sitting room. Lianne was relieved at the arrival of her things, knowing their familiarity would make Nanna's house a bit more her own.

Over the past several days she had begun the mental process of making the aristocratic old town house home, if only for an interim period. Even though Nanna was gone, Lianne had felt like a guest for the first week or so. Now she was ready to become mistress of the house.

On Sunday she had invited Nanna's closest friends, Mesdames Marthaler and Dunoyer, for coffee and cake so that she might have their counsel on disposing of some of the clocks. At her urging both women had selected pieces for themselves, and the rest, save the two she had decided to keep, she donated to charity.

With the clocks gone Nanna's house had been strangely quiet, and Mrs. Weber's face had become a death mask. The housekeeper's world seemed to be slipping away, and Lianne sensed that the woman blamed her for it.

As the deliverymen were placing the last of the cartons onto the hand truck, the postman came up the steps. Lianne watched him with vacant curiosity. Most of the mail was still addressed to Nanna. From her vantage point at the sitting room window she could hear the housekeeper and the postman exchanging a few words before the door was shut again.

*"Mademoiselle,"* Mrs. Weber said from behind her.

Lianne turned around. The woman shuffled toward her, an envelope in her hand. "This one is for you."

She took the letter and looked at the unfamiliar hand. It bore Swiss postage stamps and had been mailed locally. She glanced up at Mrs. Weber, who was obviously curious, but turned and limped from the room.

Lianne tore open the top of the envelope. Inside was a folded piece of embossed notepaper with the name Maximilian Alberte Julen at the top. She read:

My dear Lianne,
I should like to make good my promise and invite you to dine with me Saturday evening next. There is a very pleasant little restaurant in Coppet that has been a favorite of mine for many years. I think perhaps you would enjoy it. Please let me know if I may have the pleasure of your company.

With kindest regards,
Max

A smile of joy filled her face as she considered the note, rereading it twice. It was polite, courteous, yet there was a certain intimacy about it that touched her. Lianne had wondered if she would hear from Max again. After their tea, she had thought of him often, happy yet a little distrustful of the warm feelings he had engendered.

Tatiana had been delightful, as well, but meeting the girl hadn't been without its drawbacks. The experience had started her thinking about Alexandra, bringing back those agonizing memories.

Her mother and Nanna couldn't have known what scars their decision would leave, of course. And they had been right about the handicap a baby would have been to an eighteen-year-old. Their intent had been good, but the aftermath had caused her so much pain and guilt.

How did those few years of freedom compare to a lifetime of denial? Was Alexandra better off because of what they'd done? Lianne had no way of knowing. Perhaps that was the hardest part of all—the uncertainty.

Max hadn't mentioned Tatiana in his note, so he doubtless intended a dinner for just the two of them. Lianne was glad of that. It was easier not to have to deal with too much at once. On the other hand, maybe what she needed was to confront the issue head-on rather than run from it as she always had.

She sent Max a brief note, accepting his invitation, finding the ceremonial formality of European etiquette gratifying. How many people in New York did she know who were even capable of using the telephone nicely?

She'd always felt at home in Geneva. Her mother had been born in the city, and Lianne had come often when she was growing up. And yet she had always thought of herself as American, not Swiss. Comfortable as she was in Nanna's house, it was good to have her own things. And clearing out her apartment had enabled her to sublet it.

With each passing day she was becoming more content with the thought of staying on in Geneva, though she still wasn't sure what impact that might have on her career. For the moment, though, it would be enough to finish writing her dissertation.

Besides, Max Julen had given her something to think about that she had been ignoring for years—her needs as a woman. She didn't know where their budding friendship would lead, but she was sure she wanted to see him again and find out.

And it wasn't only because he was Alex's handsome brother, either. Lianne was very attracted to Max as a person. His sophisticated European manner was appealing, and there was a comfort in his presence that she simply hadn't known before, even with Alex.

Still, a part of her wondered if, at some level, Max was a substitute for his brother. All she could say for sure was that she was ready for her quiet life to come to an end. And Max Julen was the reason.

WHEN IDA LET Max Julen into the house Saturday evening, Lianne was still in her bedroom getting ready. She listened to the unintelligible sound of their voices in the hall as she put on her pearl earrings, all the while wondering about the nervousness she felt.

When she walked into the salon, Max was sitting with his legs crossed and a finger alongside his cheek, staring out the window contemplatively. He wasn't aware of her presence for a moment, giving her an opportunity to observe him.

She was aware she felt a definite warmth toward him, yet in a way it was more than that. It was hard to put her finger on exactly what it was that attracted her so. But one thing was clear—Max Julen was a change from the colleagues with whom she'd shared shallow relationships. For some reason he seemed safe.

And his friendship was a welcome counterbalance to her continuing anxiety over Alex. More and more she had come to realize that some final act or understanding was needed between them.

Just then Max turned and noticed her standing at the doorway. He got to his feet. *"Eh, voilà!* I didn't see you, Lianne."

She walked over, extending her hand. "I confess I was spying on you."

Max took her hand and kissed it. "Spying?"

"You looked so contemplative."

"Life is complicated. There's much to think about." He looked her over admiringly. She was wearing her mother's pearls along with one of her favorite dresses, a chocolate-brown cashmere that made her pale hair look like burnished gold. "I must say, you look lovely, Lianne."

She smiled at the compliment.

His blue eyes were fixed on her. Then he glanced around the room. "I see Madame Gevers's house has become Mademoiselle Halliday's."

"Yes, women like to put their own feathers in whatever nest they occupy. I had some of my things shipped over. But, as you can see, the furniture is still Nanna's."

"How's your work coming along?"

"I haven't done much, to be honest. I've promised myself to begin in earnest Monday, though." She gestured toward the velvet sofa. "Would you care to sit, Max? We can have an aperitif before we go."

"If you like."

Ida appeared moments later with two glasses of cocktail sherry. Lianne and Max sipped their drinks, seated side by side on the couch.

"How is Tatiana?" she asked.

"Fine. She's well."

"She's a lovely child. I very much enjoyed meeting her."

"And she enjoyed meeting you. She liked you. She found your American traits to her liking."

She gave a smile of amusement. "Am I that different?"

"Yes. Your French is perfect, of course. But, yes, you are different. I find you refreshing. Perhaps Tatiana did, too."

"You've done a remarkable job with her, Max."

He shifted uncomfortably. "She's a good girl. A lot of spirit. Much like you, if I may say so."

"Maybe, when I was younger." Lianne sipped her sherry.

"I knew very little about you before you arrived," Max said. "Everything I heard was secondhand."

She lowered her head. "I don't imagine Alex talked about me much."

"We did have a few conversations about you and . . ."

"My baby?"

"Yes."

Lianne felt a sudden surge of emotion. "It's been fifteen years, but ever since I've been back in Geneva, she's all I've been able to think about." There was a catch in her voice, and she tried to smile to cover her emotion.

Max took her hand, rubbing the back of it with his thumb. Lianne was aware of the intimacy of the gesture. Then he drew it to his lips and kissed her fingers. His eyes showed the depth of his compassion.

"Look at us," Lianne said. "Being sentimental over something long in the past. It's much better to think of the present. Don't you think?"

"Probably."

"I think so. There's a time for remembering. I don't think this is one."

"Do you wish to see Tatiana again," he asked, "or is it easier if you don't?"

She was taken aback. "Max, that's like asking if I want to see you again."

He nodded, acknowledging the comment. "Perhaps it is."

"Well, what do *you* think?"

"I don't want to hurt you," he whispered.

"I'm not a china doll, Monsieur Julen. I won't break."

Now he had to force a smile. "Maybe it's me I should fret about."

Lianne touched his hand affectionately. "Maybe we both worry too much."

"Yes, Lianne, I believe you are right."

THE RESTAURANT in Coppet was more suggestive of an *auberge* than a fine restaurant. The building was old and rustic with low ceilings and rough-hewn floorboards. They were seated at a corner table next to a window with flounced curtains.

Max asked Lianne to tell him about her theories on Shelley, wanting to know her mind as well as her emotions. He watched her in the candlelight, speaking in English with animation about the poet and his connection with Geneva. But it wasn't her words that fascinated him—they hardly mattered—it was her enthusiasm, and the fact that she was so keen to share it with him.

"You're a true romantic, Lianne," he said with admiration.

"Aren't you?"

"I'm a businessman, but perhaps there's a corner of my soul that's romantic, as well."

"That's not nearly so important as being humane, caring and kind."

Max sipped the last of his wine, watching her intently, savoring her beauty. She was a remarkably lovely woman. His eyes roamed her face, taking her in. He was fascinated with her mouth, the loose strands of hair that lay about her neck, and the vaguely sorrowful eyes that had grown animated.

They had finished their meal and the dishes had been cleared. The waiter dutifully swept off bread crumbs and poured the last drop of wine into Lianne's glass. Then he served coffee. Lianne continued to talk, sounding a bit overeager, like a schoolgirl just released from an imposed silence.

Studying her, Max realized how strongly he was drawn to her. The vague attraction had grown more intense. The woman had gotten to him. He felt his heart slipping away.

The past week he had thought about her often, finding himself eager to see her. And the evening was even better than he had hoped for. Lianne was now rounded, complete in his mind. In getting to know her he was finding more dimensions to her personality, more layers, and each was still more rewarding than the last.

It was all coming as a great surprise to him. Over the past few years, since losing Catrina, he had managed to desensitize himself toward women. It hadn't been by conscious intent, but rather through a plodding inevitability of circumstances. He hadn't worried about his lack of interest, though. He simply accepted it as normal, desirable even.

Lianne paused in her discourse. "I've been running on, haven't I?"

"No, not at all."

"You're being polite. You don't care about my dissertation ... and you shouldn't." He put his hand on hers. "Max, we are friends, aren't we?"

"Yes, of course."

"Friends can risk the truth, can't they?"

"Of course." He slowly turned the stem of his empty wineglass between his fingers, watching her.

"Knowing you, having you as a friend, has been very important to me. You've made coming back here much easier."

"And ...?"

"And I want you to know that my feelings for you have nothing to do with what happened between Alex and me. I consider that a separate issue." She hesitated.

"There's a 'but' coming. I hear it in your voice."

"Yes, you're right. There is. The 'but' is, I feel I have unfinished business."

"With Alex."

"Yes."

He set his empty wineglass aside. "What is it you want?"

"I'm not really sure. That's the problem. I feel the need for finality, for ... something. I just don't know what."

He listened, watching her, hating what he was hearing, without being surprised. There was no point in denying the truth, no matter how much it disappointed him. He couldn't wish away what was. "I get the feeling you would like my advice."

"I don't know. I'm not even sure if it's fair to ask. But I trust you, Max."

He winced inwardly at her words, for in fact, he felt a scoundrel. He was raising her child, the child who had tormented her for years, and he'd said nothing. She trusted him, yet he was keeping the greatest secret imaginable from her. What kind of trust did that merit? He lowered his head. "I wish I was worthy of the compliment."

"Of course you are," she replied.

He took a deep breath. "What is it you want to know, Lianne?"

"Should I try to see Alex, write him perhaps?"

He drew a long breath, considering his words before speaking. "He knows you're here."

The statement brought her up short. "How?"

"We spoke by phone the other day. I told him."

"What did he say?"

"Well, obviously the news caught him by surprise. He was unaware of your grandmother's death. Perhaps he'll come to Geneva. Perhaps not. I really don't know what he'll do."

"If you had to guess..." she prompted.

"I can't say. Honestly. Alex isn't easy to predict. He—what's that expression in English? He marches to a different drummer."

Lianne lowered her eyes. "Yes, I know." She ran her finger over the rim of her wineglass. Then she looked up, bravely trying to smile. "I'm sorry I brought him up. He really doesn't matter."

"Of course he does."

"No, why should he? Fifteen years. That's a long time, Max."

He wasn't as sure that was true as she seemed to think, but he saw no point in arguing with her. Lianne's feelings were obvious enough, although the implications were unclear. As she had suggested, many years had intervened. But she'd started out by saying Alex had nothing to do with her friendship with him. What, really, did that mean? And, more important, what did he want it to mean?

"Let's change the subject," she said, once more touching his hand.

"Your happiness is important to me, Lianne."

She smiled. "That's quite a compliment, considering how briefly we've known each other. And I want you to know the feeling is entirely mutual."

Max covered her hands with his as he looked into her silver eyes. He felt joy, but also as if his heart might break. And it was already too late to turn back. Lianne Halliday intrigued him, moved him. Already he wanted more of her.

MAX DIDN'T SAY much on the drive back to Geneva, and Lianne could tell that their conversation had put him in a mood, though which kind she didn't know for sure. Perhaps she had put too great of a burden on him, imposed on a friendship that was still fragile.

Several times she started to comment, to address the issue directly. But she decided that to say something would only lead to more of the same. Silence seemed more appropriate.

"Lianne," he said when they were nearing the rue Beauregard, "would it be too much to ask you to dine with me and Tatiana some evening?"

She considered the question, resolving to put her sensitivities behind her. "No, I would enjoy it."

"Tatiana likes you, but I don't want being around her to be a problem for you."

"Not at all."

They came to the house. Max double-parked, putting on his warning lights. He started to open the door, but

Lianne stopped him, touching his arm. "It's not necessary for you to get out. I'll see myself in."

"Are you sure?"

"Yes, really."

She looked at his shadowed face in the dim light of a distant lamppost. She could feel the emotion in him, unspoken and clawing. Alex had affected them both. A feeling of compassion and gratitude came over her. She wanted to reach out to Max.

"When we have dinner with Tatiana," she said, "why don't we do it here? I'll cook for you...if Ida will let me."

He gave a little laugh at her comment. Then he took her hand. "That would be very nice."

Lianne studied the contours of his face. There was an intensity about him that suggested an inner struggle. "It was a lovely evening," she told him. "I very much value your friendship."

"And I value yours, Lianne."

He kissed her fingers. His tenderness touched her. For a fleeting instant she wanted him to kiss her mouth. Desire for him raced through her, but she forced it aside. Instead she touched his cheek and slipped from the car and into the brisk night air.

# CHAPTER FOUR

MAX SAT in his favorite chair in the salon, looking over the financial reports of their Belgian subsidiary as he half listened to Tatiana speaking with Maria in the back of the house. The girl's voice grew increasingly more emphatic, her deliberate French phrases interspersed with an occasional word in Spanish for emphasis. He could tell Tatiana was beginning to see herself as the woman of the house, though in so many respects she was still a child.

Max had noticed a definite change in the girl in the week since his dinner with Lianne in Coppet. When he got home that night Tatiana was asleep on the sofa, having tried unsuccessfully to wait up for him. He had awakened her so that she could go to her bed, and she immediately assaulted him with a barrage of questions about Lianne, some betraying her jealousy. It was all too evident that the girl's feelings were mixed.

In the days since, Max hadn't brought up Lianne, though Tatiana found occasion to mention her. Then, one afternoon while he was in his office overlooking the Place du Rhône, Lianne had dropped by to say hello. She had been to a meeting with Pronier just up the street and said she'd decided on saving a postage stamp by coming in person to invite him and Tatiana to dinner.

Max had been delighted to see her. She had worn a business suit, and her pale hair was pulled back in an elegant chignon. She had looked remarkably lovely. He had ushered her into his large office with a view of the Pont du Mont-Blanc, but she had insisted she could only stay for a few moments.

"I wanted to make good my promise and have you to dinner," she had explained.

"It's a promise I wouldn't hold you to," he'd told her with a smile.

"I know. But it's something I want to do. I'd like to see Tatiana, as well as you."

Max had read a certain eagerness in her manner, making him wonder if Tatiana had become important to her. This would be a mixed blessing, he knew, but he could hardly stand in the way of such a development. So the engagement had been set for Friday evening, and Lianne had left almost immediately. For a long time afterward Max had sat at his desk, oblivious to the throb of Geneva's commercial district, his thoughts entirely on Lianne Halliday.

If he wasn't already obsessed, her visit and invitation had made it almost impossible not to think about her. She popped into his mind at the most awkward moments. More than one business conversation had floundered when his thoughts wandered to the appealing young American, who coincidentally happened to be the mother of his child.

Tatiana had taken news of the dinner invitation with cautious delight. She was naturally pleased to be included, but had speculated openly on Lianne's feelings toward them.

"If she was once Uncle Alex's girlfriend," she'd said, "she may have a mind to become yours, as well, Papa."

"That's rather impertinent, Tatiana. I hope you have the maturity to keep such thoughts to yourself."

She'd been miffed by his response, but it didn't prevent her from raising the subject of Lianne Halliday in the days before the dinner. Now that Friday had finally come Tatiana was in a dither.

From the back of the house Max heard the housekeeper, who was normally a rather circumspect individual, fire off a salvo in Spanish, followed by a rather precipitous exodus from Tatiana's room. He didn't understand what the commotion was all about, but it was obvious enough that Maria's patience with the girl had worn thin.

A moment later Tatiana appeared in the sitting room, her hands on her hips, a very annoyed expression on her face. She was wearing a pink silk dress, and her feet were bare.

"Father, you simply must do something about Maria."

"What has she done?"

The girl turned around to show him her back, as though that were all the response that was required. The zipper was halfway down, her hair hung with bits of ribbon interspersed in her thick brown-blond tresses.

"She wouldn't zip your dress? Come here, then, and I'll do it."

Tatiana turned around. "No, Papa," she said irritably. "My hair. She won't fix it the way I asked. She insists on doing it as if I was ten years old."

"What's wrong with it?"

She stomped her foot with exasperation and turned her back to him again. "Don't you see? I wanted ribbons, sexy ribbons, not hair like Shirley Temple."

"Sexy ribbons?"

She looked at him. "Ribbons like a woman, not like a child."

Max restrained a smile. "And what, pray tell, is the difference?"

"Oh, Father, you're no better than Maria!" She started to stomp away, but he called out, stopping her.

"Perhaps the problem is in your manner, Tatiana."

Her hands were on her hips again. "I showed her a picture of what I want. What more could I do?"

"You could learn patience."

"That won't help. Just because Mummy trusted her, she thinks she must keep things as they've always been. She treats me like a child."

"Nonsense."

"It's true!" She glared at him, shaking her head. "You don't understand. Miss Halliday will be beautiful tonight, and I must be, too."

"It's not a competition."

Now Tatiana smiled. "Father, sometimes you amaze me."

There was enough maturity and superiority in her tone that Max felt a bit the fool without knowing why he should.

"All women are in competition at all times. It's a given fact," she explained.

Max contemplated her, realizing that indeed she was growing up. "And what would you have me do about Maria?"

"Simply tell her that she's not to consider herself my *dueña*."

"Is it boys we're discussing, then?"

"No," she replied emphatically. "I believe it was me and Miss Halliday we were talking about."

"Yes, that's right. Your competition with Lianne."

There was consternation on Tatiana's face. "The problem, Papa, is that you don't understand women."

With that she retreated down the hall, pulling the ribbons from her hair as she went. "As soon as I get this hair fixed, I'll be ready to go," she called back to him. "You're going to put on a dark suit, aren't you? After all, it *is* Miss Halliday we're going to dine with, isn't it?"

Max put his report aside and sat a moment longer in bemusement as he thought about what Tatiana had said. It was a bizarre situation he'd put himself in. He was permitting his and Tatiana's relationship with Lianne Halliday to continue, knowing there was a strong possibility it could end in disaster. And yet he felt helpless to do anything else but proceed on the course he'd set.

LIANNE PUT THE BOWL of pink and yellow roses in the middle of the table and turned it first one way, then the other. She had spent the better part of the afternoon preparing dinner and getting herself ready. Max and Tatiana would be arriving soon, and she was surprisingly nervous—more about the girl than Max.

The decision to go to his office with the invitation hadn't come easily. She had thought at length whether it was wise to invite the two of them into her life. In the end she had let her instincts guide her. Now she could only hope it wasn't a mistake.

Lianne looked over the table, walking slowly around it counterclockwise, straightening the silver that Ida had spent the morning polishing. Nanna's heavy sterling candelabrum with half a dozen large candles burned brightly on the sideboard, giving the room a warm glow. There was a single candlestick in a slender holder at the end of the table where the three place settings were clustered, but it remained unlit.

Stepping back for a final glance around the room, Lianne pressed her palms against the front of her long skirt. Deciding everything was all right, she slowly backed into the adjoining sitting room, turned and walked nervously across the floor.

Nanna's console radio was playing softly as Lianne went to the fireplace, which was purely ornamental. Nanna had had the flue sealed years ago with the installation of a modern heating system. The flowers Lianne had bought gave the room a pleasant scent.

Finding everything in order, she went to the entry hall, where she caught a glimpse of her own image in the mirror over the pier table. Her hyacinth silk blouse with a small tie at the neck looked almost gray in the muted light. She touched the bow and looked at her face and hair, which was pulled up off her neck in a loose chignon.

Her cheeks felt warm and, as she moved closer to the mirror, she saw the color in them. She stared at her image for a moment, seeing a serenity that was deceiving. After all the quiescent, unremarkable years, she felt something different building inside.

Just then she heard the sound of an automobile and went to the front window. Max's Mercedes was pulling into a space nearly in front of the house. On the passenger side she saw the vaguest outlines of the girl's face. Tatiana seemed to be gazing directly at her. They stared at each other for a moment, forging an uncertain connection.

Then Max got out of the car and, as he walked around to the passenger side, Lianne pulled back from the window. For the first time her fear was as great as her expectation. But she gathered herself and, going to the door, waited until she heard them, then opened it, permitting a rush of cold air into the house.

Tatiana, enveloped in fur, had just reached the top step. Warm light from the house fell on her pale skin. Her hair was piled on top of her head, elongating her face and transforming the girlish features into more womanly proportions. The image was totally at odds with the child she had met at the Geneva Academy of Dance.

Lianne glanced down at the girl's mink-clad figure. "Tatiana, how elegant you look!" They clasped hands, and Lianne brushed her cheek against the girl's in the European manner.

"*Bon soir,* Lianne," Tatiana said breezily. "It's Mummy's coat, and Papa let me wear it this one night when I showed him I'm as tall as she was." Her French was crisp and had an unmistakable tone of maturity.

The girl went on in, and Lianne turned to Max, who was arriving at the top of the stairs. His smile was a bit weary and, despite the deep lines at the corners of his eyes, he looked so much like Alex in the dim light that it gave her a momentary start.

"Ah," he said with seeming pleasure, then added in English, "how lovely you look." He kissed her on the left cheek, and the scent of his cologne hung heavily in the brisk night air. She glanced into his eyes, noticing in the light how blue they were, and not like Alex's at all. He smiled, and they went into the house together.

"I'm afraid I've indulged her a bit with the coat," he said as they both watched Tatiana, who had moved on and was staring into the dining room at the candlelight. "I promised her she could wear it the first winter she reached a hundred and sixty-eight centimeters. We measured, and she fell only a few millimeters short. I thought you might understand my indulging her better than the society ghouls at the theater or the symphony."

"She looks lovely. Definitely beyond the dress-up stage, if still a little young for mink."

Max nodded, and Tatiana turned toward them. Seeing that they were watching her, she pirouetted in their direction, the tails of the coat flying out from her slender legs.

"How beautiful and romantic you've made Madame Gevers's house, Lianne," she said with self-assurance. She stopped in front of her father and turned her back to him so that he could help her off with the coat. "Did you go to all the trouble just for us?"

"Yes, just for you."

Tatiana looked back at her with a gamine smile as Max hung the coat in the hall closet. "Too bad Uncle Alex isn't here to appreciate it."

"We can appreciate it just as much," Max said, as he removed his dark cashmere coat.

"I didn't say we wouldn't, did I, Papa?"

He hung his coat beside Tatiana's and closed the closet door. "Don't forget our bargain," he said to the girl.

Tatiana gave him a look of annoyance but didn't comment.

Max turned to Lianne. "Personally I've been looking forward to this evening all week."

"So have I," Lianne said, glancing at Tatiana, who turned away, her chin rising ever so slightly. She wasn't sure of the emotion she saw, but there was pique of some sort. "Shall we go into the salon?" she asked. "What would you two like to drink?"

Max asked for Scotch. Tatiana went to the chair that had always been Nanna's favorite, smoothing her silk skirt as she sat.

"And you?" Lianne asked. "What would you like, Tatiana?"

"What are you taking?" she asked in English.

"May wine, I think."

"Then I shall, as well." She glanced over at Max, who had sat on the couch. "If I may, Papa."

"A little won't hurt."

"May I help with the drinks?" Tatiana asked.

"If you wish."

With a wry smile at Max, Lianne led the girl back to the kitchen. Tatiana leaned against the heavy kitchen table as Lianne went to the refrigerator and took the small ice tray from the freezer.

"You look very pretty tonight, Lianne."

She glanced back at the girl. "Why, thank you."

"I think Papa thinks so, as well."

"Do you?"

"You must have noticed yourself. And you certainly wanted him to think you're beautiful."

Lianne turned around. "I usually try to look my best. That's normal enough."

"I was telling Papa that this evening, as a matter of fact. But he didn't know that about women . . . or he pretended not to. I think men don't understand women very well, Papa included."

"I don't know that that's true, Tatiana. Your father's a sensitive and caring person. I think most women like that sort of man."

"Do you like him, then?"

"Yes. Very much."

"But you don't love him, as you did Uncle Alex?"

The bluntness of the question came as a surprise, and she realized that the girl was probably jealous. If so, she would have to deal with Tatiana very carefully indeed. "Your uncle and I had a different sort of relationship."

"Papa says the same thing. But I don't believe it."

"What don't you believe?" Lianne went to the sink with the tray, trying not to let on how unsettling she found the girl's comments.

"Don't think I'm jealous," Tatiana said, ignoring the question. "Papa thinks that. But it's not true. I know you must have loved Uncle Alex very much, because he's the type that women love."

Lianne couldn't help herself. She turned around again and looked at Tatiana incredulously.

"But you're older now," the girl went on, "Papa's here and Uncle Alex isn't."

"Tatiana..."

"I don't mean to offend you, Lianne. It's only that I've always heard Americans say what they think, and when you speak with them, you don't have to play the silly games of politeness."

"Politeness has its place...even among Americans."

"Then I offended you?"

She took a deep breath before she spoke. "Not really, but I don't think my personal relationships are a proper subject for discussion."

"I'm sorry. It wasn't something I could say in front of Papa, and I didn't know if we would have a chance to talk again tonight."

"Then maybe it would be a good idea for us to have a nice long chat sometime." Lianne turned back to the sink, dropping some ice cubes into a highball glass. She poured in some Scotch, some soda, then handed the glass to Tatiana. "Take the drink in to your father and I'll bring in our wine."

She watched the girl go, marveling alternately at the child's audacity and her insight, though Tatiana's thinly veiled jealousy concerned her. Lianne was beginning to realize that her own sensitivities weren't the only ones to be considered.

As Tatiana entered the sitting room, Max noted with amusement the rather stiff, overly careful way Tatiana carried his cocktail. She handed it to him and returned to her chair.

"Lianne is very pretty this evening, *n'est-ce pas,* Papa?"

"Yes, very."

"And she's very nice."

Max took the drink, hearing in her voice a warning note of secret thoughts. "You've decided you like her, then?"

*"Oui,"* she said, inhaling the word in the characteristically Swiss manner.

"You see. There needn't be a competition."

Tatiana smiled as though what he said was very silly. "No, Papa. There is always competition. The only question for a woman is if it will be friendly."

"Is your competition with Lianne friendly?"

She looked at him thoughtfully. "I don't know yet. It might be, but it might not be, as well. I should think it depends on her as much as on me."

"Then I recommend you do your utmost. I'm confident that she likes you and will do her part."

Just then Lianne came in from the kitchen with a bottle of wine and two tumblers on a small tray. She was smiling, and Max noticed again how radiantly beautiful she was.

"Here we are," she said. She put the tray on a side table near Nanna's chair, where Tatiana was sitting.

Max observed his daughter, who was watching Lianne very closely as she poured the wine. Tatiana graciously accepted the glass, then silently waited as Lianne went to sit on the couch next to Max.

"What shall we drink to?" Lianne asked, holding the tumbler up in front of her.

"I think to Uncle Alex," Tatiana said before Max could speak. "After all, he's the only one in the family who isn't here."

Max and Lianne exchanged looks.

"All right," she said cheerfully. "To Alex."

Max raised his Scotch silently and took a sip. His brother was the last person on earth he felt like drinking to just then, but Tatiana had left them little choice.

THE DINNER CONVERSATION was a bit awkward at first, but they got through the meal and, once the table was cleared, Lianne and Tatiana managed to settle into an easy patter. Max mostly listened as his two dinner companions worked their way through a host of subjects—ballet, fashion, skiing, American music, poetry and the immaturity of Swiss boys.

Though the conversation was polite enough on the surface, Max felt an undeniable tension—the competition his daughter had so precociously spoken of earlier. Though there were smiles and deferential sounds from both of them, there was also an edge to their voices, especially Tatiana's.

The girl's perspicacious observation about feminine competition did give him an insight into her he hadn't seen before. She had grown into a young woman almost overnight. Until now he had naively focused on the adolescent veneer, missing entirely what had developed under the surface.

As he would have expected, Lianne was handling the competition with greater maturity and a certain ironic bemusement. But there was no doubt there were intense energies at work. Max would have liked to flatter himself in thinking he was the object of the competition, but he knew that was only partially true. He was little more than a convenient excuse.

"What do you think?" Tatiana asked, turning to him unexpectedly. "You've known more Americans than I."

He had been caught, his mind wandering, the thread of the conversation lost. "What do I think about what?"

"Weren't you listening? Lianne said she's not a very typical American. I couldn't say myself because I've hardly known any."

Max considered the question, looking at Lianne, whose skin had a delicious, healthy glow in the candlelight. "I suppose it's true, in a way. She's not typical, but in other ways she *is* very American."

"How?" Lianne said, gazing at him over the rim of her wineglass.

His eyes settled on her, and he was very aware of her appeal—so much so that her question was virtually lost.

"Yes. How, Papa?"

Max looked at Tatiana. "Well . . . there's a certain audaciousness that's part of the American character. Lianne is more subtle than most, but I see the quality in her nevertheless." He turned to her. "I hope my bluntness isn't offensive."

She smiled. "No, of course not."

He felt the connection between them that had been forged the night they'd dined in Coppet. She seemed very much his ally and, as always, his friend. He regretted more strongly than ever that they weren't alone.

"How about Papa, Lianne?" Tatiana said. "Would you say he's typically Swiss?"

Lianne glanced at Max, then Tatiana. "Admittedly I don't know him well, but from what I've seen, I would have to say yes."

"I should be flattered, I suppose," Max said. "And if I had the arrogance of the French, nothing else would cross my mind. But I'm not sure what *you* mean by it, Lianne."

"All the best things, of course. My mother was Swiss, you know, so it's at least partially my heritage, too."

"And there was your grandmother."

"Yes, I was as close to Nanna as anyone in the world."

"And what about Uncle Alex?" Tatiana interjected. "Is he typically Swiss?"

"No," Lianne replied without hesitation. "Not in most ways—unless he's changed, of course."

Tatiana's insistence on bringing Alex into everything was beginning to annoy Max. He gave her a look, but she turned away. "There hasn't been so much talk about my dear brother in years," he mumbled into his brandy glass.

"I don't think he's very Swiss, either," Tatiana said, ignoring her father's comment. "Not so provincial as we usually are. He's been everywhere, done everything there is to do. And he has known many ladies, too, if you don't mind me saying so."

"Tatiana!" Max said.

"I'm sure it's true."

"What would you know about such things?"

"It's pretty obvious, isn't it?" She turned to Lianne. "Don't you think it's obvious?"

"Tatiana," Max said, "this isn't an appropriate subject of discussion. Please let the matter drop."

The girl leaned back as though she'd been stung, pouting in a way that was more in keeping with the years she'd been through than the ones ahead. With the tension in the room acute, Nanna's grandfather clock struck the half hour.

"How about some more tea?" Lianne asked Tatiana, trying to fill the uneasy silence. She lifted the pot.

"No, thank you."

Lianne poured a bit more into her own cup. "Max, can I get you some more coffee?"

"No, thank you very much. I'll just finish my cognac." He lifted his wrist and pushed back his cuff to look at his thin gold watch.

"Please don't say it's time to go," Tatiana said. "Tomorrow's Sunday. No school and no work."

"I think we may have outstayed our welcome."

"No, not at all," Lianne said.

His expression told her he would like to stay, but it was Tatiana he was thinking of.

The girl yawned, unable to repress it.

"You see," Max said. "You're getting sleepy. Between the wine and the hour..."

"Oh, we mustn't go, Papa. You've hardly had a chance to talk to Lianne. I shouldn't spoil the evening for you."

It was a generous observation, and it pleased him. His own interests had, by circumstances, been shunted aside.

He noticed that Lianne looked content enough. She had taken Tatiana in stride and didn't seem to have been as bothered by his daughter's behavior as he.

"If you're tired, Tatiana," she offered, "you can lie down. I have a guest room, so you're very welcome to nap for a while if you wish."

The girl looked at each of them, probably trying to decide between pride and the social exigencies of the situation. "Perhaps I will, then, if it's all right. I doubt very much that I shall sleep, but the wine has made me drowsy, I admit. And I think Papa would like to stay."

"Come," Lianne said, rising. "Let me show you the way."

Max rose as the two left the table.

"Pour yourself some more cognac if you wish," Lianne called back to him as they left the room.

Taking her cue, he went to the sideboard and poured himself some brandy, then wandered into the sitting room. The opera that had been playing on the radio most of the evening had given way to symphonic music. It sounded like Debussy.

Max sat at one end of the couch and thought about Lianne. He was happy to see that Tatiana's references to Alex hadn't seemed to upset her. That was good, but it did point out how fragile the situation was. And the fact remained—he was playing with fire.

Ironically he was sitting in the very room where everyone's fate had been decided. The entire family had come to Madame Gevers's to discuss the baby. He glanced over at the fireplace and could almost see his father leaning with an elbow on the mantel between two of the woman's sacred clocks, his fingers thrust into his vest pocket, the antiquated gold watch chain he'd worn longer than Max's memory, draped across his stomach.

"Marguerite," Alberte Julen had said, "I've come to make you, your daughter and granddaughter a proposal."

The old woman had waited, maintaining her dignity despite the embarrassing circumstances. Max was sitting on the couch where he was now, Catrina beside him. Alex was back in the corner, as silent and small as he could be.

"Alberte," Madame Gevers had said, "I take it you're referring to Lianne and Alex's baby."

Alberte shifted his feet and nodded. *"Oui."*

"And?"

The old man cleared his throat. "I understand your Eloise plans to put the baby out for adoption, and it occurred to me that a child of my blood—and your blood, Marguerite—shouldn't spend its life with a strange family abroad."

"Eloise won't consent to marriage, Alberte."

"No, no. They're too young. I realize that. But that doesn't mean the child should be abandoned."

Madame Gevers lifted her chin and waited.

"I think the child should be here in Geneva with us. In the family." He gestured toward Max and Catrina. "My children will take the baby...if you can convince Eloise."

Max lay his hand on the cushion where Catrina had sat that evening, remembering how she had interjected at that point.

"Perhaps you are aware, *madame,*" she had said, scooting to the edge of her seat, "that I cannot have children. Max and I have talked of adopting a baby, but we've both been reluctant. And now there is this child of my husband's blood, and the daughter of a family we know. Nothing could be more suitable for us or the child. If it will not be with its mother, better it be with me and Max."

And Madame Gevers, in her wisdom, looked back at Alex in the shadows as she spoke. "You realize you're proposing that the child's father become its uncle, and its uncle become its father. I wonder how a young, impressionable mind would deal with such a situation."

"We've discussed this at length," Catrina said. "Alex is content to be the child's uncle, and Max and I would love desperately to be its parents. There's no reason why it should ever be otherwise."

"And perhaps it would be best if your granddaughter were never to know," Alberte said solemnly. "I don't know the laws in America, but I should think all arrangements could be made by Eloise.''

Marguerite Gevers had sat in the chair Tatiana had sat in that evening, her wrinkled hands on her lap, her face a mask of reflection. After a long time, she had turned her eyes to Alex. ''And what do you think of this, young man?''

Max remembered Alex's voice as surprisingly clear and strong. He looked back into the shadowed corner where his brother had sat fifteen years before.

''If it pleases my father, my brother, my dear sister-in-law and you, Madame Gevers, it pleases me,'' he had said with a diplomatic flair that was to become the trademark of his life.

There was another long silence, then the old woman had looked first at Catrina, then at Alberte. ''I shall speak to Eloise of your proposal,'' she'd said.

Max had felt his wife's nails dig into the flesh of his arm. Now he felt his eyes fill with tears. Then he heard a voice.

''Max, you look so sad.''

It was Lianne in the candlelight, looking at him from across the room, her face as innocent and beloved as Tatiana's. He saw the girl in her; he saw the resemblance. More strongly than ever before, his guilt overwhelmed him. He was withholding a terribly important fact. Were it not for Tatiana and her feelings, he would have confessed all, right then, at that very moment.

## CHAPTER FIVE

MAX ROSE TO HIS FEET. "If I look sad, I must apologize, Lianne. I'm afraid we haven't been very good guests."

"Don't be silly. Are you all right?"

"Yes, I was just worrying about Tatiana."

She sat on the sofa beside him. "You shouldn't. She's growing up. It's natural for a girl to test her wings a bit. And I don't suppose she's much used to sharing you."

"That's true." He took her hand. "You weren't offended?"

"Of course not. Tatiana's a charming girl. I find her delightful. I just wish she didn't see me as a threat." Lianne's expression grew earnest. "I've gotten used to being around a young person Alexandra's age. The sting has worn off. I'd like very much to be Tatiana's friend."

He squeezed her fingers. Lianne looked down at his large hands, sensing his understanding and compassion.

"I'm sure you shall be," he said, barely above a whisper.

She was surprised by the depth of his emotion. The evening, it seemed, had proved difficult for them all. "My plan was to have a quiet little dinner party, but it didn't work out that way, did it?"

Max looked apologetic. "I don't know why Tatiana insists on bringing Alex into everything."

"I think the notion of Alex and me together intrigues her." She looked at Max. "You haven't told her that we had a child."

"No."

Just mentioning the subject brought tears to Lianne's eyes. She tried to smile. Max looked sad again.

"I'm sorry," she said, wiping a tear from the corner of her eye.

"I shouldn't have brought it up," he replied.

"I keep thinking how Alexandra is Tatiana's age, and the fact that they're cousins . . ."

"You and Tatiana will be friends," he said, pressing her hands more firmly. His eyes were almost beseeching, and Lianne didn't understand his emotion at all—unless it was compassion. His concern touched her, though.

"You both need each other. She has no mother," he said, "and you're without your daughter. You're a kind person, full of love. You both have a great deal to give."

Lianne bit her lip. He had addressed an issue she rarely permitted herself to consider—mother love. It was something she always repressed. Many women in her situation would think in terms of marrying and having other children as a way to fill the void. But she never had. Her love, her life, always seemed behind her, not ahead.

Max put his arms around her, and she leaned against him, her face pressed against his shoulder. Max, more than anyone she knew, could understand how she felt.

He rubbed her back with his warm hand as she softly cried. When the ache abated and the tears finally stopped, she took the handkerchief he offered and wiped her cheeks.

His arm was still around her, and he was very close. He touched her hair, and she smelled his cologne with its distinctive old-world scent. His comfort and his affection were reassuring. She looked at him through wet lashes.

He bent closer. She felt his warm breath against her cheek. Then his lips touched the corner of her mouth. They lingered, and he seemed to hesitate as he whispered her name. Then he kissed her deeply, his mouth covering hers.

It was all unexpected yet, in a way, so very natural. His affection seemed an outgrowth of his compassion, and she welcomed it, kissing him back, glad for the comfort she never experienced anymore.

When their lips finally parted, Lianne was breathless. It had been a long time since she had kissed a man with such emotion. The embrace, the contact, had become more than the mutual affection of two lonely people. She sensed it in Max, more even than in herself. There had been desire. She looked into his eyes uncertainly.

He held her face in his hands and made her look at him. "Lianne..."

There were equal parts of joy and anguish in his voice. It so overwhelmed her that she sat frozen, transfixed. His mouth hovered over hers and again he kissed her. It was a delicate, sensual kiss, and it told her more than she was ready to hear. For the first time she felt a little fear and wondered whether this was really what she wanted.

Growing anxious, she put her hand to his cheek and gently eased her mouth from his. He accepted her withdrawal, seeming to understand. They looked at each other, both of them unsure, neither wanting to speak.

As their bodies disengaged, she became aware of her surroundings again—the sitting room, the furniture, the symphonic music playing faintly in the background... and another presence.

Lianne turned toward the hall and saw her standing in the shadows, her pink silk dress and hair, her porcelain skin. Their eyes met. Then Tatiana turned silently and walked back toward Nanna's room.

LIANNE AWOKE to church bells. Nanna's house, Geneva, the world at large seemed very ancient beside the world of her dreams. Moments earlier she had been a girl, younger even than Tatiana, and she was at home, though the place wasn't at all like Weston. It was more like the Maryland countryside where her mother had taken her for several weeks the summer after her father had died.

Eloise Halliday and Lianne had visited the farm of some friends for a change of scene. For several weeks she had lived a sort of Huck Finn existence. That experience had been the apogee of her childhood. And the images of that carefree summer had frequently found their way into her dreams.

Why her subconscious mind had taken her to rural Maryland with its rolling hills, tree-lined creeks, hidden ponds and remote deserted barns, she wasn't sure. Perhaps it was for a reprieve, an escape from the mink-clad woman-child of the night before.

Lianne had lain awake the previous night, trying to convince herself that Max's overture had been a spontaneous expression of emotion—the same emotion that she felt. But the notion had been only half-convincing, and now, with the church bells ringing outside in the crystalline air, she remembered the look of desire on his face. His interest in her was romantic. There was no doubt about it.

After Tatiana had seen them kissing, Max had gone back to Nanna's room for a word with the girl. Lianne had no idea what was said, but they were in there for a very long time. When they finally came out, Tatiana was contrite, shy and seemed embarrassed. The assurance with which she had arrived only a few hours before was gone, and Lianne had immediately felt sorry for her.

Max had soon announced that they had to leave. There was a brief exchange of courtesies, with Tatiana doing what was socially correct under her father's watchful eye. And at the door Lianne had taken the initiative, embracing the girl and pressing her face against her fiery cheek. Then, as Tatiana had gone out, Max had kissed Lianne briefly and affectionately.

"I'll call you soon," he'd said, smiling. Then he had left.

Lianne rolled onto her side and stared out the window at the pale gray sky. She remembered his face in the candlelight, the glimmer of emotion in his misty eyes. She felt his lips. But gnawing in the back of her mind was another presence. Though he seemed remote, more a spiritual force than a living man, Alex was there.

It had been that way for the past fifteen years. Whatever she was doing in life, wherever she was, Alex always seemed to be in the shadows. Nanna's death and Lianne's return to Geneva had given her the opportunity to deal with his memory once and for all. The need had become even more urgent because of her growing feelings for Max. But what could she do? Alex showed no signs of wanting to cooperate—not that he had any obligation. After all, he had a life of his own.

But Lianne felt the need to do something. If Alex was to be exorcised, it was up to her. Jumping out of bed, she bathed, pulled her hair back with a tortoiseshell clip, slipped into jeans and a soft blue turtleneck and went into the kitchen for some breakfast. Ida was finishing up the dishes from the night before.

"How was the dinner party?" the housekeeper asked, a bit more cheerily than usual.

"It was lovely. I had a good time."

Ida acknowledged the news with a silent nod.

"I think after breakfast I'll lease a car and go for a ride in the country," Lianne announced.

"What a shame you decided not to keep *madame's* automobile, *mademoiselle*. It would come in handy at a time like this."

"Posh, Ida. I'm not one to be driven around by a chauffeur, and I certainly wouldn't have driven that monster myself."

"Well, anyway, it should be a good day for a drive. Not so cloudy as earlier in the week," the housekeeper replied. "What can I serve you for breakfast?"

"Just some bread and jam."

"*Du café, mademoiselle?*"

"Please."

Lianne had managed to imbue herself with a sense of determination. She quickly drank her *café au lait* from the large bowl Ida put in front of her, had a few pieces of bread with jam and a wedge of cheese, then she was off, taking her suede jacket.

"I'll be home in a few hours," she told Ida on her way out. "Don't wait lunch."

"As you wish, *mademoiselle*."

THE RENAULT SEDAN lacked the personality of Alex's old Deux Chevaux, but it was taking her where she wanted to go and gave her a sense of freedom. Lianne had been thinking of the Col de Jambaz ever since her return, and it finally occurred to her that to return to the spot where she had made love with Alex, and where Alexandra had been conceived, would liberate her once and for all.

She drove steadily toward Thonon, recognizing land-
marks, though she couldn't be sure if the recollection was
from the time she'd gone with Alex. At a wine shop she'd
purchased a small bottle of cheap brandy under the theory that the peasant, Gonnet's, attitudes would be the
same. The brandy might smooth her way as it had for
Alex.

With some difficulty she found the road leading to the
pass and, as she climbed, she began worrying about the
reception she would get. Would Gonnet even be there?
He wasn't a young man even fifteen years ago. She wondered if he would remember Alex, though it was certain
he wouldn't remember her. There had been other girls
before her, and perhaps there were others after her, too.

There were several places along the road that might
have been the turnoff point. Lianne didn't remember a
distinctive landmark. As she recalled, it was just a track
running off to the south. And the spot could have
changed considerably over the years.

Eventually she realized that she had gone too far, so
she turned around, heading back down the mountain
road. She descended the valley more slowly, this time
looking up at the collateral valleys as much as the road-
side itself. At a point where the topography looked
promising she searched diligently, finally finding a rut-
ted side road half overgrown with grass.

Turning the Renault into the track, she went less than
fifty yards before encountering a closed gate. She hadn't
recalled a gate the last time, but it could have been open
or built since her visit fifteen years earlier. It didn't look
terribly old, but it was hard to tell.

There was a sign indicating that the land was private
property. Lianne felt a deep disappointment, having
come all that way, but she still had the bottle of brandy,

which was a passport of sorts. And even if Gonnet wasn't in residence, perhaps the new occupant would be equally amenable.

Lianne got out of the car to see if the gate could be opened and found that it was simply secured by a large double loop of heavy-gauged wire. Unfastening it, she swung the gate open and returned to the car.

It was apparent that the track was little used, and the farther she went the more apprehensive she became. Eventually she arrived at the small house and found it deserted. Gonnet, Alex's wizened little friend, was gone and nobody was there to replace him.

The windows and doors were boarded up, and the grass was high all around the structure, which was in even greater disrepair than she recalled. The table that had sat under the tree was gone. There was no sign of life. No chickens, no cat. The little farmhouse that had lived so vividly in her memory all these years was abandoned and decaying. Lianne turned off the engine and let the silence of the place envelop her.

She tried to find meaning in what she saw. Gonnet, she decided, was dead, gone like her own youth. The mountain itself seemed unchanged, but it would stand forever. The mountain hardly mattered.

The house, though, was something like a living thing, like the old man. One night he had died, perhaps while she was studying for an exam or grading papers in her little rented house in Storrs, Connecticut. And the morning of his funeral, perhaps Alexandra was riding her bicycle along the sidewalk of some tree-shaded street in an unknown town, chased by a puppy whose name Lianne didn't know.

And when they came to the house to throw the old man's things in boxes and cart away his furniture, perhaps Alex was in Africa, sitting on the veranda of an old hotel reading *Le Monde* and drinking gin and tonics brought my waiters with coal-black skin.

She looked through the trees where Alex had driven the Deux Chevaux. She could see the wall along where the track had run. It was falling down in places and the grass stood high against it. Starting the car, she proceeded ahead, following the barely visible ruts where she could.

She stopped where Alex had and got out. It was too late in the season for wildflowers, though she saw a few scattered blossoms. There was no goat. She locked the car and began walking along the path leading up the mountainside.

Lianne wanted to retrace their steps, to relive it as best she could. She doubted she would find the mountain hut, though she hoped she would. Her memories of that earlier day were vivid now. The mountain under her feet, the alpine air, the vista brought it back more sharply than was possible in years of imagining and dreaming.

She looked up at the sky. Large puffy clouds drifted lazily overhead. There were no thunderheads on the horizon, no promise of anything extraordinary. But she remembered.

She began wandering off the vague trace of path across the flank of the mountain. The grass was not as lush as the summer grass, but she remembered the feel of it on her naked skin. The bittersweet memories had to be relived if they were to be properly forgotten.

Lianne never found the mountain hut, but she kept climbing all the same. She grew weary from the exertion, but she was determined. Soon she was perspiring, despite the cool mountain air. It took a long time, but finally she came to the top of the ridge line. There, on the grassy summit, she was able to look down at Lac Léman.

In the haze was Geneva, barely visible in the distance. Lianne stood with her hands on her hips, still breathing deeply. Somewhere down the slope behind her was the place where she had been with Alex; ahead was the city where she had made her home for several weeks. It was where Max and Tatiana lived, the people she had grown so close to in the brief time she'd been back to the place of her mother's birth.

Lianne was glad she'd come. It was sad to see Gonnet's little house in disrepair, ravaged by the passage of time, but it helped her to put things into perspective. Her memories wouldn't be the same. This time she had gone to the mountaintop. The future she saw looked different. Alex was far away in Africa. The present was Max.

THE HIKE BACK DOWN the mountain was much easier. On the way Lianne passed a young couple winding their way up the path, holding hands. She exchanged greetings with them, wondering if they were off on a great adventure as she and Alex had been, hoping for their sake it wouldn't end so unhappily.

But she was in a lighthearted mood, more at ease than she'd been since her arrival in Switzerland. The outing had been a very good idea. She felt liberated. Perhaps Alex's hold on her would finally be a thing of the past.

At the foot of the mountain, near where she had left her car, there were a couple of motorbikes parked in the grass. The young lovers had arrived a bit differently than she and Alex had, but that youthful expectation and excitement was undoubtedly much the same.

She drove back to Geneva, with the windows down, letting the cool autumn air blow her hair loose from the clip. She arrived back in the city in the middle of the afternoon. Despite her instructions to the housekeeper, Ida had some soup on the stove and a place was set at the kitchen table.

"I thought in case you hadn't stopped for a bit of food, *mademoiselle,* there should be something warm for you to eat."

With a bemused look Lianne sat down. The soup did smell good, and she was grateful for Ida's thoughtfulness. When the soup bowl was placed before her, she began eating with appetite. Ida cleaned the kitchen. Lianne watched her, feeling sorry for the woman. She'd been with Nanna for forty years and surely felt the loss as keenly as anyone. Poor Ida had been forgotten in the shuffle.

"Why don't you come here and sit with me so that we can talk for a few minutes?" Lianne suggested to her.

The housekeeper looked at her as though Lianne had just made a most improper proposal.

"I don't mean to make you uncomfortable, but surely it wouldn't hurt to chat for a while, woman to woman."

Ida looked completely at a loss.

"Did you and Nanna ever sit and talk?"

"Madame Gevers was my employer, *mademoiselle,* and I her employee. We both understood what that means."

Lianne wasn't going to be deterred. She pointed to the chair at the other side of the table. "Well, I should like to talk to you just the same."

The woman slowly made her way to the chair and sat gingerly on the edge, as though it were made of china. She nervously worked the gnarled fingers of one hand in the palm of the other, her face nearly expressionless as she waited.

"Didn't Nanna ever talk to you about herself? You were together for many years. Surely you shared some of your personal lives."

"Only what was necessary to do my job."

Lianne studied the taciturn countenance. "She never confided in you?"

"I was her employee, not her friend, *mademoiselle.*"

"Are the two exclusive?"

"In the way you suggest, yes, Mademoiselle Halliday."

"Because you prefer it so?"

"Because it is so."

Lianne considered the response. "Are we bound by the way it was with my grandmother, you and I?"

"I am your employee now, *mademoiselle.*"

"I'd like to make some alterations, then."

"As you wish."

"Mindful of your own desires, I'd like our relationship a bit more...democratic, for lack of a better term. Perhaps it's my American upbringing, but I feel more comfortable when things are in the open than when they're hidden."

Ida waited, her expression unchanging.

"I suppose you know little about me except from when I visited the house as a child."

"This is true."

"Did Nanna ever discuss me with you?"

Ida lowered her eyes. "Very little, *mademoiselle.*"

Lianne hesitated, but she had come this far, so she decided to follow through. "Were you aware that I became pregnant here on my last visit? That I gave up my child for adoption?"

The housekeeper nodded without looking at Lianne.

"It's just as well. I thought you had to know, considering all the gnashing of teeth that went on here. But all that's long past."

"It was a family affair and not my business."

"You knew, of course, that Alex Julen was the father."

The woman didn't look up. *"Oui, mademoiselle."*

Lianne could see the conversation was like pulling teeth, but she considered it an opportunity to find out what she could. So she pressed on. "I suppose one reason I'm bringing this up is because I want to know what my grandmother really felt. Even though I saw her regularly after that summer, I never found the courage to ask her what she personally thought. Her first obligation was to my mother, and I had a feeling she went along with the adoption, but I don't think she believed it was right."

"Perhaps."

"Tell me, Ida, what did she think should have been done with my baby?"

The housekeeper looked exceedingly disconcerted. "She never discussed the matter with me, *mademoiselle.*"

Lianne pondered the situation. "No, I suppose she wouldn't. And so you didn't know her wishes for me?"

Ida cleared her throat. "I believe Madame Gevers would have liked to see you marry."

"Marry Alex?"

"Considering your... condition, yes."

"That's the traditional attitude."

"But... if I may, *mademoiselle*..."

"Yes, Ida, what is it?"

"I believe if *madame* could have chosen for you, she would have chosen Monsieur Maximilian Julen, not the other brother. When Maximilian married, that became impossible. But she always was partial to him."

Lianne's brows lifted in surprise. "Max! Really? How do you know? Did Nanna tell you this?"

Again Ida nodded.

"How interesting."

The housekeeper began wringing her hands nervously.

"You've been around for a very long time," Lianne said, "and you know everybody. Tell me what you think of Max Julen."

"I couldn't."

"I want you to."

Ida groaned miserably.

"It won't hurt to say what's in your mind."

"He is a fine gentleman, of course. And would make a very suitable husband."

"A husband? For me? Is that what you're suggesting?"

"You are young and beautiful, *mademoiselle*. He has no wife and the child has no mother."

Lianne spoke quickly. "But that's not enough."

"Monsieur Julen has no lack of opportunity among women. He is very rich and very kind. He is every woman's dream." The housekeeper bit her lip, as though she couldn't believe what she had said. She wouldn't look up at Lianne.

"What do you suppose his desires are, Ida?"

"There is no way for me to know."

"I understand. What do you imagine Nanna would think?"

"She would think the child needs a mother and you are the perfect one."

Lianne sat back in her chair. "My, my, how far we've come! I started the day thinking of Max as a dear friend, and now look what we've come to."

"It was not my wish to say these things, *mademoiselle.*"

"I know, Ida. I've made you play my game. But I didn't mean to make you uncomfortable with my questions."

"Please, *mademoiselle,* do not make me say more!" Ida crossed herself. "Madame Gevers would not approve of this conversation. I'm quite sure."

"That may be, but I'm glad we talked."

"May I return to my work now?"

"Yes," Lianne said, smiling, "and don't worry. Nanna was fond of us both. She would want for us to be friends."

Ida retreated to the sink, shaking her head and muttering.

Lianne finished her meal, thinking affectionately of her grandmother. It surprised and pleased her that she would have chosen Max for her. But then she knew that Marguerite Gevers had always been partial to the elder Julen son. Still, it was satisfying. What would Nanna have thought if she knew that Max had kissed her granddaughter on the sitting room sofa?

After carrying her dishes to the sink, Lianne went to her room to rest. She'd gotten a lot more exercise that day than usual and her muscles were tired. She lay on her bed, hoping she might doze off, but her mind was too full of her conversation with Ida for her to sleep.

Staring at the ceiling, she found herself thinking about Max instead of Alex. In the course of twenty-four hours her heart seemed to have been turned upside down. Nanna had always seemed the wisest person she had ever known. How remarkable that she would have paired her with Max Julen. Lianne wondered if there was something in the situation that she should have seen all along. Could Nanna have known Lianne's heart better than she?

Lianne thought of Max's kiss, the desire she'd seen in his eyes. Until now she hadn't really considered Max's intentions, but it made sense that he'd want his daughter to have a woman's influence, not to mention companionship for himself. Yet Max hardly seemed the type to act on practical considerations alone.

What if he did seriously court her? The prospect was a bit disconcerting. Coming to Switzerland, nothing had been further from her mind. Her whole adult life she'd focused on the past. And now, suddenly, Max Julen was beginning to make her look to the future.

# CHAPTER SIX

THE NEXT MORNING Lianne worked on her dissertation, but didn't accomplish much. She had trouble concentrating. The romantic images of Shelley's poems brought Max Julen to mind, and she began wondering just how much she might come to care for him. It worried her that he might be nothing more than a deep-seated substitute for Alex. That, she realized, wouldn't be enough.

After lunch she decided to go for a walk in hope of clearing her mind. Nanna's town house was at the edge of Old Town, where she and Alex had passed many happy hours together. Lianne headed that way, going down the boulevard Jacques Dalcroze, past the Museum of Art and History, then into the Place du Bourg-de-Four. As expected, it looked smaller than she remembered, though the spires of the nearby Cathedral Saint Pierre did seem to rise majestically into the heavens.

She moved around the cobbled square, noticing that the outdoor tables of the cafés had been moved inside because of the autumn weather. Staring at the empty places, she remembered the umbrellas, the sunshine and being there with Alex. There had been a little fondue restaurant somewhere near the square where they had had their last rendezvous before their affair had begun to unravel. She looked for it, but couldn't remember where it was.

Leaving the square, she headed toward the rue Grand where she could look at the windows of the antique shops. After going a short way, she spotted the fondue restaurant. The sign in the window indicated it was closed. She looked in just the same, seeing the table where she and Alex had sat. What would she have thought that day had she known that fifteen years later she would be back, a single woman of thirty-two, still trying to put the events of that summer into perspective? With a sigh she went off to look at the antique stores.

By the time she made her way back to the rue Beauregard, the sun was dropping toward the gabled rooftops of the old town. For the last half mile she had been thinking of almost nothing but a hot bath and a cup of tea. A brisk wind had picked up as the day wore on, sending leaves tumbling down the narrow streets, nipping at her ears and cheeks.

When she neared the town house, she noticed Max's car parked across the street, which sparked a twinge of joy. A smile touched her lips.

She climbed the stairs, slowly turning over in her mind the possible reasons for his visit. She was fumbling with her key when Ida pulled the door open.

"You have a caller, *mademoiselle.*"

Max, in a business suit, was sitting on the couch where they had kissed the night before. A teacup and saucer were in his hand. He was just putting them down when she entered the room. He rose, looking her over happily.

"Forgive me for dropping in like this. I did call and was told you were out for a few hours, but I decided to take my chances, anyway. I hope you don't mind."

Lianne unzipped her jacket and went over to him. Max stepped forward to greet her. They clasped hands, and she offered her cheek, which he kissed. His cologne was different than the previous night, though for some reason familiar. Keeping hold of one gloved hand, he led her around the coffee table to sit beside him on the couch.

The housekeeper stood waiting at the entrance to the room. "Tea, *mademoiselle?*"

"Yes, thank you, Ida. I'd like some."

The woman shuffled toward the kitchen, and Lianne turned to Max. "What a nice surprise. I'm so glad you came." She removed her gloves and rubbed her fingers together. "I went for a long, long walk, and I think the chill finally caught up with me."

Max took her hands and pressed them between his palms. "Your fingers are like ice."

"Yours are warm."

He lifted her hands to his mouth and kissed the tips of her fingers. She watched his eyes, the way he touched her, and she wondered about his feelings for her.

"The reason I've come is to apologize," he said in English.

"For what?"

"The other night."

"There's no reason to."

They heard Ida coming, her slippered feet skimming the hardwood floor. They both fell silent.

Max waited for the housekeeper to place the cup of tea on the table. Lianne slipped off her jacket and put it beside her. When Ida was gone, Max said, "Mrs. Weber seems as dedicated to you as your grandmother."

"Under that stern veneer she's a good-hearted person. We're getting to know each other."

"For Americans that's important, isn't it?"

"I spent a lot of time in this house as a child and took Ida completely for granted. Now I'd prefer to know her as a person."

Max smiled and sipped his tea.

"She's very admiring of you, you know," Lianne said, recalling her conversation with the housekeeper that morning.

"Oh?"

Her eyes sparkled with mischief. "Told me that you were a catch."

His brow furrowed. "A...catch?"

Lianne picked up her cup and saucer. "A man highly sought after by women," she said, explaining the idiom.

Max grinned, amused. "I'm flattered. But to be honest, I would be more interested in what you think than Mrs. Weber."

She couldn't help teasing him a little. "As I told Tatiana last night, you're a typically Swiss gentleman."

He put down his cup and saucer, the corners of his mouth twitching. "I'll accept that."

"You *are* a gentleman. It's the first thing I noticed about you."

He seemed to like the comment. "Which brings me back to my apology," he said, lapsing back into French. "I hope you weren't upset by Tatiana. But I'm as responsible as she."

"Really, Max, there's no reason to apologize. Nor do I want her to feel badly."

He reached into the inside pocket of his jacket, retrieving an envelope. "This is from Tatiana...and not at my urging, I might add. She asked me to give it to you. I presume it's some sort of note of apology."

Lianne looked at her name written on the envelope in the girl's hand, then set it, along with her cup and saucer, on the table. "I wish the two of you wouldn't worry. Nothing happened that bothered me in any way."

"Well, for better or worse, we're Swiss. Certain courtesies are ingrained. But that's not the primary purpose of my visit." He looked steadily into her eyes. "I'm very fond of you, Lianne...obviously. I would like to see more of you. I came to ask if that would a be a problem for you."

"Of course not. Why would it be?"

"I'll be frank. Because of any feelings you might still have for Alex."

She studied Max carefully, but it was really her own feelings she was examining. She remembered the way he had kissed her, the way she had enjoyed the affection. And Tatiana's words came back to her as well: *Uncle Alex isn't here. Papa is.* The distinction wasn't insignificant.

"Alex has had a big impact on my life. But I wasn't even eighteen when I knew him. I'm a woman now."

"I don't mean to drag him into everything, but I had to be sure."

"I understand. Anyway, you know now how I feel."

"Well," he said, taking her hand, "now that we've gotten that out of the way, I'd like to ask you to accompany me to the flea market down in the Plaine de Plainpalais, if it would interest you. I often go down on Sunday evening and browse. I was on my way when I stopped by, thinking you might enjoy it. On occasion I've found a good antique piece or some art. There's a jewel to be found in the chaff from time to time."

"It sounds like fun. I adore antiques."

"*Bien!* Then let's go."

Lianne got her coat, told Ida she was going out and that she would see her in the morning. They drove down to the Plaine de Plainpalais, a great open parklike area south of the heights of Old Town. It was getting dark as they arrived, but the crowds were still considerable. The market took on a carnival air at night, the vendors' stalls lit by bulbs strung on electric cords. Max told her how pleasant the market was on a warm summer evening when the daylight lasted till nearly ten, but admitted he also enjoyed the brisk winter evenings when the smell of cooking sausages and hot mulled wine filled the air.

They strolled down the narrow, crowded aisles separating the stalls, Lianne with her hand on Max's arm. It was a cheery scene, and she felt happy and content in his company. From time to time they stopped to look at some of the merchandise. Lianne tried on some antique silk shawls, a couple of which she thought very beautiful, but in the end decided not to purchase either. She did buy a pair of antique cloisonné earrings, though, and she and Max spent a while looking at rare books owned by a merchant he frequently patronized.

They looked at art next. Max considered purchasing a late-nineteenth-century miniature that was very well priced, but decided in the end he didn't like it well enough to own. Laughing, Lianne told him she was relieved, because she found the piece a bit uninspired.

"Perhaps our taste isn't dissimilar," he said.

"No, perhaps it isn't."

After they had some hot mulled wine and warmed themselves in a canvas-covered tavern, they went off happily again for more browsing. They had joked and laughed a lot over their wine, and Lianne was in good spirits. Max put his arm affectionately around her shoulders as they strolled through the crush.

In a stall presided over by a little old woman in a fur hat Lianne found an antique ivory letter opener and magnifying glass that came in a velvet-lined box. Max agreed that it was a very beautiful set. But it was also rare and quite expensive.

"It looks like something a scholar, such as you, should have," he told her.

"But a wealthier one than I," she replied. "No, it's a bit too extravagant."

Max didn't want her to pass it up, though. "A gift from your grandmother perhaps?"

"No," Lianne insisted, having decided that Nanna's money, when it came, should be saved.

But Max wouldn't be deterred. "Then it shall be a gift from Tatiana and me." He handed the box to the proprietress. "*S'il vous plaît, madame.*"

Lianne objected, but Max insisted, and in a few minutes they headed off again, she with the box wrapped in paper and tucked under her arm. "Max, you shouldn't have."

He gave her a squeeze but said nothing as they headed for the parking lot.

"It's getting late," Lianne said. "Tatiana will be wondering where you are."

"No, she's spending the night with a classmate. A big exam tomorrow. They're studying together."

"So you're a bachelor for the evening?"

"In a manner of speaking."

"I haven't planned dinner yet. Would you care to have a bowl of soup or something with me?"

"You cooked just two nights ago. Why don't we go to a restaurant?"

"You've spent your money on this gift. Let me at least offer you a meal. Besides, it's cold and we both need a brandy to warm us up."

"I must confess it sounds delightful."

They drove back to the town house, which was dark when they arrived. Lianne turned on a light in the sitting room and put her gift from Max on the table where her files and manuscripts were arrayed. Then she got a bottle of cognac and two brandy snifters from the kitchen. Max had turned on Nanna's radio. She let him pour them each some cognac.

"To the woman I find more delightful and lovely each time I see her," Max said, toasting her.

Lianne couldn't help blushing. She recalled what Ida had told her about Nanna's preferring Max over Alex as a suitor for her.

The brandy was strong, and it warmed Lianne's insides. She was soon feeling quite content, if a touch nervous. She leaned back on Nanna's couch, thinking about how quickly her life had changed. Even today her relationship with Max had taken a quantum jump. Their kiss had been the turning point, but the stroll through the flea market had reinforced her growing feelings for him. She was struck again by what a warm and appealing man he was.

"How is it such an intelligent and attractive woman is still alone?" Max asked when they both become mellow from the brandy. "Hasn't there been anyone?"

"I've had friendships, of course. And an occasional romantic relationship, but nothing that ever lasted. In fairness, I suppose I never gave anyone a chance."

"Why? I thought American men had a reputation for single-mindedness in that regard. I would have thought they'd have found you irresistible and refused to let you get away."

"I guess it takes two to make a committed relationship."

"I hope you're over your shyness, Lianne."

She looked into his eyes to read his meaning. Just as she had the other night, she saw affection, maybe even a spark of love. Max took her face into his hands, leaned over and kissed her softly. She kissed him back, feeling a closeness that she hadn't felt in a long, long time.

In the past, when a relationship drifted toward intimacy, Lianne had held back. Never had she truly let go of herself emotionally since her affair with Alex. For that reason, if no other, she was hesitant about getting serious with Max. Yet at the same time her attraction to him—as a man and a person—was very strong. Now she wanted to give of herself. Max had made her want to be a woman in the fullest sense of the word.

As his passion became more intense, his desire for Lianne became apparent. She opened her mouth, permitting his tongue to slip inside. She sank her fingers into his hair, crushing his lips hard against hers.

Then she fell back on the sofa breathlessly. *"Mon Dieu!"* she exclaimed.

"Oh, Lianne, Lianne. I can't get enough of you." With that he slid his hand under her sweater and up the smooth plane of her stomach to her breasts. His fingers probed the edge of her bra. Then he rubbed his thumb over the lace covering her nipple until Lianne felt her breasts begin to tingle.

She held her breath, savoring the sharp joy. And when she couldn't deny her needs any longer, she sat up and lifted her sweater over her head. Max unhooked her bra, his hands trembling with desire. Then he leaned over and lightly kissed the tip of each breast. When Lianne moaned, he began painting moist patches over her nipples, swirling his tongue over her nubs and sucking on her until her whole body felt electrified.

Cradling her breast in his palm, Max's lips returned to her mouth. She moaned again, and he whispered his desire for her. "Lianne, *ma chérie,* I want you."

She lay back on the sofa and looked into his pale blue eyes. Her heart was thumping wildly. She was profoundly aroused, and she wanted him inside her.

Clutching her clothes to her chest, Lianne took Max's hand and pulled him to his feet. "Come," she said. "Come to my room."

MAX SAT on the edge of the bed. The room was dark. Lianne had gone off to the bath almost immediately. He closed his eyes, fighting himself for control. His desire was still burning intensely. He had been drawn to Lianne from the first day he'd seen her, and now he wanted her as he'd never wanted a woman before.

His brain kept reminding him who she was, kept warning him of the dangers, of the risk to everything he held dear. Yet his craving for her was overwhelming. All that mattered was to have her, to make her his beloved.

He heard her in the hallway and turned to see her naked silhouette as she appeared in the doorway. The faint light behind her exposed the elegant curves of her body. She seemed perfect, flawless, and yet so much more than just the physical being he beheld.

She moved toward him, the moonlight from the window behind him casting a silvery glow on her skin. She stopped in front of him, and he felt his loins engorge. He wanted to take her into his arms, to bury his face in her tender flesh. But at the same time he wanted to go slowly, to savor each moment. He stood up and placed his hand alongside her face in a gesture of affection.

Lianne smiled, her teeth glimmering in the faint light. Then, slipping past him, she climbed onto the bed, sitting up against the headboard, her arms wrapped around her knees. She stared at him with the intensity of an uncertain doe.

Max calmly began undressing. By the time he had stripped, she had lain back, stretching out her long legs. He crawled onto the bed and lay next to her. The softness of her skin, the vision of her waiting for him, naked and willing, aroused him even more. As he leaned over and kissed her lips, his hand found her breast once more.

"Go slowly, Max," she whispered. "It's been a long time."

"You're protected?" he asked, his lips grazing the corner of her mouth.

She nodded, but rolled her head away slightly. In the faint light he could see the shimmer of tears in her eyes. He was sure she was thinking of her child, and the realization made much about her clear to him. "Are you okay, darling?"

She gave a half nod, but he could see she wasn't.

He kissed her tenderly. "What's the matter? Are you afraid?"

She hesitated, then in a shaky voice said, "Oh, Max... I'm not sure this is right."

He stroked her head, liking the feel of her silken hair against his palm. "It's all right, *chérie.*" He could see her blinking back tears. "If you don't want to make love, we needn't. I thought it was what you wanted."

She pulled his head down, pressing his cheek against hers. "It is. I mean, I thought it was what I wanted...."

"I'd rather you be sure," he said, smiling gently.

"Just hold me for a while, will you?"

He gathered her still closer, and she put her head on his shoulder, just under his chin. Her satiny softness aroused him, and Max felt himself rise against her. He swallowed hard, trying to calm his passions, trying to concentrate on his love for her.

The truth was, it had been a long time for him, as well, though perhaps not as long as for her. There had been women since Catrina, but very few—a hostess for Swissair, a Flemish girl in the law firm in Brussels, the sister-in-law of his banker in London, the widow of his university classmate in Zurich. Only the relationship with Yvonne Helbling, the widow, had lasted more than a few nights, but it, too, had ended when honor demanded it.

This wasn't the same. Their acquaintance was young, but Max already felt an undeniable love for Lianne. Still, though his feelings were pure, he was plagued by a definite guilt for what he had failed to tell her, the truth he had withheld. But he also knew there was no way he could tell her about Tatiana now, not without Alex's consent, and then only if his daughter wouldn't be hurt by it.

Max could feel his heart pounding. He felt Lianne's warm breath on his neck. She cuddled close to him and murmured his name. He kissed the top of her head.

She lifted her face, looking at him with wide eyes. "I do want you so very much," she purred.

He covered her lips with a long kiss, and she stirred, running her hand over his hip, inciting him more. Their kiss deepened, and he felt her relax in his arms. He was sure now she wanted him to take her. But she had asked that he go slowly, and he was determined to fulfill her in every way. Max wanted this to be the first of thousands of times he would make love with her, and he wanted it to be perfect.

So slowly, ever so slowly, he brought her along, caressing her lips and neck and breasts. When she finally parted her legs, he let his hand drift to her inner thigh. He could feel her tense, so he didn't move until she seemed to relax once more. Then he touched her center. Finding her curls heavy with liquid, he slipped his finger inside and began rhythmically massaging her.

Within minutes Lianne was begging him to take her. Her legs parted still wider, and Max moved over her. He found her opening and slowly eased inside.

Lianne's breath wedged in her throat at the sensation. He felt her body tense. As he slowly began sliding in and out of her, she held onto his shoulders. He sensed she was tentative, so he kissed her to allay her fear. As their love-making progressed, he felt her body begin to grow more supple. Gradually her surrender became more complete. Then her excitement started mounting along with his. She began writhing under him, lifting her hips to effect a deeper penetration.

Max could wait no longer. His climax came suddenly. Lianne cried out, the timbre of her voice poised between pleasure and joy.

At his final release he collapsed onto her, spent. Lianne went slack. He kissed her neck, feeling the heat of her body against his lips. He wanted to tell her he loved her, but it somehow seemed wrong to say that so soon.

"You're wonderful," he told her instead, his forehead pressed against hers. "The most wonderful creature I've ever known."

She pressed her cheek against his but said nothing. Max couldn't be sure what she was thinking. Maybe it was insecurity on his part, but his intuition told him that his brother wasn't as completely expunged from her heart as Lianne would have him believe. From the beginning his greatest fear had been that she would love him as a substitute—a substitute for Alex.

IN THE MORNING, after Max left, Lianne ran a bath and sat thinking about what had happened. They had shared a good deal more than sex—of that she was sure. Max wasn't the sort of man to play games with a woman.

Still, it had all come so suddenly that she didn't know what to think. One day she was living a solitary life, working hard on her career, and the next she was intimately involved with a man whose feelings for her were serious indeed.

At breakfast Max had told her he had been considering selling his town house and finding a place in the country with a garden and some land. Did she like the country? he'd asked her. Lianne hadn't known how to respond, and so she'd acted as though the question had no implications for their relationship. Max was clearly the sort who knew his mind and, once decided, plunged ahead with assurance.

Of course, he'd made no direct reference to marriage, but he was giving her a chance to spurn the suggestion. And although the whole thing was shocking, Lianne didn't find the idea offensive. To the contrary, she was happier than she could ever remember, if a bit nervous. Max was simply the sort of man with whom a woman could find contentment. How else could she explain the warm, happy feeling he evoked?

But to protect herself from disappointment she tried to keep it all in perspective. She tried to think of it as just another relationship, an intimate friendship limited to her time in Geneva. And yet she knew there was a lot more than just her pleasure and his at stake. There was Tatiana. Max had to have given some thought about how a serious relationship would affect his child.

The bath was hot, and Lianne sat upright to cool her chest. Her pale hair was pinned on top of her head, and her arms rested on the smoothly rounded edge of the ancient porcelain tub. She looked at her toes protruding from the water and, remembering the pleasure of the night before, couldn't help a smile.

But Tatiana came tumbling back into her mind again, and Lianne wondered how much of a role the girl was playing in her feelings. There was no way to deny that she regarded her as a substitute for Alexandra. What she didn't know was if that would help ease the pain she had carried all these years, or if it would only make it worse.

Then Lianne remembered the note that Max had brought. She hadn't yet read it. Getting out of the tub, she dried herself, donned her terry robe and went to the sitting room, where she'd left the envelope the night before. Passing through the hall, she heard Ida Weber, punctual as always, in the kitchen.

The bottle of cognac and their glasses from the night before hadn't yet been cleared away, and Lianne considered gathering them up herself, then decided there was no point in trying to hide the truth. Ida might even be pleased to know that she had entertained Max Julen. But none of that mattered now. Tatiana's note was on the table. She picked it up, studying the careful handwriting.

Images of the girl went through her mind. She saw her in her leotard and ski parka, in her mother's fur, in the gray silken shadows of Nanna's hallway. Lianne carefully opened the envelope and slipped out the note.

Dear Lianne,
I hope you will forgive my rudeness last evening. I was more a child than the woman I wish to be. And I wasn't truthful about my jealousy. Papa has never cared for another woman apart from my mother and me. The idea that he cares for you is not an easy one to accept.

I realize that it is not your fault, and it is not my place to blame. The honest truth is that I like you very much and I hope that we shall be friends. If you can forgive me.

Yours affectionately,
Tatiana

Lianne read the note twice more, then tucked it back into the envelope. The girl's candor touched her. Lianne believed Tatiana when she said she liked her. It gave her an unexpected joy.

"Of course we'll be friends, Tatiana," she whispered. "Of course."

# CHAPTER SEVEN

TATIANA RAN UP the steps to the house, her overnight case in hand, calling goodbye to her friend Suzanne-Elise. "*Ciao!* See you tomorrow!" She dug her door key from the bottom of her book bag and let herself in. Judging by the cooking smells, Maria already had dinner ready. "*C'est moi!* I'm home!"

There was no immediate response from the kitchen, but Tatiana wasn't surprised. Maria took note of such things without comment.

The girl dumped her book bag on the floor, hung her coat in the hall closet and went into the sitting room. There she made a circle around the room, taking a chocolate mint from the bowl on the mantel. Her mother had loved mints but had always kept them from Tatiana's reach when she was little, knowing it was easy to eat too many. Maria kept the mints where they had always been, though it was rare that anyone took one. Even as she'd grown older Tatiana had never developed much of a taste for the candies, taking one only when she was very hungry and didn't feel like going to the kitchen.

Squeezing the foil wrapper into a small ball, she slipped it into her pocket and plopped into her father's chair. Curiously, not only was the evening paper on the side table, waiting for him, but the previous night's newspaper was there, as well, folded neatly and untouched.

Tatiana found that odd. Her father always read his paper as soon as he came home. Why would he have neglected his reading? Rising, she sauntered back to the kitchen, where she found Maria chopping vegetables.

"*Hé,* Maria. How are you?"

"I'm well, *señorita.* How was school?"

"Just fine. The headmaster pitched me out for smoking in class, but otherwise things are great."

"Good." Maria continued her work without looking up.

Tatiana never was sure whether the maid missed her jokes completely or chose to ignore them. Either way the pattern was always the same. The only time Maria paid much attention was when they fought over something or Tatiana refused to cooperate.

The squat dark-headed woman was in her early forties and had been with the family since Tatiana was a baby. Catrina Julen had personally gone to Spain to select her from an agency that specialized in employing domestics abroad. Maria was chosen because she had almost no family and was eager to leave the country of her birth. Catrina had wanted someone who would be with the family at least until Tatiana was grown.

Wandering near where the woman was busy working, Tatiana snatched a carrot stick from the cutting board, narrowly evading Maria's cautionary slap. Neither of them bothered to say a word. Tatiana went and sat at the table.

"Why didn't Papa read his paper last night, Maria?"

"What?"

"Father's paper from last night is where you always put it. Why didn't he read it?"

"How should I know? I am only the maid, señorita. Ask God, not me."

"God isn't available at the moment."

Maria crossed herself, mumbling something in Spanish.

"Papa isn't on a trip," Tatiana said.

"Perhaps he went someplace else."

"Where?"

"I don't know this," Maria replied impatiently. "I am only—"

"Yes, I know. You're only the maid."

"So don't ask me these questions."

"Are you sure he wasn't home last night?"

Maria rolled her eyes. *"¡Dios mio!"*

"Papa always reads his paper unless he's away on a business trip."

"Well, he didn't sleep in his bed last night because it was still made from the day before. So he went someplace else, no?"

Tatiana blinked. "He wasn't here at all?"

"He is a man, not a child, *señorita*. He can go where he wishes. You were away, were you not?"

It suddenly dawned on Tatiana what had happened. Her father had obviously been with a woman. Lianne Halliday! He had spent the night with Lianne!

Tatiana felt her cheeks turn crimson. A terrible jealousy welled up. How could he? In a way, after seeing them kiss at Lianne's the night of the dinner party, she wasn't surprised. Still, hearing proof of it was almost too much to bear!

For the past few days Tatiana had been struggling with her feelings, resenting her father for chastising her about snooping on him. He'd promised her he wouldn't marry Lianne, and now it was perfectly obvious that he would!

Fuming, Tatiana got up and stomped out of the kitchen. She went to her room and sat on her bed, feeling completely betrayed. She liked the American, but there was no need for her to worm her way into their home. They were perfectly happy without her.

But until she asked him she couldn't be absolutely sure her father had spent the night with Lianne. It was possible he'd gone somewhere else. Finding out would be easy enough, she decided.

Tatiana went to the telephone in her father's bedroom and dialed his office. His secretary told her he was on an international call, but Tatiana insisted she would wait. Finally, after five minutes, he came on the line.

"Papa, I worried about you all day? Where have you been?"

"What are you talking about, Tatiana?"

"Last night. I tried calling you until the small hours and there was no answer."

"Oh, what were you calling me for?"

"To ask a question about math. Suzanne-Elise and I couldn't figure something out and her father was no help. He knew less math than we do."

"I'm sorry I wasn't home to help." His voice was very calm, even.

"Where were you?"

"It's not important."

"But I worried so. I thought maybe you were sick and in hospital. Suzanne-Elise and I even called the Hôpital Cantonal to see if you were there on an emergency."

"Tatiana, how silly. There was no emergency."

She pressed harder. "Then it was something you were ashamed of. That's why you aren't telling me."

"Of course not. Why these questions? What's gotten into you?"

"I was only worried, Papa...." She let the emotion in her voice show, hoping he might yet tip his hand.

Max remained mute for several moments. "Well, I'm quite busy now, Tatiana. Perhaps we can talk more when I get home."

"It doesn't matter. Now that I know you're safe, nothing matters."

"That's good."

"I guess it's fortunate I didn't disturb Mademoiselle Halliday last night by inquiring about you. It only would have gotten her upset, as well." When Max didn't say anything immediately, Tatiana added, "Unless, of course, she knew where you were...?"

"I think we've discussed this quite enough. You may pay a bit too much attention to my business than is healthy, Tatiana. If there's need for concern, you'll be notified soon enough."

She let the rebuke be the last word, but she learned what she wanted from his reaction to her questions. Her father *had* spent the night with Lianne. There was no doubt. "Yes, Papa," she said, letting the receiver slide back into the cradle.

For a long time she sat on her father's bed—the one he'd shared with her mother—and brooded. The problem was obvious enough. Lianne couldn't have Uncle Alex, because he was away in Africa, so she took Papa instead. She was very pretty and nice, so of course her father would instantly fall in love with her.

Well, she thought, if that was the problem, then the solution was just as obvious. If Uncle Alex returned, Lianne would fall in love with him again, and things would be back to the way they were.

After a few more minutes of reflection, Tatiana decided that it was up to her to right a situation that had gone wrong. She might not be a math genius, but she was grown enough to understand the way the world worked.

Taking her father's leather address book from the drawer in the bedstand where he kept it, she paged through it until she found Uncle Alex's number. Phoning Africa wasn't like calling Lausanne, but it could be done. She needed the international operator. Any school child knew that. In three minutes she had the Red Cross office in Lagos. Alex Julen soon came on the line.

"Tatiana, what a surprise!" His voice was cheery. Tatiana always liked that about Uncle Alex. He'd been good fun as long as she could remember.

"I was thinking you haven't been home for Christmas in two years, Uncle Alex, and I wanted to say I hope you come this time."

"How thoughtful of you to invite me."

"I decided if I wrote to you the letter might get stuck away in a drawer, but this way you have to promise you'll come."

"*Tiens!* You have grown up, haven't you? Only a woman could come up with such a scheme."

"I *am* a woman, Uncle Alex. You've been away so long, you don't know it, that's all."

"Perhaps that's true."

"This might be an especially good year to come home," Tatiana cooed. "Your girlfriend from the old days, Lianne Halliday, is here in Geneva. I think she'd like to see you."

There was a stunned silence on the line, and Tatiana waited.

"Uncle Alex, are you there?"

"Tatiana, where did you get this idea?"

"From Lianne, of course."

"She told you that we were . . . friends?"

"Yes, Uncle Alex. It's not a secret, is it?"

"No, not exactly."

"Well, I told you I'm a woman now. So why shouldn't she talk about you? Anyway, we're good friends."

"Apparently you are. What else has she said?"

"Nothing special. Just the things women talk about."

"Such as?"

"Well, I know she would like to see you, for example. She talks about you quite a lot."

"I see."

"She hasn't said she still loves you, of course, but I think she does. Papa likes her very much and Lianne likes him, too. But I know it's really you that she cares for."

"This is all very surprising," her uncle said.

"You won't tell them that I told you, will you?"

There was a short silence on the line before he answered. "No, but why have you told me?"

"I guess because Lianne wouldn't tell you herself. She's American and they're different, you know."

"Yes..."

"Anyway, if you come, Lianne can be sure it's you she loves, not Papa."

"This is interesting, Tatiana, but I wonder if you shouldn't be talking to your father about this instead of me. In case you're wrong about Lianne he might be able to help."

"Oh, I'm not wrong. She told me!"

"I see."

"Will you come for Christmas, Uncle Alex? I think it's very important. It's you she loves, not Papa."

"I won't make any promises, but I'll consider it," Alex replied.

"Please do. But whatever you do, don't tell anyone I invited you. Papa will be very angry with me. And so will Lianne. I think it's better if you simply come. Make it a surprise!"

"We'll see, Tatiana."

"And if you do come, don't forget to bring me a present!" She giggled, not being able to resist. One of her greatest joys growing up was the presents Alex brought her whenever he came back to Geneva.

"Of course I'll bring you a gift," he said. "Have I ever forgotten you?"

She laughed. "I love you, Uncle Alex." She hung up the phone, wondering if her ploy would work. There were two possibilities. She had either scared him off, or she had managed to intrigue him. Men weren't as easy to understand as women, but if she had to guess, she'd say Uncle Alex would show up. Men had their own type of competition—different from women, of course—and Tatiana had known since she was a little girl that Uncle Alex was jealous of Papa.

MAX HAD THOUGHT about Tatiana's call the rest of the day, and wondered if it wasn't time they had a long talk. The girl was precocious. There was no denying that. It ought to have been easier to get away for an evening alone with a woman, but until he and his daughter had an understanding, it was apparent problems could arise at any time.

When he got home that evening, the house was full of cooking smells. Maria was hard at work in the kitchen, but there was no sign of Tatiana. He went back to her room, but her door was closed. Max knocked softly.

"*Oui?*"

"It's me, Tatiana. Can we talk?"

"Yes, Papa. Come in."

She was on her bed, a schoolbook open on her lap. She was already in her nightgown. Max sat on the edge of the bed.

"Aren't you feeling well? Dinner will be ready soon."

"I don't think I'll eat tonight. I'm not very hungry, Papa."

"What's the matter? Is it the telephone call this afternoon?"

"No. If you want to spend the night with Lianne, there's not very much I can do about it. It's not my business, as you say."

"Tatiana, your words say one thing, but your voice says another. The truth is Lianne and I *are* fond of each other, and we will be seeing each other a lot in the future."

"I'm not surprised."

He drew a deep breath. "It's our right."

"You promised me you wouldn't marry her."

"No one has said anything about marriage yet. Lianne and I are still getting acquainted."

Tatiana scoffed.

He could see that under the bravado she was truly threatened. "Why does the prospect upset you so? Because of your mother?" he asked gently.

"I don't think Lianne loves you the same as Mummy."

"Well, this isn't something to speculate on. You know I loved your mother. But it's been a long time, and life does go on."

Her eyes narrowed. "So you will marry her!"

"I said no such thing. For the moment we're friends. Very close friends."

Tatiana looked away, a dour expression on her face.

"I'm sorry if you're displeased," he said. "Perhaps we should change the subject."

"You brought it up, Papa."

"So I did. But there are other things to discuss."

"Like what?" she asked, turning to him.

"Well, I've been thinking it might be nice if we started looking for a big house in the countryside."

Her face screwed up. "What for?"

"We've been here a long time. And the country is most pleasant. I'm thinking someplace just outside Geneva. A place with a garden. And we could get a puppy! You've always wanted one."

"Honestly, Papa, you treat me like a child. Don't you think I can see what you're doing? You want a new house to live in with Lianne because this one belonged to you and Mummy. A new home would be better for a new wife. And, as for me, I get a dog."

He sighed, his exasperation showing. "Tatiana, I was thinking about this long before Lianne came along."

"But now it's more urgent."

"You know, the problem is you aren't willing to give Lianne a chance. I think you could learn to like her if you'd try."

"I do like her. That's not what we're talking about."

"Is it that you're jealous?"

Tatiana's mouth narrowed to a thin line, and she looked away again. "You're trying to make it my fault."

The telephone rang in the other room, and Max turned his head toward the door momentarily. But he knew the maid would get it. "Let's not get into fault," he said to his daughter. "We'd all do well to show each other a little charity and understanding."

Tatiana still groused.

"Is that unreasonable?" Max asked.

"What if it's Uncle Alex Lianne truly loves?"

"If so, then we'd all simply have to accept it. But that was a very long time ago and things are different now."

"You still love Mummy, don't you? And she died a long time ago."

"That's different, Tatiana." There was a knock at the door. "It's not the same."

They both turned to the door.

"*Señorita,*" Maria said from the hallway, "the telephone is for you. Miss Halliday wants to speak with you."

Max chuckled. "What timing."

Tatiana climbed off the bed. "You may not believe it, Papa. But I do like her." With that she skipped off to take her call, closing the bedroom door after her.

Max sat on his daughter's bed, thinking. There was no doubt that Tatiana was no longer a child. The problem was she was just enough of an adult to be dangerous. And unfortunately she was feeling her oats at a most unfortunate juncture.

Still, he was glad Lianne had called. If Tatiana were ever to come to accept things, it would be because Lianne had won her over. And that, Max realized, was the supreme irony. What would the child think if she were to learn the woman she was so jealous of was her real mother? For that matter, what would Lianne think?

The situation was getting more complicated by the day. Max wondered if perhaps he shouldn't give Alex another call. Somehow it had to be sorted out. In the end the truth would be known, but the dangers in between were formidable.

The bedroom door opened and Tatiana came strolling back in, a self-satisfied expression on her face. "On Saturday," she announced, "Lianne and I are going shopping, and we're having a ladies' lunch."

"Well, *that* should be fun."

Tatiana smiled with amusement. "You still don't understand, do you, Papa? I really do like Lianne."

LIANNE FOUND the little bistro where she was to meet Max without any difficulty, but he wasn't yet there when she arrived. It was on the Place du Molard in the heart of the shopping district and not far from his offices. She took a table in the back corner, telling the waiter a companion would be arriving soon. When Max still hadn't showed up after ten minutes, she ordered a glass of May wine.

The bistro was rapidly filling with the noontime crowds of shoppers and office workers. Such places had a certain bustle and cheer at mealtimes, particularly in the winter months. It was a cold day and the warmth of the bistro was welcome to anyone who'd been outside for long.

Finally Max came in the door and, seeing her waving to him, made his way back to where she waited. He squeezed onto the banquette beside her, smelling fresh and of the outdoors.

"Sorry to be late, darling," he said, kissing her cheek, "but a flurry of cables came in just as I was leaving."

She took his hand, rubbing his cold fingers. "I understand. You must look after your business."

He caressed her cheek, smiling. "It's only been a day since I've seen you, but I missed you terribly."

Lianne leaned her head on his shoulder. "I've missed you, too."

The waiter appeared. Max asked for a glass of wine, and they each ordered a large bowl of soup.

"I wish you didn't have to go to London," she said. Max had called that morning to tell her that urgent business was taking him away, but he wanted to see her for a quick lunch if she didn't mind coming downtown to meet him.

"I'd much prefer to stay," he said, kissing her temple.

"Did Tatiana tell you we're having lunch on Saturday?"

"Yes," he said, "she was pleased. But there's another problem that's come up that I'm sure she didn't tell you about."

"What's that?"

Max recounted his conversation with Tatiana and her discovery that he hadn't come home the night she was away.

"I suppose she's at the age where things aren't easily hidden," Lianne said.

"True. But her insistence on bringing Alex into everything is particularly trying. For some reason she's fastened on to that. Perhaps we were too candid at the beginning."

"It's not a good policy to hide things," Lianne said. "It only leads to trouble."

Max lowered his eyes, looking terribly distressed.

"It's not your fault," she assured him. "Perhaps if I'm able to become friends with her, she won't be so upset by our relationship."

Max pulled her hand to his lips and kissed her fingers. "I want you to know, Lianne, that you are very, very dear to me. And I won't permit any of this to come between us."

The sentiment warmed her. Max was becoming an important part of her life. And though it had all happened quickly, she was happy, happier than ever before—certainly since she'd become an adult, with adult understanding. "That means a great deal to me," she said.

The waiter brought his wine. Lianne had hardly touched hers, but she picked up her glass. Max touched his tumbler to hers. "To the most beautiful woman in Geneva, and probably all of America, too!"

Lianne laughed. "That's covering a lot of territory."

"To me you are."

They sipped their wine.

Soon the soup was brought and they ate together happily. Lianne thought about Tatiana bringing up her Uncle Alex again. It was strange how the girl had fixed on that.

"Maybe it would be best for everyone if Alex were to come back," she said thoughtfully.

Max looked over at her. "Is that what you want?"

"Don't you think it would clear the air?"

"It seems to me you're the principal party with an interest in this, Lianne."

"I was really thinking of Tatiana more than myself." Again she noticed a strange expression on Max's face. He looked positively morose. "Did I say something that upset you?" she asked.

Max drew a deep breath, obviously considering his words carefully. But then he sighed, shaking his head. "No," he said. "It's just that I hate to see you suffer."

"I'm not suffering, Max. I've never been happier in my life than I have been the past few days."

He smiled at her, but there was pain in his eyes. And Lianne simply couldn't understand why.

"YOU'RE JUST TOO MUCH!" Tatiana said in English, placing the emphasis on the wrong part of the phrase.

Lianne laughed as she squeezed into the chair on the other side of the small marble-topped table. They were both inundated with packages, boxes, all the things they had accumulated in the course of four hours of shopping. The café was crowded and there wasn't much space to stow their purchases. Tatiana's chin was barely topping the boxes and sacks on her lap. She looked exhausted but happy.

"*Tiens*. You really think Papa can be bought off by one little tie, Lianne? I've spent hundreds of francs. I've never done this before."

"Women do run over budget. He'll just have to understand." Lianne began placing her things under her chair and around her feet.

Tatiana was still looking over her Grand Passe shopping bag. "In the past when I've needed something Papa has taken me. Or if it was small he would give me the money and I would go get it."

"That's the way a man shops. With women it's different."

The girl let her things slide to the floor. She leaned her elbows heavily on the table and looked at Lianne. "Do you think he knows this?"

"Certainly."

"Then he won't be upset?"

"I can't guarantee that, but he'll come to accept the fact that as a young woman you'll be behaving like one. In any case, I'll talk to him and explain that I was the one who corrupted you."

Tatiana laughed. "If you want the money back that you loaned me, you'll *have* to talk to him."

"Let's not worry about that."

The waiter came. Tatiana ordered a hot chocolate. Lianne did, as well. They slipped off their coats.

Tatiana had had such a good time that she almost felt badly about her effort to undermine her father's affair with Lianne. The day had been the most fun she'd had in a very long time, and she regretted the things she'd said to Uncle Alex. Now she almost wished he wouldn't come to Geneva for Christmas.

She looked into Lianne's beautiful silver eyes. "Papa tells me he's taking you to a concert at Victoria Hall tomorrow."

"Yes, he has two tickets, but if you would like to go, he may be able to get a third."

"No, I don't like concerts so much, but thank you, anyway. Victoria Hall is a dank old place and the seats are very uncomfortable. Anyway, I'm sure Papa is going to be with you, not for the music."

"Is it a problem for you, Tatiana?" she asked lightly. "Your father has said he wants to take me to parties and dinners, to meet his friends and so forth. I'll be seeing a lot of him. I don't know if he's told you that."

"Yes, I know. I've decided that it's his business . . . and yours. If I was jealous before, it was only for Mummy's sake."

"Don't you think your mother would want him to go out and have a good time?"

"That isn't the point, Lianne. Mummy's gone, and you're the one he cares for now."

Her words brought a vacant silence. Tatiana felt brave saying it, but deep inside it still hurt. It would be so much better if it was Uncle Alex that Lianne loved. Tatiana could still be friends with her, and it was a friend she really wanted, not a stepmother.

Their hot chocolates came, occupying the moment. Lianne fingered the handle of the heavy earthenware mug.

"Don't worry about me," Tatiana volunteered. "I hope everybody is happy in the end."

"You're being quite mature about this." Lianne smiled warmly, impressed by Tatiana's attitude, but still not sure what conclusions to draw. The girl's desire to be friendly seemed sincere enough. She knew, though, that real friendship would have to be built on trust, the kind of trust that came with sharing a confidence. "Your father hasn't told you much about your Uncle Alex and me, has he?" she said.

"No, not really."

"If we're to be friends, and understand each other, perhaps you ought to know a little about my past."

"I already guessed that you and Uncle Alex were—" she lowered her voice and leaned toward Lianne, glancing at the nearest table "—lovers."

Lianne smiled openly. "That's true. But I'm sure you don't know that we had a child."

Tatiana's eyes rounded and she put her fingers to her open mouth. *"Vraiment?"*

Lianne nodded.

"But... you didn't marry... ?"

"No, the baby wasn't intended. I was very young. Too young."

"But where...why...?" Tatiana's mouth was still half-open.

"Your Uncle Alex and I were lovers, even though I was only seventeen. When I got pregnant, my grandmother sent me home. My mother packed our bags as soon as I arrived, told everybody I was going to spend the school year in Switzerland and took me to Boston. We rented a small house until the baby came. Then, when I recovered from childbirth, we went on a trip around the country, seeing all the national parks. I was miserable."

"What happened to the baby?"

"She was put up for adoption."

"It was a girl?"

"Yes," Lianne replied, looking away as her voice quavered. "A little girl." She had managed to relate the story with a certain detachment and control, but the emotion had caught up with her. It wasn't easy to look into Tatiana's eyes.

"Oh, Lianne..." she whispered, her tone sympathetic.

"I hope I haven't shocked you. That wasn't my purpose. It's just that our friendship means a great deal to me. You're the closest to my own daughter I'll ever come. You're her first cousin, you know." Lianne took the paper napkin from in front of her and dabbed the corner of her eye.

"Thank you for telling me. I know it must have been hard."

"Well," she said, trying to effect a cheerful demeanor, "what do you think about having a cousin somewhere out there in the world?"

"You don't know where?"

"Someplace in New England. But I don't know her name. I call her Alexandra, though, after your uncle."

"You don't see her, then?"

"I've never seen her."

Tatiana bit her lip, feeling a rush of sadness.

Lianne reached across the table and patted the girl's hands, finding it difficult to be brave. "I didn't tell you to make you sad. I thought you should know so that you'd understand the situation better."

"Papa knows all this?"

"Yes."

Tatiana bowed her head. "I'm very sorry. It's a sad story. I wonder what the girl must think. Is she still young?"

"She's a week older than you. Her birthday's April 10."

"Oh, we're almost twins! Of course she's not little. How stupid. You haven't seen Uncle Alex for many years. And what about him?'' she asked, her expression growing cross. "Why didn't he marry you?"

"My mother wouldn't agree to it. Nor would your grandfather. We were so very young. Looking back, it's just as well, though if I could do it all over again, I'd keep Alexandra. My mother made all the decisions. I was given little choice."

"And Uncle Alex agreed?"

"He didn't have much choice in the matter, either."

Tatiana suddenly looked upset. "So this is why he hasn't come home to see you. I didn't know, Lianne."

"I don't know if that's why. But it's a very painful situation for everyone."

As Lianne watched, Tatiana blushed deeply. She looked up at Lianne with a mournful expression on her face. "I feel dreadful," she said.

"Don't, Tatiana. That isn't why I told you."

She shook her head. "You don't understand," she mumbled.

Lianne looked at her with perplexity but said nothing.

"Sometimes a person does something very foolish without knowing it," Tatiana said.

"What do you mean?"

"Oh, nothing. Nothing I can say." She tried to smile, but inside she was hurting. She wondered what she had done. Calling Uncle Alex had been foolish. Now she could only hope he hadn't listened to her, that he would stay away from Lianne.

# CHAPTER EIGHT

MAX SMILED at August de Koning through the cloud of cigar smoke billowing around the prosperous-looking Dutch businessman.

"These Cubans certainly know how to make a cigar," de Koning said contentedly. He turned the brandy snifter in his other hand. "And the French know their cognac."

Max sat on the corner of his desk, fingering his own glass, though he'd hardly touched the brandy after they had their traditional toast. He knew Lianne was waiting patiently for him in his outer office, but the de Koning deal was a very important one, and there was custom to be considered.

Max and his marketing people had worked for over six months for their German subsidiary to become the supplier of the electrical components used at the giant de Koning plant in Rotterdam. Max had finally swung the deal by helping the Dutchman obtain a major block of capital from a Swiss banking syndicate in order to retool his Rotterdam operation.

It was hardly the time to offend the man. And so Max tried to maintain a pleasant demeanor, even though he was terribly eager to see Lianne.

At long last de Koning, a heavyset, bald man of sixty, got up from his chair. "You've been most hospitable, Julen, and I should like to invite you to dinner."

"You're very kind, but I'm afraid I already have an engagement. But you'll be my guest for dinner on your next visit to Geneva."

"The luncheon today was delightful. I'd hoped to reciprocate."

"I'm very sorry."

"Undoubtedly I'm keeping you from your engagement."

"No, it's no problem. She understands."

"Aha!" the Dutchman exclaimed. "A woman. Now I truly see I must go. You shouldn't keep a lady waiting." Without hesitation de Koning closed his alligator briefcase, got up and ambled toward the door to Max's office. "You should have told me," he mumbled apologetically.

The staff had gone home, but Lianne was seated in the waiting area of the outer office. She was in an electric-blue wool suit with high black boots. Her hair was up, her cheeks rosy. Max thought she looked quite sophisticated . . . stunning really.

"Oh, good heavens," the Dutch businessman said, seeing her. "Julen, if this is what was waiting for you, you should have thrown me out an hour ago."

Lianne rose to her feet. Max made the introductions, and de Koning kissed her hand chivalrously.

"*Madame,* a thousand pardons. We've kept you waiting."

"Not at all," she replied. "I hope your meeting went well."

"We made our deal," the man said, beaming. "I would say it went well, wouldn't you, Julen?" Without waiting for a reply he patted Lianne's hand and said he had to go.

"Why don't you join us?" Lianne asked politely.

De Koning glanced at Max. "It would be a pleasure, but I'm afraid Julen here would never do business with me again. No, I leave you to your pleasure. But thank you all the same." He saluted them, took his coat and went out the door.

Lianne turned to Max. He immediately took her into his arms, inhaling her fragrance.

"I thought he'd never leave," he whispered. "I hope you weren't too terribly bored."

"Of course not, Max. I understand how important your business is."

He still had his arms around her. She was so lovely and she'd handled de Koning well. Lianne was beautiful, intelligent and socially adept. She would make a wonderful wife.

They still hadn't talked about marriage, though. Not directly. But the past month or so had been a terribly happy time for them both. They had seen each other nearly every day that he wasn't out of town. And once or twice a week they managed to be alone together, even if he wasn't always able to stay the night.

As for Tatiana, there had been a sudden change in her attitude. Whenever she spoke of Lianne, the reference was favorable, though he sensed an underlying problem of some sort.

Of course the major stumbling block remaining was the truth about Tatiana's parentage. Several times he had come close to blurting out the story. But he had an obligation to Alex, and Tatiana's happiness had to be considered. Besides, he was convinced that somehow he would know when the time was right to tell Lianne—certainly before their relationship progressed much farther.

But in spite of the fact that he knew Lianne loved him, Max still had misgivings. He wasn't entirely convinced that her love for his brother was a thing of the past. And neither could he be sure how the truth about Tatiana would affect her feelings for him. The longer Max kept the secret the harder it became. And yet he had his responsibilities to others.

If they did marry, he wanted to be sure that Lianne had wanted him for himself. And if the truth about Tatiana came out before she accepted a proposal, then he would never be sure how much the child had been a factor. Then, too, there was always the possibility that Lianne would hate him for keeping the truth from her. The dangers in the situation were limitless.

Lianne looked up at him. "You must be exhausted. The negotiation lasted all afternoon, didn't it?"

"Yes, I am tired. But all I need is some air. Is it too cold out to walk to the restaurant? Judging by the color in your cheeks, it must be pretty chilly."

"It is cold, but I don't mind. Perhaps we can walk up the rue Grand and look at the windows of all the antique shops."

"Let's," he said. "I'd enjoy that."

Max got his coat and they went off arm in arm, crossing the Place du Rhône and making their way up to the rue Grand, a narrow cobbled street in Old Town that was full of history and elegant shops. Christmas was only days away and all the stores were decorated for the holidays. Though most of them were closed, there were a number of people in the street, looking into the display windows just as they were.

"What's Tatiana up to this evening?" Lianne asked as they strolled.

"She's not feeling too well. Has a little cold or something. I asked if she'd like to go out for a fondue with us, but she said she'd prefer to stay home."

"I'll give her a call tomorrow and see how she's doing."

"You're always so thoughtful," Max said.

Lianne squeezed his arm.

"So tell me," he asked, "how was your day?"

"I called Professor Brockmeyer in New York and told him I'd be mailing my dissertation to him after the first of the year."

"You've worked very hard on it. I'm sure it'll be a big success."

"I hope so. But once it's approved my work will be over. I also talked to Pronier. The final settlement of Nanna's estate will come soon in the new year, as well."

Max stopped walking and turned to look at her. "Are you trying to tell me you're running out of reasons for staying in Geneva?"

She shook her head. "No, but I do have to think about the future. I have a career, Max. With my family's money I'm hardly poor, but there's my self-respect to consider. I want to make a contribution."

They began walking again.

"You'd talked about looking into a teaching position here in Switzerland," he said, feeling suddenly threatened by the conversation.

"I have."

"And?"

"I have an appointment at the American School next week. Of course, English Literature is a limiting specialty outside the English-speaking countries, and I really want to work in my field."

"I understand," he said, "though I'd certainly like to see you find something here."

She smiled up at him. "Now why in the world would you feel that way?"

He pinched her nose with his gloved fingers. "I should have fallen in love with a Swiss woman. They don't worry about silly things like careers."

"You can always move your company headquarters to the States," she replied. "Perhaps to Connecticut, or somewhere near where I'll be working."

*"Touché,"* he replied.

They came to one of the finer antique shops on the rue Grand and looked into the brightly lit window. "Oh," Lianne exclaimed, "look at that beautiful *secretaire!*" She was pointing to a lovely high-top desk and bookcase made of a rich dark wood with pane glass windows covering the bookshelves.

"It's a handsome piece," Max remarked.

"It's gorgeous! Look at the proportions. What do you suppose it is, Max?"

"I'd say English probably. Late eighteenth or early nineteenth century. Sheridan maybe. That's rolled glass. You can tell by the waves. An older technology."

"I love it."

She admired the piece for a minute longer. Max made a mental note and they strolled on. A cold wind blew down the street, and Lianne shivered. He put his arm around her and held her close.

"A nice hot fondue will be welcome, *n'est-ce pas?*" he said.

"Fabulous!"

As they made their way up the street, Max again worried about the future. The next step was up to him—that much was pretty obvious. There had been no word from his brother, and that was what had been keeping him from taking action. But it was probably a mistake to rely on Alex to phone. No, not probably—it was surely a mistake. Seeing that at last, Max knew what he had to do. He had to give his peripatetic brother another call.

AFTER THEIR DINNER, they went to Lianne's. The house was a bit chilly, so they went off to bed immediately. All through the evening he had been thinking about holding her in his arms. He kissed her hungrily when at last they were together.

Lianne was silent during their lovemaking, though more passionate than usual. At the moment of her pleasure she cried out, clutching him to her with surprising force. Then her body slackened and she turned as soft as a kitten.

Afterward she lay naked in his arms, her big down comforter covering them. Max stroked her head. "These moments with you are so precious to me," he whispered. "They mean so much."

Lianne snuggled closer, always appreciative of his affection. But he sensed that she, too, knew there were outstanding issues. Each of them had been living day to day, happy with each other's company and love, but with secret reservations. He kissed her temple, wishing he could end the smoldering anxiety with a stroke.

"I'm going to have to leave you now," he said. "I must get home."

"Are you worried about Tatiana?" she asked, rousing herself from her dreamlike state.

"A little. I should go."

"That's one thing I admire about you, Max. You're such a devoted and conscientious father. Far too many people are selfish about their lives. But you aren't."

The comment was meant as a kindness, but Lianne couldn't know how much it hurt. He didn't feel honorable in the least. His damn secret was keeping them apart—that and Alex.

Lianne didn't talk about Alex anymore, and Max didn't bring him up, either. Still, the younger Julen was hanging there above them, a sort of Damoclean sword. Ever since he had resolved earlier in the evening to get hold of Alex, Max had been restless. Lianne had wanted him to stay with her a while, and so he had. But he would go home now, though not just to check on Tatiana. He would call his brother and get it over with.

After holding Lianne a few more minutes, he slipped from her bed. She had half drifted off to sleep again, hardly noticing that he was leaving. He dressed in the dark, then quietly left, descending the stairs with his shoes in his hands. When he got downstairs, he put on his shoes, got his topcoat from the closet and stepped outside into the chilled December air.

Ten minutes later Max climbed the stairs to his own house. It was dark inside. He went first to Tatiana's bedroom. She was sleeping peacefully, so he got his address book and returned to the parlor. He dialed his brother's home number in Lagos. Alex had gone to bed early and answered groggily.

"Max, what time is it?"

"Nearly midnight. I'm sorry to call so late, but I had to talk with you."

"What's happened now?"

"Nothing new. It's Lianne. We've got to make a decision, Alex."

"Now? Tonight?"

"You were going to let me know what you wanted to do. I haven't heard from you."

"Funny you should call now. Only today my request for leave was approved. I plan on coming to Geneva for

Christmas if I can work it out. I intended to call you tomorrow.''

Despite it being his purpose in calling Alex, the news came as a surprise. Max's heart sank. It was what he wanted—to get matters cleared up once and for all—yet a part of him feared Lianne seeing Alex again.

"Good," he said, wanting to show confidence, even if it was lacking. "It's for the best."

"I've thought a lot about the situation," Alex said. "Perhaps Lianne and I need to talk. Things ended awkwardly between us, perhaps unfairly.''

Max heard something in his brother's voice that he found disturbing. "What about Tatiana?"

"That's part of it, certainly. What do you think should be done? As you said last time, we're both affected."

"I think the truth must be told eventually."

"To them both?"

"I see no other way," Max replied.

"The question is, who is to tell them, and when?"

"Yes, that is the question."

Alex hesitated. "As I said, I've given this a great deal of thought. I wonder if, before they're told, it wouldn't be best if Lianne and I made our peace. It seems to me a logical first step."

Max searched his brother's words for a hidden agenda, feeling badly because of his suspicion. It was silly of him, he knew, because both Lianne and Tatiana loved him. And yet the fact remained that Max was a pretender of sorts. Alex was Tatiana's biological father and Lianne's first lover.

Max brushed those thoughts aside. The truth was the truth. "If you feel it's important, Alex, then talk to Lianne first. I should like to be involved in telling them, though."

"Yes, of course."

"It's settled then. When are you coming?"

"I don't know for sure. Before the holidays, with luck. Unfortunately we're badly shorthanded at the moment, and we're at the critical point in two major programs. The exact timing will be a last-minute thing."

"I see. But I can tell them you're coming, in any case."

"Perhaps it would be better if you didn't, Max. If I make it for Christmas, then I do. No point in making Lianne anxious unnecessarily."

Max didn't like the uncertainty, Alex's vagueness, but he wasn't going to argue. "I guess it isn't important one way or the other. It's the truth about Tatiana that will be the emotional blow."

"Right."

"All right, then," Max said, still feeling uneasy. "We'll wait for you to come."

Alex cleared his throat. "I take it you and Lianne are still friends."

"Yes, we are. I'm very fond of her, Alex. And she's very fond of me."

"You *are* in an awkward position, aren't you?"

"Putting it mildly, yes."

"Well, in a few weeks it will be behind us. We're simply paying the price for decisions made years ago, Max."

"I wish I could be as philosophical about it as you," he muttered.

"Cheer up, big brother. The holidays are upon us. Now if you'll excuse me, I'm bushed. I've got an early-morning meeting. Thanks for the call."

Max said goodbye and hung up. He sat in his chair for a long time then, uncertain whether he felt better or worse.

THE ENGLISH DOOR CHIMES that young Miss Halliday had the electrician install sounded in the entry hall. Ida Weber got to her feet, the pain in her ankles shooting through her like a knife. The chimes were ending their musical song by the time she made it to the front of the house.

She pulled the heavy door open to a gush of cold December air. Several ambient snowflakes swirled in with the wind. Max Julen was standing bareheaded in the light from the house. His dark hair was speckled with snow. He was smiling as always, his cheeks red from the winter air. In his arms was a bouquet of long-stemmed red roses wrapped in florist paper.

*"Salut, madame!"* he said with undue conviviality.

*"Bon soir, monsieur."* She stepped back to admit him into the house.

"The air outside has the feel of the holidays. You can almost smell it," he said zestfully. He laid the flowers on the pier table and unbuttoned his topcoat. "I hope you're in good health," he said. "The arthritis isn't acting up too much, I trust." He handed her his vicuña topcoat and glanced down, noticing Lianne's small overnight case against the wall. He smiled, then took a peek at his black tie in the mirror, straightening it before smoothing the lapels of his dinner jacket.

"I am well, thank you," she said without looking at him directly. She took his coat to the closet.

Max had picked up the roses again and extended them to her. "For Miss Halliday."

Ida took them and gestured toward the sitting room. "*Mademoiselle* will be a few minutes. Please sit down."

It was a rite they'd been through many times. Max was already headed for the couch.

Ida made her way slowly to the kitchen where she gave one of the buds a cursory sniff before placing them on the counter. Since Monsieur Julen had begun the ritual of bringing flowers on each visit, the vases had been moved from the back of a lower cupboard to an upper one. But, looking in, she found only one left, the Baccarat.

She thought. Baby yellow roses from Tuesday in the Limoges, chrysanthemums from Thursday in the antique bronze, the orchids were on the piano in Madame Gevers's Waterford crystal, the out-of-season tulips were in the Delft in the sitting room. Hopefully something would die before she had to resort to the plain glass in the storage room.

After she trimmed the roses, placed them in the vase and added water, she carried them to Lianne's door. *"Mademoiselle,"* she said, knocking, *"monsieur* has arrived. Here are your flowers."

Lianne opened the door and beheld the roses, showing her delight. "Aren't they lovely!"

"Where shall I put them, *mademoiselle?"*

Lianne was grimacing, struggling to get the back on her black pearl and diamond earrings. "Leave them here with me. The fragrance is so nice."

Ida placed the vase on the nightstand and headed for the door.

"Tell Monsieur Julen I'll be there shortly."

The housekeeper paused at the door, secretly noting the glow on the young woman's cheeks. It gave her pleasure to see it, because it would have given Madame Gevers pleasure. Ida had little doubt now they would marry. Once the flowers started coming regularly, the die was cast.

Lianne saw the tiny smile of contentment on Ida's mouth as she withdrew and closed the door. Her relationship with Max had been a source of satisfaction for the housekeeper, which Lianne found endearing. Everybody assumed now that they would marry, including Tatiana. Lianne herself had finally begun to think of the future, looking at last beyond the happiness she had found in each day. And yet a part of her doubted they would ever get beyond the flowers, the intimate dinners, the stolen moments alone. She loved Max, but she sensed a problem, a hidden concern.

At first she was convinced it was Tatiana, but that concern seemed to fade. Her relationship with the girl was growing better by the day, though there, too, she'd detected a lingering sadness. It couldn't have been Catrina. Max had long ago put his wife's passing into perspective. Whatever was holding him back, Lianne didn't think it was doubt. It seemed almost as if he was afraid of something.

Once, a week or so earlier, she'd asked him about it, but he had insisted he loved her and that that was all that mattered. He'd begun speaking of the future of late, but always vaguely and with unspoken qualification.

Lianne certainly couldn't fault him, because like all mature people in love, she had questions of her own. At times she wondered if it might not be wise for her to return to New York for a month or two in order to put her feelings for Max into perspective. Time apart was a good test. But her happiness was too hard to deny. All too vividly she recalled the loneliness in her life before Max had come along. And, after all, wasn't that the comparison that mattered?

But there had been one other thing that occasionally crept into her thoughts. Alex. Recently he had become most noteworthy because no one spoke of him. Not Max, not Tatiana, nor had she. Accordingly Alex had become a sort of ghost, inhabiting her consciousness by his very absence. Occasionally she had the urge to mention his name, if only to measure the effect on Max, if not on her own feelings. But she avoided the issue instead.

It was all very silly, because Lianne had no doubt about her love for Max. Yet at the same time things weren't completely right. Could it somehow be Alex?

Checking her makeup in the mirror, she decided to put all that out of her mind. It was to be a very special evening. Max was taking her to a society ball, a large party given by socially prominent friends. It would be a coming-out of sorts for her.

Lianne had met some of his friends over the past month or two, but *genevois* society was closed and formal. One didn't introduce an outsider lightly. Until now Max had kept her largely to himself. Taking her to this party was his way of announcing their relationship to the world.

She had wondered if convention wouldn't have dictated a formal engagement first, but she was afraid to ask. There were nuances of *genevois* custom that Lianne wasn't privy to. She had learned a great deal about life in Switzerland, both during childhood and in the past months. But the exact significance of this evening was one she'd have to discover as it progressed.

Lianne didn't let it worry her, though. Since falling in love with Max, she had made a point of taking each day as it came, loving their time together and the happiness he gave her.

There had been one curious twist in their plans for the evening that she still hadn't figured out. Max had told her to pack an overnight bag because he wouldn't be bringing her home after the ball. He wouldn't say more, though. The rest was a surprise. With a final sniff of her roses Lianne took her evening bag and went downstairs to find Max.

He was in the front room, admiring the tree she had put up a few days before with Tatiana's help. Most of Lianne's Christmas things were in storage in Connecticut, so she had taken the girl with her on an outing to purchase decorations for the house. They'd found what they needed in the shops along the rue du Marché, and Lianne had purchased enough to create the effect she wanted. Christmas had been one of her happiest childhood memories, and she had wanted to show Tatiana what it had been like.

The result wasn't entirely American in flavor, but it was close enough. Some of the things they'd bought were similar to what Lianne had had at home, most of the American holiday customs having been brought over from Europe.

As they'd decorated, Lianne had played Christmas tapes on her stereo, and Tatiana had tried to sing the carols with her, though many of the tunes were unfamiliar and some of the words incomprehensible to the girl. They'd had a lot of fun, though, and Tatiana had told her she was anxious for her father to return from Brussels so that she could tell him all about it. Ever since the lunch they'd shared, Tatiana had seemed much closer to her.

"So this is the magnificent tree I've heard so much about," he said, smiling.

Lianne made her way to him, and he took her into his arms.

"You look lovely as always," he whispered, "but in a way more beautiful than ever." He inhaled her and kissed the corner of her mouth.

"You, too," she said, placing her hand against his cheek.

Max stepped back to admire her dress. It was a strapless smoky gray chiffon with a full floor-length skirt. It was sexy and very, very feminine.

"The roses are lovely," she told him. "Thank you."

"There just isn't anything that says what I wish to say."

"I don't need anything but you, Max."

He kissed her softly on the lips. "Shall we go, then?"

They went to the entry hall, Max holding her hand. "I see you've got your case," he noted.

"When are you going to tell me what you've got planned?"

"Not until we get there."

He helped her on with the chinchilla jacket she'd inherited from Nanna, taking the opportunity to kiss her on the nape of the neck. Ida came out as Max slipped on his coat.

"You go on home," Lianne told her. "And don't bother to come tomorrow. Take the day off."

Ida nodded her assent. Max picked up Lianne's case and they went to the door. "Look after that arthritis, Mrs. Weber," he said to the housekeeper.

"*Oui, monsieur. Merci.* Have a nice evening."

And they were off with a gust of swirling snowflakes. Ida closed the door, shivering a little at the pocket of cold air that had filled the entry hall. She heard the couple laughing as they descended the steps. There was joy in their voices. Ida knew what it meant. Very soon Maximilian Julen would take Madame Gevers's granddaughter as his wife.

## CHAPTER NINE

AT THE SOUND of a horn Tatiana dashed from her room and down the hall, nearly colliding with Maria. She entered the sitting room, traversing it in four or five strides, and slid over the highly polished floor to the window. She pulled back the sheer curtains, looked down at the pavement out front, up the street in one direction, then back the other way, her long tawny hair swishing with each rapid movement of her head.

It was dark and snow was falling, but there was no sign of a taxi anywhere. Tatiana sighed with relief. "It's not him!" she called out. "I still have time to change."

She turned around, managing only a step or two before she saw Maria blocking the doorway, her hands on her hips, her resolute countenance as imposing as the walls of Avila.

*"Mademoiselle,"* the housekeeper said in heavily accented French, "your father is only gone from the house for an hour and you treat the place as if it were the refuse pit of the city. Look," she said, pointing, "books and magazines on the divan, records on the table. And your room is a disaster. If I permitted it, even my kitchen would be in shambles. *¡Dios mio!"*

Tatiana drew herself up to her full height, though in her jumper, which came a good four inches above her knees, she had the look of a girl. She put her hands on her hips in defiance. "Maria, I don't have time to argue with you. Uncle Alex called from the airport, and he'll be here anytime. I have to get changed.''

"If you don't respect your father, if you don't respect me, at least respect your visitor.''

"He's not a visitor! He's family. He's my only uncle and Papa's only brother.''

Maria glared. ''Does this mean you cannot show respect?''

"Oh, sometimes you're impossible.'' Tatiana went to the couch and picked up the books and magazines that had been so offensive. There were quite a few, so it took her a while to gather all of them. Then she walked past the housekeeper, lifting her chin as a parting shot of defiance. ''If I'm still changing when he arrives, you'll just have to explain.''

*"Bastante,"* the housekeeper said, throwing up her hands in resignation. ''Okay. I'll bring the other things, but it is the last time. I do it now only because your uncle is coming, and he mustn't see a house fit for... *cochons!"*

Tatiana dropped the books and magazines onto the floor in her room, then kicked aside the jeans and sweater she had worn the day before as she made her way to the large mirrored armoire. It was crammed so full that she could hardly see a thing.

What she had been fearing so long had finally happened. Ever since her lunch with Lianne she had regretted inviting her uncle back to Geneva. Finding out about the baby, and seeing how Lianne had suffered had made Tatiana see her in a new light. Of course, she still wasn't thrilled with the notion of her father marrying again, but if it had to be someone, at least she liked Lianne.

And now Uncle Alex had returned and he was sure to make a mess of everything. Tatiana felt terrible because she knew it was her fault. But at the same time she did love her uncle and always found his visits exciting. Perhaps, if she was lucky, she could convince him that he shouldn't see Lianne. No, she decided, that would never work. He had come all the way from Africa to see her. The best she could hope for was to find out what he had in mind.

And, of course, she could try and warn Papa. As soon as her uncle had phoned from the airport, Tatiana had called Lianne's, but there was no answer. They'd already left for their party in Gland. Fortunately Papa had left a telephone number in case of an emergency, so she would call him there as soon as she was alone again.

Uncle Alex rarely stayed with them when he came to Geneva, preferring the privacy of a hotel. Tatiana hadn't understood when she was younger, but now she knew why. He wanted to be able to share his bed, and that he couldn't very well do if he were in their house.

There were one or two ladies in town who still loved Uncle Alex, Tatiana was quite sure, though by necessity it was now from afar. The only one she knew by name was Claire Jacquet, a rich divorcée with big breasts who had also shown an interest in Papa a few years earlier, though he had never reciprocated.

But Tatiana knew Madame Jacquet still adored Uncle Alex, because the last time he was in Geneva she'd called the house asking for him. Nobody had ever told her so, but Tatiana even suspected Uncle Alex had been Madame Jacquet's lover before her divorce. In her maturity Tatiana now realized that might have been another reason why Uncle Alex had stayed away from Geneva for so long.

Of course, none of that mattered now. It was Uncle Alex and Lianne that concerned her. What was she to do about that? The first thing was to get herself dressed so she'd be presentable when he arrived!

She began pulling clothes from the armoire and spreading them out on the rumpled bed so that she could select what to wear. Lianne had shown her how to put on mascara and had bought her a little lip rouge, which she had begun wearing over Papa's initial objection, though, by agreement, not to school. She decided to take the time to add makeup. Fortunately she'd already bathed and washed her hair. She didn't want Uncle Alex to have to wait too long.

Tatiana continued rifling through the armoire until she had a dozen outfits spread out before her. What a shock Uncle Alex's call had been. When she found out he was phoning from the airport and not Africa, she'd sputtered with surprise. No, she'd told him, Papa was away for a few days. She hadn't known whether or not to tell him he was with Lianne, so she hadn't.

"Then may I come to see you?" he'd asked.

"Of course you can. Why shouldn't I want to see my favorite uncle?"

He'd laughed, the way he always laughed. She did love him and found him wonderfully exciting. But she wished now he hadn't listened to her plea to return to Geneva.

Their telephone conversation had been brief, and he hadn't mentioned Lianne, though Tatiana was sure it would be a major topic of conversation once he arrived. What if he asked her a lot of questions? What would she tell him?

Tatiana sat down on the bed, right on a wool plaid skirt, trying to sort out the dilemma. Adrenaline began flowing as the terrible possibilities began occurring to her. *"Mon Dieu,"* she said, half-aloud.

The doorbell sounded and she jumped to her feet. "Oh, no," she cried, glancing down at herself, knowing there was absolutely no way she could go to the door looking as she did.

Grabbing the brown dress that Lianne had helped her pick out the month before, Tatiana went to her dresser and took out a pair of beige tights, then held them next to the dress, trying to picture the effect. It would be close enough, she decided, and tossed the dress onto the dresser, knocking a little stack of loose photographs to the floor.

*"Merde!"* she said with exasperation as she grabbed the hem of her jumper and pulled it over her head in a single motion. She was peeling off her white tights, balanced precariously on one foot, when there was a knock at the door.

*"Oui?"*

"Your uncle is here, Tatiana," Maria said.

"I'll be right down. Three minutes!" She remembered her mascara. She had to put on her mascara. "No, ten minutes. Tell him just ten minutes!"

The housekeeper went away, and Tatiana quickly dressed. Then she began rummaging through the bottom of the armoire, looking for shoes that would go with the dress. She only had a couple of brown pairs. Where were they? Finally she found the ones she was looking for, but there were ugly scuffs on them. She groaned. Too late now.

She looked at her watch, but it had stopped. She'd forgotten to wind it again. She stuck her head out the door and, seeing the hall empty, dashed into the bath. Her hair didn't look bad; it simply needed to be pulled back on the sides and clipped with barrettes. The mascara would take the most time.

She quickly found it in her little box of makeup. Pulling out the mascara wand, she leaned close to the mirror, just as Lianne had showed her. Opening her lids as wide as she could, she began stroking her lashes. When she finished, she applied some lip rouge. She looked fine, except for the scuffs on her shoes. She'd simply have to keep her feet out of sight.

She headed for the sitting room, forcing herself to slow down to keep from skipping. When she entered the room, Maria was just placing the tea tray on the table. Alex was at the window in a light linen suit, his tie loosened and the top button of his shirt undone. One hand was resting on his hip, the other holding back the sheers so that he could see out.

It was snowing hard. Tatiana could see the swirling flakes against the black of the windowpane. She cleared her throat, loud enough for him to hear. He turned his head and looked back into the room.

"Hello, Uncle Alex. You're looking well."

His mouth curled with amusement. He let his eyebrows rise. "Uncle Alex, you say? Do I know you, *mademoiselle?* I was under the impression this was the home of my little niece, Tatiana Julen."

"Uncle Alex! Don't you recognize me?" She knew he was teasing.

"Tatiana?"

She couldn't help herself. She skipped across the room and into his arms. He embraced her, twisting her back and forth as they hugged. Then she offered him her cheeks, and he kissed them.

"My God, how you've grown." He held her by the shoulders at arm's length, looking her up and down. "What's Max been feeding you? Fertilizer?"

"Certainly not," she replied, giggling.

"Don't laugh. Some folks in my part of the world don't eat much better sometimes."

"Uncle Alex, this is your part of the world. You're not African, for heaven's sake!"

He smiled at the quasi-adult lilt to her voice. The child had grown up without him even knowing about it. "No, I suppose you're right. It's been a while since I've been back. And I'm glad now I couldn't resist your invitation."

Tatiana managed to smile, but the words made her feel positively dreadful. "How long will you stay?"

"That depends," he said, taking her arm and leading her back to the sofa. They sat down in front of the tea Maria had set out.

"Shall I pour?" she asked.

"If you like."

As she leaned forward on the edge of her seat to pour the tea, Alex lightly touched her hair, marveling that the child he'd spawned was already very nearly a woman.

"What does your staying depend upon?" she asked.

"I've accumulated a few months of leave, but I haven't yet decided whether to take it now. And, of course, it depends upon the needs of the Red Cross. We're pretty shorthanded in Lagos right now. I'll be meeting with my superiors at the beginning of the week. So we'll see."

She handed him a cup and saucer. "I hope you won't have to go away."

Alex reached out and patted her cheek. "It's really good to see you, Tatiana."

She looked over the handsome man who, second only to her father, she had always loved more than anyone in the world. Uncle Alex was a tease. He made her laugh. Ever since she could remember their relationship had been very special.

He smiled at her, his soft brown eyes always a little mischievous. There were wrinkles at the corners of them, deeper than she had remembered, and his hair had touches of gray, more even than Papa. His tanned face looked a little older and more drawn, and it had been a day since he had shaved, but he was still terribly handsome. Perhaps Papa had aged just as much, though seeing him all the time she didn't notice it. Tatiana sipped her tea.

"Oh," Alex said, putting his cup down, "I nearly forgot. Your Christmas present." He reached behind the divan and picked up a large rectangular box from the floor. It was perhaps half a yard long and wrapped in paper painted with brightly colored primitive figures of a Madonna and child. He handed it to her. "Shopping's a bit limited in Nigeria. Hope you like it."

"I can't open it now. Christmas is a week away."

"Well, I'd planned to get you something else, as well. We'll make this the gift I brought you because you're my... niece."

"If you think that's all right."

"Of course it is."

Tatiana examined the paper. "Looks African."

Alex laughed. "It is."

She gently shook the box. It was fairly light, but there was a solid object of some sort inside. "It seems suspiciously like a doll," she said. "The box is the right size. I hope you know I've outgrown dolls, Uncle Alex."

"It's not a baby doll."

She gave him a mildly displeased look and began removing the paper.

"I told you, shopping's limited. But now that I see you're a grown-up lady, perhaps I can bring you some jewelry in the future. They've some lovely handmade ivory and semiprecious stone pieces.''

"I'm sure the doll is very nice.'' She had the paper torn off and was breaking the tape that held the lid in place.

"It's not exactly a doll, mind you.''

Tatiana managed to get it undone and lifted the lid. Inside she found a carved wood figurine, a rather dramatic piece. "Oh . . . how lovely.'' She lifted it out of the box.

"It's not quite museum quality, but I'm told it's a very fine example of primitive art. The dealer claimed it was a hundred years old.''

"Uncle Alex, how wonderful! It's not a doll at all. It's art!'' She leaned over and kissed him on the cheek. "It's beautiful and I like it very much.'' She turned the figure around and looked at it from each angle. "Is it used for something special or just decoration?''

He chuckled. "It's a fertility figure, I'm told. But don't tell your father that.''

Tatiana blushed. "No, Papa wouldn't understand at all. He's very stuffy about some things, and he worries about me all the time, though of course there's no reason. If it wasn't for Lianne, I wouldn't even be able to wear—'' She stopped abruptly and put her hand to her mouth. "Oh . . .''

"What's the matter?'' Alex said. "Would you prefer not to talk about Lianne?''

She prevaricated. "I didn't know if you'd want to.''

"Why shouldn't we? You called me about her, didn't you?''

She took a deep breath and drew herself up. "That was when I was very emotional on the subject. Since then I've thought I might be putting my nose in business that wasn't mine. I hope you didn't come to see her on my account, Uncle Alex."

"Don't worry, Tatiana. That isn't why I came."

She gave an audible sigh. "Really?"

He shook his head.

She felt tremendously relieved. Why hadn't he said that from the beginning? "So you won't see her then?"

"To the contrary. I do plan to see Lianne, if she's willing."

Tatiana's heart rose into her throat again. "Oh..." She glanced down at her gift, toying with it, avoiding her uncle's eyes. Then she looked up at him. "I think Papa and Lianne are in love, Uncle Alex. I think they'll get married."

Alex blinked. "Max and Lianne?"

Tatiana nodded, watching the strange expression cross his face. He didn't say anything, and after a while he loosened his tie a little more. "Hmm. That's a surprise, isn't it?"

"I hope I didn't upset you." She watched him very closely.

Alex shook his head. "Why would it upset me?"

"I know everything, Uncle Alex."

*"Everything?"*

"Lianne told me about the baby, about the two of you. It's a very sad story. I cried when I heard. Poor Lianne."

"Oh, yes, that. I see. It was a difficult time, true. Surely she's over it by now, though. I mean . . ."

"I'm sure she thinks about it. But the important thing is that she's happy now."

"So it seems. So are your father and Lianne engaged?"

"I guess not officially."

"But they told you they'll marry? Is that it?"

"Not exactly, Uncle Alex. That's my impression. I mean, they see each other all the time."

"That's a bit different, Tatiana. It could be that you're seeing more than there is." Alex picked up his teacup. He stared out the window at the snow.

Tatiana noticed the strange expression on his face, and she could tell he was thinking about Lianne. It was possible that he still loved her, but there was really no way to know for sure. "Would it upset you if they got married?"

"Of course not." He smiled, but it wasn't very convincing.

Tatiana shrugged, but she was beginning to think her suspicions were right. Perhaps Uncle Alex loved Lianne, too. What a terribly complicated situation it had become!

"What about you, Tatiana," Alex asked, "how do you feel about all this?"

"I like Lianne. And I want everybody to be happy. Beyond that, I try not to think about it too much."

"Yes, I suppose one doesn't change mothers like shoes, does one?"

"What?"

He patted her hand. "Oh, nothing, just sort of muttering to myself."

She looked at him and could tell that his mind was already somewhere else. It was like that when he visited. He always seemed to be off in Africa or South America or some other place in the world. Uncle Alex never really came home. But this time Geneva was a different place. Lianne Halliday was here. Tatiana could tell that much by the vacant, dreamy look in his eyes.

GLAND WAS A VILLAGE in the canton of Vaud, about halfway between Geneva and Lausanne. There were a number of small châteaux and grand houses in the district. That night the countryside was a fairyland, dusted white with a thin glaze of snow. As they made their way along a country lane in the Mercedes, crystalline snowflakes still swirled in the air. Lianne rested her hand on Max's shoulder.

"We'll be at the Barots in a few minutes," he said. "I suppose I ought to tell you what I've got planned for the evening, so you won't be upset if I take you away early."

"What do you have planned?" she asked. Her voice had a lilt to it.

"I've rented a villa on the mountain above the lake near Montreux. It's not ostentatious—part chalet, part manor house—but we'll have total privacy. I thought it was an ideal place for the two of us to get away...alone."

"It sounds lovely, Max. Was this a spur-of-the-moment decision, or have you planned it for a while?"

"I've been thinking about it. I know the place and I want to share it with you."

She reached over and patted his knee. "I'm sure it's wonderful."

"The weather worries me a bit. We normally don't get much snow at the lower elevations. The villa is partway up the mountain." He smiled at her. "But I'll get you there if I have to pull you on a sleigh myself."

"How gallant!" she teased.

He took her hand. "Lianne, I love you."

She kissed his fingers, and when she spoke, her voice was low, serious. "Each morning I wake up happier than the day before. Does that tell you how I feel?"

"This will be a special weekend for us, darling. Very special."

She looked out at the snowflakes dancing in the head-lights. At times the visibility became impossible, but she wasn't alarmed. She trusted Max completely.

In a few minutes they entered the gates of a large estate. The manor house, a small château, was aglow with lights. Numerous cars, all luxury vehicles, were parked about the grounds. A valet stepped out to greet them.

*"Bon soir, monsieur, dame,"* he said, opening Lianne's door. He helped her out and Max came around, offering her his arm. They hurried to the door where a butler admitted them instantly.

Pierette Barot, fiftyish, wearing heavy emerald satin, came hurrying to the door as the maid was taking their coats. *"Voilà!* You made it! And I was worrying about the snow." She let Max kiss her on the cheek, and he introduced Lianne. "Aren't you stunning, though! *Ravis-sante!"* There was a smile on her pretty round face. "Max deserves you, my dear. I needn't tell you what a wonderful man he is, though, I'm sure."

Roger Barot arrived to greet them. Tall, gray-headed and proper. Understated, compared to his wife. "Welcome, Miss Halliday. We've heard so much about you." He spoke in English.

"Oh, Roger," Pierette protested, touching her dark hair. "She'll think we've been talking about her all evening!" She took Lianne's arm. "Of course, it's true." Then she laughed. "Come along, *ma chère.* We'll get the introductions over with so you can get back to Max. Roger," she called over her shoulder, "show Max to the bar, will you, dear?"

They made the rounds then, Lianne certain by the way she was watched that they had all been waiting to meet Maximilian Julen's American friend. She had already met a few. She and Max had shared a box with one couple at the theater and another she'd met at a restaurant off the Place du Rhône. But most were new to her. She was introduced to the grandson of Nanna's friend, Madame Dunoyer, and his wife. They were one of the few younger couples. Many were older—matrons in out-of-fashion gowns and heavy diamond necklaces, white-haired gentlemen with creaky voices and creakier backs.

"So," Pierette said after they pretty well covered the salon and ballroom, "that's done. I wouldn't have put you through it, but otherwise you'd be pestered all evening."

They were standing on the dais at the end of the small ballroom, looking over the crowd. The chairs nearby appeared to be ready for musicians, but none were yet in evidence.

She saw Max at the far end of the room, moving through the crowd toward her, and she smiled. He'd only gone a few steps when a redhead with large breasts intercepted him. Pierette had introduced her earlier, but Lianne couldn't remember her name.

Pierette saw her noticing. "Claire Jacquet," she said, anticipating the question.

Lianne watched the animated conversation, noticing Claire shifting her bare shoulders as she spoke. It was almost as if she were gesturing with her bosom. When Lianne was introduced to her earlier, the conversation had been subdued. If anything, the redhead had been sullen to the point of dour. "They seem to know one another well," she observed to Pierette.

"Claire was probably the most disappointed woman in Geneva when your friendship with Max became common knowledge."

"Pity." Lianne noticed a decided twinkle in Pierette's eye.

"Her papa owns stores, all kinds of them in Switzerland and France, and he's always wanted to expand the family horizons. He's had his eye on the Julens for twenty years. It broke his heart when Max married Catrina, so he set his sights on Alex—have you met Alex?"

Lianne nodded.

"Of course, your grandmother knew them for years." Pierette toyed with her diamond lavaliere as she spoke. "Anyway, for a while Monsieur Jacquet had Claire paired up with Alex, but he went off with the Red Cross—God only knows why. Claire married unwisely and was divorced after a few years. It looked hopeless for her until Max was widowed. Then the Jacquets put on a campaign like you've never seen. Papa all but proposed to Max himself."

"Poor Claire."

"She's spoiled and utterly boring in my opinion. Max was wise not to let her turn his head. Hasn't he told you any of this?"

Lianne shook her head.

"He's a modest man. Of course he wouldn't. Claire's of no consequence, though. You needn't worry about her. If you want my opinion, it's Alex she still loves."

Lianne felt her curiosity rise, though not the tiniest part of her felt jealous. "And how does he feel about her?"

"Well, he's hardly ever in Geneva. I suppose that's an answer in itself. Alex has a train of broken hearts across the map. But listen to me gossip! That's hardly what you're here for."

Lianne liked Pierette. She was less staid than most Swiss, and clearly easy to talk to. As they watched, Max broke away from Claire and resumed his trek toward them. "Ah, here he comes," Pierette said.

They watched him moving through the crowd, stopping every so often for a word or two with someone. He had a glass of punch in each hand and looked at them whenever he was stopped.

"Poor Max," Pierette said. "All he wants is to be with you."

"You think so?"

"But of course, my dear."

He finally made his way to them, handing Lianne a cup of punch. Then he leaned over and kissed her cheek. "Sorry I took so long."

"Why Max," Pierette teased, "we hardly noticed."

He looked at her suspiciously. "What's going on, you two? Judging by your faces, a feminine conspiracy is brewing."

"That must be your guilt talking. We saw you chatting up your bosom buddy," Lianne replied coolly, using English.

Max turned red.

*"Qu'est-ce que c'est?"* Pierette didn't understand.

"Nothing," Lianne replied. "A feminine retort to Max's feminine conspiracy."

"Remind me not to leave you two alone," he said, sipping his punch.

"It's apparent *you* shouldn't be left alone," Lianne said, teasing him.

Max looked amused. "You aren't jealous of Claire, are you?"

"Yes," she replied, and then laughed.

He put his arm around her. "Delicate but deadly these American women," he said to Pierette.

She patted his cheek. "You have nothing to complain about, *mon chéri*. I haven't seen you looking so fit and happy in ages."

"Lianne may have something to do with it, you're right," he said wryly, and gave her a sly wink.

Pierette noticed the moment they were sharing. "Well, dears, I must attend to my other guests." She gave Max a perfunctory kiss, then Lianne. "I'm off. Perhaps I can breathe a little life into this séance before it's through." She hurried away.

They were silent for a while after her departure, sipping their punch.

"So what did you and Pierette discuss?"

She bit the inside of her cheek to keep from giggling. "Claire Jacquet's breasts. Did you notice them, Max?"

He smiled at her game. "Perhaps."

"I would hope you did. You aren't blind."

"True."

"I understand she has a predilection for Julen men."

"So you heard the whole story."

"Enough of it. So...why didn't you marry her?"

"I didn't love her."

"Her father's very rich, I understand."

He reached over and tweaked her nose. "I had no desire to marry him, either."

Lianne laughed. "Claire must not care much for me."

"We hardly discussed you, as a matter of fact."

She cocked her head, clearly interested in the details. "Hardly, but you did."

"A little."

"And what did she say?"

"That you're very pretty."

"It was a ploy. You didn't believe her, I hope."

"Oh, but I did. She was very convincing on the point."

Lianne gave him a playful nudge. He squeezed her. She liked the feel of Max's arm around her.

"Come on. Let's find a quiet spot where we can... spoon," he said.

"Darling, we have to update your vocabulary."

They moved off through the smiling crowd, arm in arm. Strange how relative everything was, she thought. Only a year ago she had been to a faculty mixer at NYU where a young art history professor had told her how remote and untouchable she seemed. He'd been willing to change that, but Lianne hadn't given him the chance. Without knowing it she must have been waiting for Max. She was still smiling to herself when he got her alone in a quiet corner.

"What's so amusing?" he asked.

"Perhaps I was remembering the roses you brought me this evening."

"Liar."

"You can't know everything, even if Swiss gentlemen are used to being master."

"I think it's time to go to Montreux."

"We can't be impolite. Besides, Claire and I might want to talk a little. Compare notes perhaps."

*"Mechante!"*

She laughed gleefully.

"I'll give you half an hour more. Forty-five minutes maximum. Then I'm taking you to Montreux."

A few minutes later one of the maids found them. "Oh, here you are, Monsieur Julen. You have a telephone call. It's your daughter."

He looked startled. "Is it an emergency?"

"I don't believe so, *monsieur.* But the young lady said she would like to speak with you."

"Very well." He glanced at Lianne. "If you'll excuse me, darling."

Lianne watched Max go off with the maid. What could have gotten into Tatiana? she wondered. It seemed of late the girl had gone out of her way not to interfere. Her jealousy seemed long past. Hopefully there wasn't a problem.

As she stood sipping her punch, the Charavays joined her. They were the couple she'd met at the theater with Max. Gilbert was in his mid-fifties with deep-set, penetrating eyes that seemed to dance. He had a well-trimmed goatee that he stroked as he exchanged anecdotes with Lianne about Shelley, whom he had read extensively in English.

Stella, his wife, was Austrian, at least fifteen years younger and very effervescent. She was tall, with a pleasant figure and the palest blue eyes Lianne had ever seen. Stella painted while Gilbert was away trading commodities and dabbling in other types of business.

"You're the talk of the ball, you know," Gilbert said, speaking in English as always. "Noticed for your beauty and charm and for the man who brought you. A lot of tongues are wagging."

"Oh, Gilbert," Stella said, admonishing him. Then to Lianne she said, "He always wants to be the first to know when an important announcement is forthcoming."

"There are no announcements I'm aware of," Lianne said, feeling a bit embarrassed.

"It's terribly rude of us to pry, but it's only because we're so fond of Max. I hope you won't resent us."

"Of course not."

"Then the subject is closed." Stella looked relieved.

Max made his way through the throng to where Lianne was standing with his friends. She immediately noticed the troubled expression on his face. He greeted the Charavays.

"Is everything all right?" Lianne asked.

"Yes, yes, it was nothing." He glanced at the other couple. "A phone call from Tatiana," he explained. "But nothing to worry about. She wanted to be sure we made it all right with the snow. Apparently it's coming down pretty good in Geneva."

"Unusual storm," Gilbert said.

"You know, Lianne," Max said, "I think perhaps we should be on our way. The longer we wait the worse driving conditions will be."

"Whatever you think, Max."

"You aren't taking her away," Stella protested. "Lianne's the loveliest flower at the ball."

"You'll be seeing her at others," Max replied. "Many others."

Stella looked at Lianne with a knowing smile. Then she leaned close to her. "I believe our intuition was right," she whispered. "And if I may say so, Max couldn't do better."

Gilbert was shaking Max's hand. "What's this?" Max said, turning to the women. "More machinations?"

"I was just telling your young lady how much she is admired," Stella said.

"By none more than I," he replied.

"No, Maximilian dear," the woman said. "That's readily apparent."

# CHAPTER TEN

THEY FOUND LAUSANNE asleep when they entered it, a village already curled up for the night. There were a few small groups of young people out in the snow near the cafés, laughing, throwing handfuls of slush or sliding on the frost-slickened pavement. But most of Lausanne was at the family hearth, or already sleeping under down comforters.

Max drove through the dark streets, the cathedral sitting on the hill above them, its spires and gray towers lit up in the night. The Mercedes moved purposefully, tires hissing through the half-melted snow. By the time they left Lausanne, large, wet semicrystalline flakes had begun falling. They were rain as much as snow, forcing Max to turn on the windshield wipers so they could see through the glaze of slush.

Lianne had grown quiet, curled up in her chinchilla, even though it was warm enough in the car. Max looked over at her, his heart aching. Not only had Alex arrived, but the time for telling the truth was upon them. Now Max deeply regretted that he'd promised his brother a chance to make his peace with Lianne first.

Perhaps it was his own fault for not making it clearer how much Lianne meant to him or what his intentions were. Still, that didn't mean he had to sit by and let Alex take the lead. His own feelings weren't in doubt. He loved Lianne as much as a man could love a woman, and he believed she loved him the same way. But how would her feelings be affected by what she was to learn about Tatiana? That was the unknown.

He had been thinking about the problem ever since his daughter's call. Even if the truth had to wait, his plans for Lianne didn't. Alex's unexpected arrival made what he intended to do all the more urgent.

They quickly passed through the villages of Lutry, Cully, St-Saphorin and the small town of Vevey. The rain turned to snow, soft full-bodied flakes, then back to rain again.

It was nearly midnight by the time they reached Montreux at the foot of the Bernese Alps. The streets were coated with a blanket of white frosting, broken only by dark grooves where vehicles had passed. When the tires of the Mercedes began slipping a little, Max drove more slowly than before, though it would take a hard freeze to turn the pavement to ice and become a real danger.

The Villa Saint Maurice Aumont was high on the mountain above Montreux. Max had been there before—always, it seemed, at critical times in his life. His mother had taken him there as a young boy to recover from a bout of rheumatic fever. And he had returned again for a week several months after Catrina died. He always thought of it as a restful, salubrious place. A place for reflection.

The setting was beautiful, with a sweeping view of Lac Léman. It inspired one, almost like one of the Shelley poems Lianne loved so. She, of all people, would appreciate what he saw in it.

When Max decided to take her away to some special place to propose, he had immediately thought of the Villa Saint Maurice Aumont. He knew their love was strong, but he also knew it would be tested by the secrets that stood between them. So it seemed doubly important to make such an emotional occasion as romantic and special as he possibly could.

Alex's arrival had added pressure, but Max was determined not to let it spoil things for Lianne. He wouldn't tell her about it until the next morning. Then, once she'd seen Alex—assuming she even wished to—he would tell her the truth about Tatiana. If their love survived all that, then and only then would he know that marriage was right.

So, when Max thought about it, he decided Alex's arrival had changed nothing. It simply meant that things would be happening very quickly now. The next few days, it appeared, would be among the most critical in all their lives.

He looked over at Lianne and found her staring at him. She smiled, and her innocence in the affair struck him once again. A pang of doubt shot through him, and he hoped she wouldn't resent or hate him for the secret he had kept.

"Tell me about this place you're taking me to," she said.

"There's not a lot to talk about. I've been here a few times before."

"When?"

He related the circumstances of the prior visits.

"It seems it's special to you," she said.

"I wanted to share it with you especially."

That seemed to please her.

"This is a very special time," he said obliquely. "I want you to remember it always."

They were going up the twisting mountainside. Max had to drive carefully. At the higher elevation the snow was thicker. In not too many hours more the road would become impassable. They encountered no other vehicles, adding to the sense of isolation and adventure. The snowy night would make the villa seem all the more inviting. Despite the lateness of the hour, Max was glad he had brought her.

Soon they pulled into the entrance to the villa, passing under an arch of snow-veiled branches. They had arrived none too early. The snowfall was heavy now, making driving difficult.

They traversed the short distance along the drive to the front of the dwelling, which was nestled in a copse of trees. By night, in the snow, the villa looked magical. Soft, warm light came from the windows.

Lianne was delighted. "What a lovely place, Max."

He didn't say anything. He just smiled and got out, going around the car to help her. She stepped out into the icy air, scented with the faint perfume of evergreen and wood smoke. There was no wind. The snowflakes drifted down around them, spinning slowly as they fell.

He led her to the entrance and thumped the heavy knocker. The door opened, and a slight middle-aged woman greeted them. "*Bon soir, monsieur, dame.* Please come in."

They went inside, the woman noticing their evening dress, though she didn't comment on it. She made cheerful sounds of greeting. Lianne let the woman help her with her coat, shivering as the satin lining slid over her arms.

"We're a bit later than I expected, *madame,*" Max said, removing his own coat. "I hope you hadn't given up on us."

"Certainly not, *monsieur.* Everything is as you requested." She pulled the cardigan she wore over her chest. "Do you have baggage?"

"In the trunk, yes."

"Give me your keys, *monsieur*, if you would. I'll see that they're fetched."

Max handed the woman his car keys. She then led them into the adjacent sitting room, sunken a few steps and dominated at one end by a large rustic fireplace made of stone. A couple of logs were blazing, giving off considerable light. Lianne went to it, holding out her palms and rubbing them together. She looked back at Max, who stood at the entrance, watching her. She smiled like a child giddy with joy. He beamed at her, then talked to the proprietress for a moment about the arrangements for breakfast. The woman left to see to their bags.

Max waited for a moment where he stood. Lianne turned to face him, letting the fire warm her backside. She could feel the heat of it through her gown. They looked at each other for several moments with bridled anticipation.

In the firelight Max's hair seemed darker, his face more distinctly contoured. He looked terribly handsome in his formal attire. And yet, whenever Lianne looked at him, his gentleness and kindness came through. To the world he was a wealthy and powerful man, but to her he was foremost a considerate, tender lover, devoted both to her and to his child.

"How do you like the Villa Saint Maurice Aumont?" he asked.

"It's delightful, Max. Wonderful."

He made his way to where she stood, stopping before her. The fire made the shadows dance on his face. Lianne felt goose bumps rise on her arms despite the warmth of the blaze. Max rested his hands on her bare shoulders, and she began trembling from the sheer romance of the moment.

"Are you still chilled?"

She slipped her arms around him and held herself against his body. "No, but I want you to hold me."

He did, rubbing her back and her narrow, chiffon-covered waist. Then she turned in his arms so that she could look down at the fire while he held her. His hands were clasped over her stomach. She felt warm and secure. It was a glorious feeling.

Still, she was a little startled when his lips touched her skin at the curve of her neck. She lifted her shoulder, rolling her head against his. She put her fingers against his cheek.

"I've been waiting to kiss you all evening," he said.

Lianne caressed his jaw with her fingers, feeling the faintest prickle from his closely shaved beard. He kissed her neck again, his moist lips making her shiver, though they were more warm than cold.

She wanted to feel his mouth with her own, so she turned around, raising her chin and offering him her lips. He kissed her then, fragilely, lightly, one hand at the back of her waist, holding her against him.

They heard the proprietress of the villa out in the hall-way. She appeared at the door. *"Pardon, monsieur,"* the woman said as they moved apart. "Your valises are in your room. Shall I bring the champagne before I go?"

"Please."

There were two large chairs covered in a bold French floral print facing the fireplace. Lianne went and sat down in one, Max in the other. The woman brought a bottle of Cliquot in an ice bucket and placed it between them on a small table, along with two champagne flutes. Then she bid them good-night. A moment later, they heard the heavy front door first open, then close.

"I hope she hasn't far to go," Lianne said as Max removed the protective foil from the champagne bottle.

"No, she lives in a cottage a few meters along the road." He popped the cork. "I shouldn't worry about her."

"She looks after the villa?"

"Yes," he said, pouring the wine. "This place will accommodate a dozen people and is often rented to groups. But I wanted it for us alone. There's no one else here." After he filled each flute half-full, he handed one to Lianne, then took the other. Raising it before him so that the bubbles sparkled in the firelight, he said, "To you, my love."

Lianne sipped the champagne, amused by the tickle of the bubbles on her nose. The room felt warm to her now, and though she would have liked still to be in Max's arms, she did feel content and happy.

For several minutes they sat in silence, together yet apart, looking at the fire, aware of each other, feeling companionship and all the contentment it suggested. It was amazing to her how much her life had changed, what new and wonderful feelings Max had brought to it. Her existence had been so removed from real life before—much like the poetry she studied, full of nostalgic remembrance, sorrowful emotion and regret.

That had all changed now. The passion she'd longed for had become immediate, a part of her daily existence. And the difference was Max's love.

"I'm terribly happy," she told him, a dreamy smile of contentment on her face. "Thank you for bringing me here."

"I was hoping you'd like it. I want us to be happy together, always."

She glanced at him, her eyes glistening, seeing that his were, too. She could tell that he wanted to say more. And she sensed that he would when he felt the moment was right. It was no accident he'd brought her to such a romantic spot to profess his love—that seemed obvious. He sipped his champagne, and so did she.

After they had a second glass, Max asked, "Shall we go upstairs now? Unless the snow is too heavy, you'll see a remarkable view. This place is renowned for it."

She said she was ready to go and, after Max put the protective screen across the fireplace, they went upstairs hand in hand, the wooden steps creaking under their feet. At the top of the stairs they traversed a wide hall running the length of the second floor. Windows looked out onto the wooded park in front, the snow-laden boughs reminding her of the white-flocked Christmas trees of her childhood.

The snowfall had let up, only an occasional flake descending the night sky. The air had cleared and was crystalline now. It was so beautiful.

"Max," she said, stopping him, "look out there. Isn't it magnificent?" And he stood with her, watching petals of snow drifting down. "It's like a fairyland," she whispered.

He put his arm around her. "It's real. Very real. And it's all for you."

She turned to him, and he kissed her more demandingly than before. Desire for him rose within her.

"*Viens,*" he whispered. "Come to our room."

She went with him toward the end of the hall where a flickering glow reflected off a polished wooden door. She entered ahead of him, her eyes drawn to a fire burning in a small fireplace at one side of the room.

At the opposite side was a four-poster canopy bed. It wasn't large—no bigger than her bed at Nanna's—but it was very tall, and the heavy brocade of the canopy looked quite old. The dust ruffle and tufted headboard matched the canopy, but the bedding was mostly white—a white lace blanket cover and great puffy lace shams and pillows propped against the headboard. A thick down comforter the color of patina gold was folded at the foot of the bed.

Opposite them was an alcove with a large bay window, its glass black like an ebony mirror. Lianne could see the muted lines of their reflections—Max standing beside her, little more than the white of his shirtfront, his face and hands visible. But her bare shoulders rising from the smoky gray gown and the burnt gold of her hair were reflected in the glass.

"What's out there? The lake?"

"Go see."

As Max closed the door, she went across the room to the alcove, which was like an observation deck affording a breathtaking perspective. The snowy mountainside dropped away, revealing a vast midnight panorama. In the void, beyond the snow-flocked treetops, she saw the faintest suggestion of light, a smudge of illumination below the horizon, like distant stars spread out along a taut invisible string.

Max came up behind her, and she took his hand. "Is that the lake out there?"

"Yes, and the lights you see are St-Gingolph at the French border."

"It's beautiful, in an eerie, mystical sort of way."

Max pulled the heavy velvet curtains closed behind them, cutting off the light from the fire and the other reflections on the glass. The scene outside the windows became more distinct now, the profiles of the mountains discernible from the night sky above and the ebony surface of the lake far below them. She gasped at the dramatic effect.

Lianne put her arms around him, hugging him close as they stood together in the intimate space, their nocturnal observatory. "What an incredible sight."

"And always different. I've never seen it quite like this."

Lianne stared out, resting her head on his shoulder. "Oh, Max, what a lovely, lovely moment." She felt her eyes fill. He kissed her forehead.

"Darling, darling, I love you so."

"And I love you."

Max turned her around to face him. She could see his eyes shimmering in the faint light. "Do you, Lianne? Do you really?"

"Yes. Yes, I do."

Max reached into his pocket then and pulled out a small velvet-covered box. He opened it, revealing a huge emerald-cut diamond ring. "Enough that you would be my wife?"

She felt her heart trip at his words, like a faltering engine. Her mouth dropped open as she stared down at the ring in the dim light.

"Will you have me?" he asked.

Tears flooded her eyes and started running down her cheeks. "I can't believe it," she murmured.

Max took the ring from the box and slipped it onto her finger. She touched it, looking at it in the near-darkness. It felt so large, so substantial. Then she pressed her face against his neck.

"Oh, Max, Max." And she began to cry.

"Is it a reason for sadness?" he asked.

She shook her head, managing to smile as she looked up at him.

"Does that mean the answer is yes or no?"

"It's yes, but..."

"But what?"

"Well...I can't say it's unexpected but..." She glanced down at the ring on her finger, not quite believing what she saw.

"I know there's a great deal to think about," he said.

"I love you so much, but to be frank, I'm concerned about Tatiana."

Max stroked her cheek adoringly. "Tatiana is very fond of you, Lianne."

"Yes, as a friend. But if I were to be her father's wife, it would be quite a different thing."

He grew silent then, and she sensed a hesitation. Max didn't say anything, but she could tell there was something troubling him. She had sensed the same thing in him before.

"You have your doubts, don't you?" she said.

"About us? No. Not at all," he replied.

"About Tatiana, then?"

"I know she cares for you, Lianne. Very, very much. That's not it."

"Then what?"

"Let's just say there's much to work out. Things we haven't yet faced."

"What do you mean?"

He wiped away her tears with his thumbs. "We can discuss it later. We can talk more in the morning. What matters is that we want each other, darling. I can't tell you how happy it makes me that you want to be my wife."

"I do want to marry you, Max, though I know you're right. There's a lot to consider."

He kissed her tenderly. She clung to him, feeling the ring on her finger. A whole lifetime was being set. And yet she felt joy more than fear.

"And now there's only one thing I want," he said. "At this moment, I want most to make love with you."

She kissed his lip. "And I want to make love with you," she whispered. "But I want to be alone first. Will you wait here while I undress?"

He looked bemused. "Why? Are you suddenly shy?"

"No, I just want to be in the bed waiting for you. Is it all right?"

He smiled. "If that's what you want."

She kissed him again, then slipped through the heavy curtains. It wasn't a virginal game she had in mind, but if she were to make love with a man who'd just asked her to be his wife, the lovemaking would be a kind of marriage itself. It would be more than simple intimacy—more even than intimacy with love.

The notion of undressing alone appealed to her, especially knowing Max was near, just behind the curtains. She went to the fireplace, noticing the lively sparkle of the diamond on her finger. She held the ring up to the light of the fire, able to really see it for the first time. It was fabulous. A well of pride rose in her.

For a moment she stood at the fire, warming herself. She glanced toward the alcove. "You won't cheat, will you, Max?"

"Not if you don't wish for me to," the disembodied voice replied.

She stepped out of her shoes, then reached back and found her zipper, unfastening it so that her gown fell away, shimmering down her body. She removed Nanna's black pearl necklace and the earrings, placing them carefully on the mantel. Then she removed her undergarments, tossing them onto a nearby chair.

She looked again at the curtain. The thought of Max being there, just behind the heavy fabric, was strangely arousing. "What are you doing?" she asked.

"Waiting. Thinking about you."

It was so strange to hear his voice, to be naked and yet not see him. The fire quickly warmed her legs. She turned toward it, rubbing her thighs, stomach and breasts with the palms of her hands. She was aware, too, of the ring on her finger. When she looked at it, it seemed to dance in the firelight.

"What are *you* doing?" he asked when she didn't reply.

"I'm standing before the fire."

"What do you have on?"

"Just my ring."

"Nothing else?"

"No, nothing else."

Max pulled the curtain open and stepped into the room.

"You weren't supposed to come in yet," she protested.

He stood, taking her in, her golden hair a halo around her shadowed face, the magnificent curves of her body silhouetted by the fire. She folded her hands demurely before her. Max walked toward her.

As he drew near, she saw the desire in his eyes. His jaw was taut as he reached out and touched her face. There was wonder in his intense expression. Wonder and awe. It was as though she were a spirit and he could only satisfy himself of her authenticity by touching her.

He ran his hand down over her naked shoulder, then lightly along her arm. His fingers made her skin come alive. He grasped her hand and brought it to his mouth, kissing her fingers, all the while his eyes locked on to hers.

She felt weak with sensation, as though the champagne she'd drunk had suddenly gone to her head. But it wasn't the wine; it was Max's adoring look.

"I'm going to the bed now," she whispered. "When you've undressed, come join me."

His fingers grazed her breast as she turned and moved across the room to the four-poster bed. Carefully removing the shams and pillows aside, she pulled back the covers and slipped into the bed, the chilly sheets making her muscles tense. It was like jumping into a cool pond on a warm summer day. She shivered.

He hadn't moved from where he stood. But then he started walking slowly toward the bed, slipping off his dinner jacket as he came.

He laid the coat on a straight-backed chair by the bed, then began removing the diamond studs from his dress shirt. When he was naked, he climbed into the bed beside her. His body was warm, and she practically climbed on top of him for the warmth. But it was more than that. Since he had kissed her in the alcove, her body had been throbbing for him.

After a tender kiss, he held her. She clung to him, relishing his protective embrace. They lay together that way for a long time, their breath and body heat warming their cocoon.

Lianne had never felt so close to anyone in her life. The world seemed not to extend beyond the bed. And nothing outside it seemed to exist, let alone matter. There were only his kisses, his hands on her face and her bare skin, slowly arousing her to the point where she felt herself begin to moisten.

Before long their breathing became heavy. The warmth they shared turned to heat. His fingers made her nipples hard. After a while his kisses were no longer enough; she had to have him in her. She begged him to take her, and he complied, the urgency of his own desire apparent.

They were breathing heavily, their tongues probing, searching as he slid on top of her. His hands roamed over her, his fingers biting into her flesh. She opened her legs to him, wanting him desperately.

When Max sank into her core, she cried out, her voice throaty, urgent. They began undulating against each other then, their bodies moving in a kind of desperate, rhythmic harmony. But it wasn't until she dug her nails into his back, wrapped her long legs around his waist and cried out his name that he finally let go. Her climax came then, and she shuddered as wave after wave rippled through her.

Afterward she clung to him, having given him her body completely, knowing now he was much more than a lover. "Max, oh, Max," she said breathlessly, holding his head against her.

"I love you, Lianne. I love you."

There was love in his voice, intense emotion. But she heard something else, as well. Except for the fact that it made no sense, she would have thought it was anguish. And so she stroked his head, holding him, letting herself wonder for the first time if this was what it was like to be a wife.

SHE AWOKE rather suddenly. Max's arm was still across her breast, as it had been when they fell asleep. It was still dark and the fire had burned down. His leg was over her, the down comforter over them both. She could feel his breath ruffling her hair.

Though they were both naked, it was warm in the bed. Too warm. So she scooted away for some space. It was then that she noticed the perfume of their skin, the scent of their lovemaking, wafting from under the comforter. It aroused her and made her feel close to him. Then she was aware of the large diamond on her finger and recalled what had happened before they'd made love. He'd given her the ring and asked her to be his wife.

Lianne slipped her left hand from under the covers and looked at the ring. Her body clenched with excitement as the implications sank in. A buzz of happiness went through her.

She was awake now. And he slept quietly beside her. For a time she lay still, trying to put everything that had transpired into perspective. The memories played in her mind like a dream.

Lifting her head, she looked at the alcove, but saw that the curtain was drawn. She wanted to see it, to recall what had transpired there. And so she got up. She had nothing to wear, so she grabbed Max's jacket, hung neatly over a chair. The satin lining felt cool on her skin, but the air was cold and she was glad for the coat.

The fire had burned down to a bed of coals, barely glowing in the darkness. Hours must have passed, but she had no idea how many. She had no watch. Only the daylight would tell her when the night had ended.

She tiptoed to the alcove and looked through the curtains. It was still quite dark out, though there seemed to be some promise of daylight. She closed the curtain behind her.

There was a narrow padded bench on each of the three sides of the bay window. Lianne sat on the middle section, put her feet on the bench and pulled her legs up against her chest, wrapping the coat around them for warmth.

As she looked out the window, she realized that the sky had cleared. The lights of St-Gingolph were much more distinct, and the line of demarcation between the lake and the mountain was plainly discernible. The sky was lighter than it had been—not yet gray, but neither was it opaque as it had been in the night. And there were stars!

Lianne surveyed the scene, wondering if Shelley had ever beheld the lake at such a moment, if he might have gone out one night, restless, and surveyed the same splendor that she was witnessing now. But she doubted there were ever two moments in all eternity that were alike, and knew she would never experience anything like this again.

As she stared at a bright star over the Alps, lines from Shelley drifted into her mind, heightening her emotion. She hugged herself against the night, against her fears.

Pressing her forehead against the windowpane, she let the cold penetrate right to her skull and remembered how painful her life had been until Max had come along. Then she lifted her head from the glass and rubbed the moisture from her skin.

Looking out, she noticed the black had blushed deep purple, and the snowy spine of the mountain had turned pink. In the passing of just a few minutes most of the stars had disappeared without her noticing. Only two or three remained. The lake, far, far below, assumed the most primitive shade of indigo. The dawn was only minutes away.

She wondered why the precise moment of change was often imperceptible. When did it become light and cease to be dark? When was a person old and no longer young? Were the inadequacies in language or perception?

And even as she pondered the question, France had come into focus across the lake, visible in detail when only a moment earlier it had been tenebrous and vague. The first splash of ocher began washing across the horizon, revealing the jagged profiles of the distant snowy peaks with utter clarity.

It was then that Lianne realized she must be looking at the ridge line above the Col de Jambaz—Alex's mountains. She recalled going there a few months back. It was then, she realized, that she had finally said goodbye to Alex. After that day she had been free to love Max.

Now that they were betrothed, Alex seemed all the more remote. Yet the fact remained that he would be her brother-in-law. She hadn't really come to terms with that and didn't much like the thought. What would he think? she wondered.

She rested her chin on her knees and stared out wistfully, wondering how providence would provide for them all. Alex was no nearer to her now than those distant snowfields, barely visible by the light of dawn. Those summer days were long gone. Max was the one she loved. It was *his* ring on her finger. She could look out and see the universe, yet know she wasn't alone. That had been his most important gift to her.

Shivering, she pulled the coat tightly over her chest, but it was too cool in the alcove to stay much longer. She took a final look at the dawn from her little observatory. The lights of the village of St-Gingolph had already disappeared in the daylight.

Lianne stepped back through the curtains, closing them behind her. The room was dark, but enough light slipped through the gaps to permit her to find the bed. Max was just as she had left him.

She removed his jacket, placing it where it had been. She lifted the comforter and slid into the bed. The sheets were cold, so she inched her way over to his body. She pressed her length against him, seeking heat, trying not to shiver, trying not to awaken him if she could help it.

For a while Max didn't move, but then, in his sleep, he flopped his arm across her chest, encircling her, binding her to his side. Lianne lay very still. Thoughts of their life together floated through her mind. The warmth of his body brought her a sense of deep commitment, and she slowly began drifting off to sleep. As the world of dreams enveloped her, she realized there was no substitute anywhere for what Max had already given her—not in poetry, not in memories, not even in the forces of her own heart.

## CHAPTER ELEVEN

MAX DECIDED to wait until after breakfast to tell her about Alex. She had been so happy—looking down at her ring every few minutes, squeezing his arm or putting her head on his shoulder—that it almost broke his heart to have to tell her. He suggested they go for a walk, seeing that it was a bright, sunny morning.

Lianne agreed and they got their coats. The air outside was fresh and pungent. They walked along the drive past his car, listening to the clacking of a small group of sparrows in the melting snow.

Max inhaled deeply, letting the chilly air fill his lungs. He glanced down at Lianne, who was holding his arm. There was a little smile of contentment on her face. He hated what he had to do, but there was no way to avoid it.

"I've got some news," he said as they started along the road. "Alex is back in Geneva and he wants to see you."

Lianne stopped in her tracks. He turned to her. There was utter shock on her face.

"Alex is in Geneva?"

"Yes, he arrived yesterday sometime. That's what Tatiana called the Barots about. She wanted me to know. I didn't tell you right away because I didn't want to spoil the evening I had planned. I hope you don't mind."

She took his arm again and they resumed their walk. But now her head was down. She wasn't smiling anymore. "No," she finally said, "I understand."

They went a bit farther. "Are you upset?" he asked.

"Not upset exactly. Surprised, I suppose." Lianne seemed to be measuring her steps. "He said he wants to see me?"

"To make his peace with you, I think. I'd talked to him about it weeks ago." Max was sorry he had, but he wouldn't tell her that.

Lianne sighed. "Maybe it's just as well. In the back of my mind I've worried about him, how our relationship might affect him . . . and how he might affect us."

"Yes, I suppose it's for the best."

"What do you think he'll say, Max?"

"I don't know for sure. Alex can be very predictable in one sense, but totally unpredictable in another. We aren't as close as we once were. Poor Alex is both master and slave to his destiny, just as our father was. His yearning for freedom always subjugated him, made him his own victim. But I don't think he's ever seen that."

"None of that has much to do with me," she said.

"Perhaps not." Max didn't say it, but he suspected Alex's problems had as much to do with him as with Lianne. There had always been an underlying tension between them, a subtle competition. "In any case there should be ample time for the two of you to work things out. He should be here through the holidays, and I shall be away most of this coming week until just before Christmas."

"Must you?"

"I'm afraid so. I'd have let you know sooner, but I just worked out the details myself. We're in need of technology, and the simplest way seems to buy the company that has it. Now we think we've found the right outfit. In America. California, actually. But I must act quickly or else I'll lose it." He sighed. "It's another reason why I wanted you to have the ring now. Something to remember me by while I'm away."

"You said another reason. What's the other?"

"Alex, to be honest. He should know my feelings toward you and my intentions. That wasn't why I proposed, of course. I bought the ring long before I knew he was coming. I may have been negligent in not telling him sooner that I love you, but my intentions aren't secret anymore."

"Alex only matters because he's a member of the family. And for no other reason." Her voice was firm, resolute.

"There's still the past."

"But the past is just that," she replied. "The past."

He smiled and put his arm around her. The mountain road was damp but mostly clear of snow. It was a lightly traveled byway, an excellent place to stroll. From the various vantage points there were views of Lausanne, the high Alps, even the northern shore of the lake and the Jura beyond.

Max took a deep breath, letting the air sting his lungs. Lianne pressed her body against him, but she remained silent, staring across the lake at France.

"If you don't mind, darling," he said, "I'd like to go back to Geneva a bit earlier than we'd planned. I must leave for America first thing in the morning, and I think it's important that I talk to Alex before I go. Also, I've got another little surprise for you—something to go with the ring."

"What sort of surprise? More jewelry?"

"Not exactly. But I shan't tell you. It wouldn't be a surprise."

"And I thought for a Swiss you were terribly open, Max Julen. Now I learn you're full of secrets."

He tried to smile at the remark, but there was a wound in it she couldn't know. "I'll leave it up to you how you wish to deal with Alex," he said, changing the subject. "Once I'm gone you and he can make your own arrangements to meet."

"Wouldn't it be better if we saw him together?" she asked.

"If it's important to you, we can. I didn't want to force it."

"I would prefer it, Max. It needn't be for long. If you wish to see him in private, I can always go."

"We'll see. I don't even know where he's staying. But I'm sure Tatiana will know. As soon as we get back, I'll call him." Max leaned down and kissed Lianne's cheek.

She gave him a smile, but it wasn't as radiant and happy as before. He'd suspected it would be this way. With the mention of Alex the joy had faded some.

THE DRIVE BACK to Geneva wasn't hampered by weather. The skies and roads were clear. Max noticed that the mood in the car seemed to ebb and flow. Lianne was touching her ring and looking at it. She talked about their life together, the problems they faced, worrying what they would say to Tatiana.

Though he wanted to badly, Max couldn't yet tell her the truth. When he did, it would be a much greater shock than anything thus far. But at least now he knew that Lianne wanted him for himself. And when she learned that Tatiana was her daughter, she would see that their marriage provided a bonus, as well. Only Alex remained an unknown agent. For that reason Max was eager to get that past them.

But he had his other treat for her, a surprise he'd hoped would lighten her spirits again. When they came to Versoix, just outside of Geneva, Max exited the highway.

"Why are we getting off here?"

"I told you there was something to go with your ring."

"In Versoix?"

"Perhaps."

They went along a country lane until Max stopped the Mercedes in front of the gates of a large estate. Lianne looked at him with perplexity. "Who lives here?"

"No one at the moment. But let's have a look around." He got out and opened the gate.

When he climbed back into the car, she asked, "Max, are you thinking of buying this place?"

"No."

They drove up the circular drive to the front of the large house. It was in the French style, perhaps a hundred years old, stucco, with a mansard roof and great tall windows. The landscaping was formal and well maintained.

"If you aren't thinking of buying it, why did you bring me here?" she asked when he set the hand brake and turned off the engine.

"Come inside and you'll see."

They went to the door, and Max opened it with a key. He motioned for her to step inside. The place was completely empty, though neat as a pin. The hardwood floors were highly polished, gleaming in the sunlight. "Max...?"

He took her arm and directed her into the great salon to one side of the entry hall. There, sitting alone against one wall, was the beautiful Sheridan *secretaire* they had seen in the antique shop window on the rue Grand.

"Oh, my!" she exclaimed, turning to him. "It's the piece I admired."

"It will be your wedding present," he said.

"But why is it here?"

"It's my house. Why shouldn't it be here?"

"Your house? I thought you said . . ."

"You asked if I was thinking of buying it. I'm not. I already have."

"For us?"

"For you, me and Tatiana."

Lianne spun around, looking with awe. "It wonderful! Just beautiful."

"Much more comfortable when we've furnished it," he said with a laugh. "But I didn't want to do that without your help. After all, you'll be the lady of the house."

She threw her arms around him. "Max, darling, what a marvelous surprise! Something to go with my ring, indeed!"

"Would you like a look around?"

She was eager, and he gave her a quick tour, but she lingered here and there, calculating the decorating plans that seemed instantly to form. It was apparent she was considering furnishings, wallpapers, carpets and drapes. The joy had returned. He was pleased.

But there was still Alex to contend with. After she had a chance to savor the house for a time, he took her arm and led her back to the car. "We'll come again as soon as I get back from America," he said. "If you'd like a key to come out with a decorator, that would be fine, too."

"Max, we haven't even talked about the wedding and you're already moving me into your house."

"That's the American way, isn't it?"

She gave him a sly wink. "Not in all quarters."

He laughed, and they set off for Geneva again. When they arrived at the outskirts of the city, Lianne told him she would like to go home first, and when he'd made arrangements with Alex, he could call her.

"Are you upset, Lianne?"

"No, but I'm very tired and this promises to be a rather emotional evening. I want to rest and prepare myself."

Max felt a twinge of despair, though he kept telling himself the important questions had been answered. Lianne wanted to be his wife. That was all that mattered. He hoped, even as he doubted, that it would be as simple as that.

MAX WASN'T ABLE to reach his brother until late that evening when he returned to his hotel on the Quai du Mont-Blanc. He had just gotten back to his room and answered on the first ring.

"Well," Alex said, "been off with the lady fair, eh? Tatiana made it sound as if you were practically off on an elopement."

The irony of the remark amused Max, but he wasn't about to go into it on the phone. "I'm leaving for California in the morning," he told his brother. "Lianne knows you're in town. I told her. She's willing to meet with you, but I thought you and I ought to talk first. Originally she wanted to come with me, but when I had trouble tracking you down, she decided to wait. You can phone her in the morning, if you like."

"My, with all this formality, you'd think I was in town for an international conference or something."

"There's a lot to discuss, Alex."

"Why do I sense such concern? At first everybody seemed to want me back right away. Now I feel like an interloper."

"It's Tatiana who I worry about," Max told him. "But let's not go into it over the phone. Can I come to your hotel?"

"Certainly."

"I'll be there in half an hour."

"I'll meet you in the lobby."

Max hung up and went to Tatiana's room to tell her he was going out for a while. She had been happy to see him when he got home that afternoon, but was otherwise circumspect. For some reason that he didn't understand, she seemed distressed by Alex's return, which wasn't like the girl at all.

She was lying on her bed, reading a book when he came in. "I'm going out for a while," he told her.

"To see Uncle Alex?"

"Yes."

"Will he see Lianne?"

"Probably."

She rolled onto her back and stared up at the ceiling.

"Why does that upset you?" Max asked.

"I'm afraid Uncle Alex will mess up your friendship with Lianne, Papa."

He smiled. "Don't concern yourself."

"Uncle Alex is very hard to resist. And Lianne was in love with him once, wasn't she?"

"It's different now." Max went over and sat beside the girl on the bed. He pushed her hair back off her forehead. "Lianne and I care for each other a great deal."

"I know, Papa. She loves you now. Still . . ."

He contemplated her for a moment. "This might be a good time to tell you that I've asked Lianne to marry me.

And she's accepted. I was going to wait until after I got back from America to tell you, but somehow it seemed you ought to know."

Tatiana looked over at him, a faint smile on her lips. "I knew you would. I'm not surprised."

"Are you upset?"

Tatiana sighed. "No, not really. But I do think of Mummy. It will be hard thinking my father has another wife, but I'll adjust."

"That's very mature of you to take that attitude," Max said.

"I want you to be happy. And I do love Lianne. Honestly. If you must marry someone, I would want it to be her."

"I'm happy you feel that way."

Tatiana rolled onto her side and propped herself on her elbow. "Are you going to tell Uncle Alex about your engagement?"

"Yes."

She nodded.

Max said, "Before he may not have known Lianne and I were serious, but I believe he will now."

"That's good. Perhaps he'll be a good sport about it."

"Let's hope so." Max leaned over and kissed her on the cheek. Then he stared at her for a moment, picturing in his mind how she might react when they told her the truth about Alex and Lianne being her parents. A lump formed in his throat. There was no question it would be traumatic. "I'd better go," he told her. "Don't stay up too late."

"No, Papa."

Patting her face, he told her goodbye. Then he got his coat and left the house immediately. Having this all hanging over his head for so long had been a tremendous burden. But the end was in sight. Max just wished he knew better how everyone would react.

THE HOTEL BEAU RIVAGE was a grand old place on the lakeshore. On those rare days when it was clear enough, the guests were afforded a view of Mont Blanc. In the winter it seldom was that clear. The Geneva skies were more commonly overcast, the cloud cover and fog sometimes lasting weeks at a time.

As Max arrived at the hotel, the night was indeed foggy. He left his car with a valet and went up the steps and into the grand old building. Alex, wearing a bulky sweater, was sitting on a plush velvet chair, reading a paper in the lounge. Seeing Max, he rose. The brothers shook hands, embracing briefly.

"You look good," Max told him.

"It's the tropical climate. One doesn't move fast enough to wear out. How are you, Max?"

"Fine."

They sat down, facing each other. There was no one else in the lounge, though a hint of cigar smoke lingered in the air, undoubtedly from a prior occupant. Max looked at his brother.

"I thought you ought to know right off that Lianne and I are engaged to be married."

Alex's brow rose slightly. "It's official, then."

"Yes. She accepted my proposal."

"I suppose congratulations are in order."

"Thank you."

Alex contemplated him for a long moment. "I see why you're concerned over Tatiana. The situation is a bit messy, isn't it?"

"Very. What child would want to discover that her father is her uncle, her uncle is her father, and her prospective stepmother is actually her mother? Not to mention the fact that the mother whose death she'd mourned for years actually was no blood relation to her at all."

Alex sighed. "Maybe it's easier to leave things as they are."

"No," Max said, shaking his head. "I can't possibly let Lianne go through life living with her own child and not even knowing it. And it would be impossible to inform her without telling Tatiana."

"I suppose you're right. I take it, then, you haven't told Lianne."

"No, you wanted to talk to her first, remember?"

"So I did."

"It isn't imperative as far as I'm concerned. I thought it was what you wanted."

Alex sighed in resignation. "I do have a responsibility in this. I fathered her child and put her in a mess she lives with to this day. If I'm to be her brother-in-law, I ought to at least set things straight."

"I understand. But I have one condition. I want to be the one to tell her about Tatiana. I figure the proper time will be when I get back. I'm leaving on a very early flight, so there'll be no chance before I go. Besides, I wouldn't want to tell her that, then get on a plane. I still haven't figured out how she'll take the news."

"I don't see how she could be bitter, Max. It was a long time ago. And the decision was made by others."

"Yes, but I've had a relationship with her for months."

Alex shrugged. "So the time has come to reveal all."

"Yes, it has. Just honor my wishes. Please."

"All right. You have my word."

Max sank back in his chair. He was exhausted. So much had happened and so much was yet to come. But they would get through it, one way or another.

Alex looked as though he were off somewhere, perhaps wishing he were back in Africa. Max knew it wouldn't be easy for him, either. "What do you plan to say to Lianne, if you don't mind me asking?"

"I don't know," Alex replied. "Since you're practically her husband, I realize you're entitled to know, but I haven't figured it out. I suppose it'll depend on what her attitude is."

"I don't believe Lianne bears you any ill will. She's a very considerate, sensitive and loving person."

Alex shook his head. "It's remarkable, but I don't feel I know her at all."

Max took secret joy in the comment, but he didn't say anything. It was terrible to be at odds with one's own brother over a woman. And if the woman had been any other in the world, Max would have had no trouble. But he couldn't forget the fact that Alex, Lianne and Tatiana were a natural family. *He* was the outsider. Only the decision of his father and Eloise Halliday had made it different. He shuddered to think what would be in Tatiana's mind whenever she looked at him once she knew.

"Why so glum?" Alex asked. "I'm the one with the problem. You'll be off in America."

"My bitter pill will come soon enough."

LIANNE AWOKE the next morning with a strange feeling of foreboding. She was terribly anxious at the prospect of seeing Alex and was upset with Max for going off to America and leaving her to face his brother alone. In a way that seemed cowardly and immature, but she would have preferred he be at her side.

On the other hand, Alex was the father of her child. And though they had never married, until Max had come along, Alex had been the only man of consequence in her life. He had occupied a mystical place in her heart—half hero, half villain, always a bittersweet symbol of torment and unrequited love. Max hadn't changed that; he'd only pushed it into the background.

It was Ida's usual day off so, when the telephone rang at about ten, Lianne answered it herself. As she feared, it was Alex.

"I trust you were expecting my call," he said in English. "Wouldn't want to send you into shock. A voice out of the past and all that."

The voice was vaguely familiar, but, oh, how his speech had changed. Alex's accent was flawless—British rather than American. Lianne had to strain to pick out the French origins. Max spoke fluent English, but with a distinct accent. When they were together, they tended to speak French. Alex practically waved the Union Jack.

"How are you, Alex?"

"Damn nervous, if you want to know the truth."

His candor made her laugh. She felt a bit more at ease. "Me, too."

"We've got to talk," he said, sounding more serious. "But not on the phone. What would you like to do?"

Somehow she didn't want to have him come to Nanna's. "We can meet somewhere. How about in the Jardin des Bastions?"

There was a slight pause before he spoke. "Where we last saw each other."

"Yes, that's right." It had been where she'd had Monsieur Pronier's chauffeur take her that day she'd arrived in Geneva. "Do you think you could find the bench?"

The lilt in his voice told her he was amused by the thought. "Ever the sentimentalist, eh, Lianne? The *jardin*'s not all that large. I suppose I can."

"It'll be cold, I'm afraid. This isn't exactly an autumn day."

"We can go somewhere and have a cup of tea."

"Yes," she agreed. "That would be good."

They set the meeting for noon. Lianne hung up, feeling very strange. She lingered for a moment in Nanna's sitting room, thinking about the conversation. Alex sounded so different, yet she detected in him the same spirit. They had communicated well fifteen years earlier, and seemed to now. He still had his charm, his easy manner. Now, though, he was a mature man, a sophisticated one, not a boy. She sighed. It would be interesting to see him, if nothing else.

THE RUE BEAUREGARD WAS between the Ecole des Beaux Arts and the Promenade des Bastions, an easy walk to the park. Lianne left the town house at a quarter to the hour, which would allow her time to get to the park and find the bench.

It was a relatively clear day with small tufts of clouds dotting the pale blue sky. The wind was brisk, though, and chilly.

As she walked along the leaf-strewn promenade under the barren branches of the trees, Lianne thought of the last time she'd come here to meet Alex. She'd taken much the same route that day, leaving the town house under Nanna's watchful eye. Tears had glistened then, her world teetering on the brink of disaster. Now she felt emotion, but it was controlled emotion. Her destiny didn't turn on the conversation she was about to have; its purpose was quite different. Old demons were to be put to rest. Her destiny had been determined a few days earlier when Max asked her to be his wife.

There was no one at the bench when she arrived, and so Lianne sat. She was a few minutes early, but worried that Alex might have trouble finding her. Perhaps that earlier day was not burned into his consciousness so deeply as it was burned into hers.

Lianne held the collar of her black wool coat closed at her neck because of the bite of the wind. The leaves on the walk had been soaked by the recent snow, and so nothing but an occasional scrap of paper blew through the park. An elderly man, bundled against the wind came by, walking a dog. A young couple traversed the promenade some distance from her. Lianne heard the bells of the cathedral begin to chime at noon.

And then she saw Alex, making his way toward her along the walk. He was in a camel-colored topcoat with a fur collar. He wore gloves, but his head was bare. When he drew near, she was able to see his face better. As she had expected, there were wisps of gray in his dark hair. He was tanned. Lines scored his face where there had been none before. But the wry expression was the same, a touch of bemusement in his chocolate-brown eyes. Lianne stood as he came up to the bench.

"Here you are, then," he said, smiling, "just where I left you!" Alex took both her hands, kissing her on each cheek as Europeans were wont to do. "You look marvelous, Lianne." He took in her pale hair, his eyes skipping over her features.

"How are you, Alex?"

"I'm living as I choose, which is the point, after all, isn't it?"

They sat down on the bench. Alex rubbed his gloved hands together.

"A bit colder than the last time, *n'est-ce pas?*" It was the first French phrase he'd uttered, but he seemed to disdain it, because he continued in English. "So you shall marry my brother, shall you?"

"Yes."

"Ironic turn of events, wouldn't you say?"

She shrugged. "It's a smaller world than we realize."

He took a moment to look her over, mentally traversing the years that had intervened from the time they had been in love as kids until now. "You're more beautiful a woman than you were a girl," he said. "I understand my brother's great passion for you."

The remark was almost too frank. Lianne blushed. But she managed to look him in the eye. "I'm glad we're seeing each other, Alex," she said. "Things were left unfinished, and it's bothered me."

He sighed, looking unhappy for the first time. "That's my fault, I'm afraid."

"My purpose isn't to assign blame. We were both young. What happened, happened."

"It's best to be stoic about it, I suppose," he said.

"I never got your letters," she said. "Not until years later. My mother didn't want me to see them. So at the time I didn't know you'd written. After she died, and I saw them, I wrote to let you know. Nanna had told me you were abroad, so I sent it to your family."

"Yes," Alex said. "I did get that. There didn't seem anything to do about it at that point, so I didn't answer you. You had your life, and I had mine. I believe I was in South America at the time. Connecticut seemed pretty far away."

"I didn't really expect a reply. I just wanted you to know what had happened. Not having had any communication with you, I had no idea what burdens you might carry. Myself, I often felt guilty about those events.''

Alex had been leaning his elbows on his knees, looking at his hands. ''It's long over, Lianne. All in the past.''

''I feel better for hearing you say it.''

''Yes,'' he said, venturing a smile, ''I'm glad we're meeting to talk.''

Lianne stared off across the desolate park, robbed by winter of its vitality and lushness. How often over the years had she thought of Alex, had had imaginary conversations with him. And now that he was there with her, words seemed so inadequate to express the emotion that had accumulated with the passing of time.

''Have you ever thought of her, Alex?'' she asked abruptly, moving on to the topic that had tortured her most.

''Her?''

''Our baby.''

His head dropped. ''Yes,'' he said simply.

''I've never forgotten her,'' she said. ''I think of her daily. I still sometimes cry myself to sleep over her.''

Alex stared at his hands.

''I'm not saying that to make you feel badly. Don't misunderstand. It's just that there's no one in the world who might appreciate what I'm saying as much as you. Not even Max. She was our child, Alex. She still is.''

''Maybe there are fundamental differences between the feelings of a father and a mother,'' he said, ''which is not to say I don't care. But in life I've learned to put some things behind me.''

''Don't you ever wonder about her? The way she looks, whether she's happy? I tell myself she's in the bosom of a good family, that she has her life, but when I think she might wonder about me and ask herself why I abandoned her, I nearly die!''

"Don't torture yourself...."

Lianne couldn't help the emotion that suddenly overwhelmed her. Her eyes flooded. The wind stung them and she cried for a moment. But she got control right away. "I'm sorry, Alex. I didn't mean to do this to you."

"You can't blame yourself for anything that happened," he said. "Our families made the decisions. You and I were practically bystanders."

She wiped her eyes. "I suppose we were."

Alex rubbed his hands together briskly. "This cold is brutal. Why don't we find a tearoom?"

The little place in the park that served drinks and snacks was closed for the season, so they walked to the Place Neuve and found a café just off the square. It was a very ordinary sort of place, but it was warm, cheery and fairly crowded.

"Would you like a sandwich or something to eat?" Alex asked, taking off his topcoat. He had on a tweed sport coat and a dark turtleneck sweater. Alex was in good shape, handsome in his prime, the sort of man who turned women's heads.

"I'm not really hungry. A pot of tea would be wonderful, though."

The waiter came to the table. *"Oui?"*

"How about a cognac to warm your insides?" Alex said to her.

She shook her head.

"If you don't mind, I believe I will." He ordered a pot of tea and a brandy. The waiter went away.

Alex leaned back in his chair, studying her, though she had no idea what he was thinking. The more she was with him, the more he seemed the same to her. Hidden under the veneer of experience and years was the same person. Lianne wondered if he could say the same of her.

She had taken off her gloves, and Alex saw her ring. He reached over, taking her hand for a look. His fingers were warm compared to hers. "Quite a stone," he said, fondling her hand absently.

"Thank you," she said.

"Well, it seems that now you're to become my sister-in-law." He pulled his hand away from hers.

"We'll be related," she said. "I hope it won't be a problem for you."

"No, why should it?" he replied. But he almost sounded defensive.

"No reason. There will be more of a past between us than most brothers- and sisters-in-law, though."

"We managed to be lovers once," Alex said with a certain calculation. "Why not friends?" He crossed his legs, looking a touch self-satisfied.

Lianne shifted in her chair. "I suppose you're right."

"Tell me, what was it about Max that made you want to marry him?"

"I love him, of course," she replied, surprised by the question.

"Yes, yes, but I'm curious about the attraction."

"Your brother is a sensitive, caring person. He's warm and kind and giving."

"A saint in other words."

"There's no reason to be sarcastic," she shot back.

The waiter came with the tea and Alex's cognac. He promptly left.

"I wasn't being sarcastic," Alex said. "At first, when I heard, you and Max struck me as an unlikely pair. I don't mean that critically, understand."

"How do you mean it, then?"

"Never mind," Alex replied, abandoning the line of thought. He picked up the brandy glass and saluted her silently before taking a sip.

Lianne poured tea into both cups that the waiter had brought. "You and Max were always in different worlds, weren't you?"

"Perhaps."

"I remember how much you admired him. Yet at the same time I don't believe you identified with him."

"I don't think my brother understands me," Alex said, sipping his cognac again.

"Why's that?"

"Do you wonder? Look at the lives we lead. I'm the sort to have a child who doesn't know me, a former lover who resents me, a home I never see. Max isn't."

She studied him, trying to understand the true feelings behind the words. Alex was, she decided, the same man he was before, but she wasn't the same woman. That was the difference. He was a more mature version of the same boy. And she—despite living so much of her life in remembrance—was very much a different person than that seventeen-year-old girl he'd gotten pregnant. And yet his appeal was undeniable. Alex was one of those men who inveigled, even as a woman saw through him.

"Why haven't you married?" she asked.

"Because it never fitted in with my plans."

"And what are your plans?"

"To live, Lianne. Just to live as I wish. I cherish the freedom to be myself."

"There must have been someone along the line," she prompted.

"I've had lovers, if that's what you mean."

"But no one you wanted to share your life with?"

"You might find this shocking," he said, "but the closest I've ever come was with you."

That did surprise her. She picked up her teacup and drank. Alex was watching her with seeming amusement.

"It's true, you know."

"I feel sorry for you, then."

"Apart from Max, have there been many men in your life?"

"No."

"Well, perhaps we aren't so different, after all."

There was a twinkle in his eye as he took another quaff of brandy. It was the first clear impression she had that he was flirting. She found it a bit disconcerting. Max had told her that Alex wasn't entirely predictable. She was seeing firsthand that it was true.

"I'm glad we've had this conversation," she said, trying to return to a more serious vein. "With our feelings expressed we should be able to deal with each other more easily when the occasion arises."

"Perhaps." He studied her over the rim of his glass.

Lianne was beginning to feel uncomfortable, particularly when he let his eyes drift down her blue knit dress. It was an outfit that showed off her figure to good effect without being provocative. She unconsciously fingered her ring.

"Well, I have some errands to run this afternoon," she said, taking a hasty sip of tea. "I'd better be going."

Alex reached over and took her hand. "I'm glad we talked."

She gave him a tentative smile, pulling away her hand to slip on her gloves. "I'll tell Max it went well. He was concerned."

"Concerned?"

"He loves us both, Alex. It's important to him that things go well. His family is very important to him."

Alex smiled. "Max is a saint, Lianne. And I say that with the utmost respect. But there are dimensions to him of which you're doubtlessly unaware."

She wanted to ask what dimensions he was referring to, but decided Alex was just being provocative. "All of us have our secrets," she said instead. "No one is totally known by others."

"That," he said wryly, "is certainly true."

Lianne knew there was more in his words than she could discern, but she wasn't going to continue the game. They had accomplished what she personally intended. There was no need to linger. She got to her feet, and Alex helped her with her coat. They stood facing each other. He took her hands.

"I'm sorry for what happened to us," he told her. "Maybe I should have asserted myself more and made it end differently."

"And if you had, where would we be?"

"Perhaps happily married. Who knows?"

He seemed sincere enough, but Lianne didn't share the conviction. She and Alex were oil and water. If she didn't know it before, she knew it now. "I have only one regret," she said, "and you know what that is."

He stared into her eyes, looking more thoughtful than he had during most of their conversation. "And what if one day we found her, our daughter?"

The unexpected question sent a curious chill up her spine. "I do want to see her, Alex, but somehow I can't believe it will ever happen."

He said nothing in reply; he simply stared into her eyes. Lianne took her purse and left the café.

# CHAPTER TWELVE

MAX HAD TOLD her he would call, and she waited all afternoon, calculating in her mind the time in California—when he would be arriving, when he would check into his hotel. Lianne didn't know whether he would sleep first or telephone right away. She hoped he wouldn't wait.

These long trips were difficult on him, she knew, especially the jet lag. And he had probably worried about her meeting with Alex. She would have if their positions had been reversed.

When Lianne got tired of sitting, an unread book on her lap, she would get up and pace. She hated it that Max wasn't with her. He should be. They should be together.

Though she tried to think about Max—their life together, the new house, Tatiana, the family they would make—Alex did creep into her thoughts. What bothered her most was what he'd said about Alexandra. What could he possibly have meant when he made reference to them finding her? Was he suggesting that he actually wanted to look for their child?

She wondered if it was possible Alex was as nostalgic about everything as she. After all these years, seeing her might have sparked something in him. He might have let the pain out at last. If that was true, she felt sorry for him. One thing was undeniable—they would always have Alexandra in common.

When the telephone did ring around seven o'clock, Lianne jumped at the sound. She answered it quickly.

"Darling," he said.

His voice was so clear that for an instant she thought he had changed his mind and come back to Geneva. He sounded as if he could have been across town or at the airport. But then she remembered the wonders of modern technology. The days of the transatlantic cable with the sound of the ocean on the line were over.

"Max, I'm so glad you called."

"Are you all right?" he asked.

"Yes. Of course." She decided to spare him asking. "Alex called this morning and we had tea."

"It was okay?"

"Very polite, yes. We each said some things that were on our minds. There were apologies, regrets. I think we got out what had been bottled up. I think we can coexist in the same family."

"Oh, that's wonderful." He sounded relieved.

"A chapter closed," she said, wanting to believe it a bit more than than she did.

"There's something else you should know," he said. "I talked to Tatiana last night and told her about our plans to marry. She was concerned about Alex and you. I thought it would put her mind at ease."

"How did she take it?"

"Well. She's awfully fond of you, Lianne. You and Tatiana getting along doesn't worry me. You're so much alike."

"Maybe we are. That's fortunate, I guess."

"It'll make all the difference." He sounded positive.

"I'm glad you told me, though. I should talk to her, shore things up."

"That's an excellent idea," Max said.

"The poor little thing. I feel for her so. I want to run over there right now."

Max was silent.

"You know what," she went on, "maybe it would be nice if Tatiana and I went out to the new house and had a look around—did some joint planning perhaps. She's seen it, hasn't she?"

"Yes, I took her once after signing the contract. She didn't say anything at the time, but I think even then she knew I intended it as our home."

"And hers, too."

"Right," Max said. "Hers, too."

"Every child cares about their room in a new home. It would be good to involve her in the decorating."

"An excellent idea."

"How can I get a key?" she asked.

"I left one at the house. On the mantel in the sitting room. Tatiana knows where it is."

"Then, if you don't mind, I'll take her over there. Tomorrow, if she wants to. Her school's on holiday break, isn't it?"

"Yes. Call her. I'm sure she'd love it."

Lianne sighed. "I'm so glad you phoned. I feel much better."

"Weren't you all right before?"

She realized she'd made a slip. "It's been an emotional day."

After a pause, he asked, "Where were things left with Alex?"

"I don't know, to be honest. Just left. He didn't speak of his plans at all. I assume he'll be here for Christmas."

"I suppose he will."

"Do you want me to talk to him?" she asked.

"No, Alex knows he's welcome. He likes to see friends. And he's fearfully jealous of his independence. In the past he's had dinner with Tatiana and me Christmas Day. He'll let us know."

"Whatever."

There was silence on the line.

"I wish this trip could have been avoided," Max finally said. "I'd much rather be there with you."

"You've got your work. That's important, too. Where are you, by the way?"

"At the Clift Hotel in San Francisco. I must give you the number here. I'm glad you reminded me."

"The Clift," she repeated as she grabbed a paper and pencil.

He gave her the telephone number.

"How is San Francisco? It's been years since I've been out to the West Coast."

"It's foggy at the moment. Just like home. There's a pigeon cooing on my window, not unlike at my office. The bridges are a big more grandiose, of course, and... well, America is America."

She smiled at the observation. The States were home, and although Geneva had been her second home for years, she was confident she would never have to give up the country of her birth. Max was Swiss, but he was very cosmopolitan. The most important tie to America wasn't her home, however. It was her daughter. She couldn't think about Boston or Philadelphia or Hartford, without first wondering if Alexandra lived there.

"Max," she said, "we haven't talked about this much, but do you really want more children?" There had been one vague conversation a few weeks earlier when he'd teased her about preferring a younger woman so that he could still have the houseful of children he'd always wanted. They hadn't taken the topic any further at the time, but Lianne had assumed he'd been serious.

"I think that's much more up to you than me," he replied.

"No, we both have to want them."

"I do, yes, but when and how many is up to you."

That was so like Max. He was considerate to a fault.

"I love you," she said.

"Darling, why did I let myself be talked into wanting this damn company out here?"

"I don't know. I wish you hadn't."

"We'd better not discuss it further," he teased, "or I'll be getting on the first plane home."

They ended their conversation then, and Lianne sat for a long time in her grandmother's chair, thinking about him. But Tatiana was in her thoughts, too. Poor little thing, learning her father intended to remarry, then being left alone with the maid to deal with the news. Lianne decided to contact the girl right away. She dialed the Julens' number. The Spanish maid answered and called Tatiana to the phone.

"*Ciao*, Lianne."

She seemed in good spirits, which was a relief. "How is life as a bachelor girl?" Lianne asked her.

"It's a nice change to be on my own, but then I'm not exactly on my own with the *dueña* looking over my shoulder."

"You hadn't planned any wild parties, had you, Tatiana?" she teased.

The girl laughed. "No, with Maria on watch I'm destined to be a virgin bride, perhaps at age forty."

"*Alors,* I've got a proposal for you then. How would you like to go with me out to your father's new house and plan the decorating?"

"You've seen it then?"

"Yes, he took me by for a brief visit."

"Papa told me about your engagement, you know. Before he left."

"Yes, he told me."

"Congratulations, by the way," she said, trying her best, it seemed, to sound sincere. "I'm very happy for you both."

"Thank you, Tatiana. We'll all have some adjusting to do, but I'm sure it'll work out. I'm very fond of you, *chérie*."

"Thank you," the girl replied, sounding pleased.

"So, shall we go to the new house and see what difficulties we can cause your father's bank account?"

Tatiana laughed. "That sounds like a lot of fun. We could be a dangerous pair to a poor man, couldn't we?"

"But of course! That's a woman's duty! Shall we make it tomorrow? Lunch first, then house decorating? What do you say?"

"Lianne, you're my kind of woman!"

THE NEXT MORNING, before Ida arrived, Lianne went to some shops in town for wallpaper and paint samples. She also picked up fabric swatches for draperies and curtains, deciding it would be nice to have some things to consider as she and Tatiana went through the house.

Shortly before noon she dropped by the Julens' to pick up Tatiana. Lianne had bought a Peugeot a month earlier, but she had hardly driven it. The bus system in Geneva was excellent and parking was always a problem. But to leave town for the countryside made a car essential.

Tatiana was in good spirits as she came bumping down the steps to greet her, the key to the new house in her hand. They embraced and the girl congratulated her again on the engagement. They decided to lunch in the village of Versoix.

Lianne drove through town, crossing the Rhône on the Pont de la Coulouvreniere. Once through the congestion around the train station, they moved swiftly out the rue de Lausanne, past the botanical gardens and the various United Nations buildings and into the countryside.

"Oh, Lianne," Tatiana exclaimed, "your ring! Let me see it please."

Lianne held out her hand as she drove. Tatiana took it, examining the diamond closely. "*Superbe!* Isn't it enormous! Papa must love you a lot, Lianne. It's the most beautiful ring I've even seen."

"I hope he does," she replied, laughing.

Tatiana turned thoughtful. "It will be strange having a stepmother . . . after all these years alone with Papa."

"We'll all have to adjust. Having a family will be new to me."

"I bet you wish it was Alexandra living with you instead."

"And I'm sure you'd like having your mother back, too," Lianne said, "but one must make do. Besides, I'm very fond of you, Tatiana."

The girl smiled. "And I'm fond of you, too, Lianne."

She reached over and held Tatiana's hand, feeling a kinship toward her. It brought tears to her eyes, and when they looked at each other, she saw Tatiana's eyes were glossy, as well. They both laughed.

"Maybe we'll be good for each other," Lianne told her.

"Especially if you're good at math!" the girl replied.

They had a delightful lunch in a small restaurant, looking right into the main street of the village. The decor was simple, the food plain but tasty. Their conversation became intimate. Tatiana confided some things about her personal life—the usual teenage passions and emotions involving friends, but nevertheless events critically important to her. Lianne took the confidence as a true indication of friendship. To reciprocate she talked about her own experiences growing up.

"You probably don't want to talk about Uncle Alex, considering you're engaged to Papa," Tatiana said at one point, "but I'm really curious what he was like when he was young. Was he much different than he is now?"

"Less mature, of course. And his English wasn't nearly so good," she said with a smile. "But, on the whole, I think he's the same person."

"And you really loved him then?" Tatiana said, scraping the last of the sauce from the *crème caramel* from her plate.

"I thought I did." Lianne hesitated. "No, that isn't right. I did love him as a girl of that age loves. That's not to demean it. But at different ages, different qualities in a person matter."

Tatiana thought. "I'm not sure I understand you. Love is love, it seems to me. I've always loved Papa and Mummy, for example, no matter what age I've been. And I don't believe the love has changed. Only the way I see it. If you loved Uncle Alex once, and he's essentially the same, why don't you love him now?"

"Maybe what I loved before I still love, but it's no longer so important to me. I don't know how else to explain it, Tatiana."

"If you don't mind me asking, do you think Uncle Alex still loves you?"

"Not the way you're thinking. Probably he feels the same as I do."

"You're the parents of my cousin Alexandra. You had a baby together, Lianne. I would think that means something."

She shrugged. "It means that once we did have that experience together. That's all. I love your father now. And if your uncle doesn't love someone else, he certainly loves his life, his career."

Tatiana sighed. "I guess that's true. But he's so wonderful. If he wasn't my uncle, I could be in love with him—have a crush, I mean. He's better than a lot of film stars."

Lianne smiled. "Be happy to count him in your family, then."

"Yes, once you've married Papa, we'll have a very interesting family indeed. Won't we, Lianne?"

"Yes, Tatiana. A very interesting family."

After Lianne paid the lunch bill, they left the restaurant and headed to the house. Along the way they made a wrong turn and had to ask a farmer for directions. A few minutes later they made a second mistake, but finally arrived at the gates to the house, laughing.

"Papa will never let us leave for the market," Tatiana exclaimed. "We might not make it home!"

"Don't you dare tell your father this happened! We've got an image to maintain."

Lianne drove close to the front door and parked. Tatiana got out and ran up the steps with pure joy. She was peering in the windows of the house as Lianne unlocked the door.

The rest of the afternoon was a combination of fun and work. They accomplished a lot more than Lianne had expected. Tatiana, she discovered, had surprisingly sophisticated taste for a young girl. They liked many of the same things, though Tatiana was a bit more traditional, given the limits of her experience.

For a long time they sat in the middle of the salon, looking at decorating magazines that Lianne had brought, getting ideas for redoing the place. They had a wonderful time, especially when they discussed Tatiana's room. Lianne had a few suggestions that the girl thought were wonderful.

With the short winter day it was already getting dark as they drove home. But there was definitely a spirit of camaraderie between them. It seemed to Lianne they'd passed onto a new plateau. She couldn't have been happier about it.

"I can't tell you how much fun this was today," Tatiana told her as they pulled up in front of the Julens' town house.

"For me, too!" Lianne said sincerely.

"I don't think I've been this happy since Mummy died."

Lianne knew it was the best of compliments. "Having you as a daughter will be like having my own Alexandra."

Tatiana embraced her, holding her a long time. And when the girl finally let go, her face was streaked with tears. *"Ciao,"* she whispered, then jumped from the car and dashed up the stairs of Max's house.

Lianne sat there in her Peugeot long after the door to the house had closed. She was crying, too. But for once there was as much happiness in her tears as sorrow.

LIANNE ARRIVED AT HOME, her arms filled with the decorating samples, to find Ida in a dither, waiting.

*"Mademoiselle,"* where have you been? I've been so worried."

"I left you a note, Ida. Didn't you..." Then she remembered. She'd intended to write one but had completely forgotten. "I'm sorry. I meant to leave you a note saying I'd be out all day but home for dinner."

The housekeeper saw Lianne's tear-streaked face but seemed confused by her happy smile. "What's happened, *mademoiselle?* Are you all right?"

"Ida, I couldn't be happier!"

The housekeeper took the samples from her, and Lianne hung her coat in the closet. She told the woman to put the things down and took her into the sitting room.

"I've got some wonderful news. Over the weekend Max asked me to marry him!" She held out her hand with the enormous emerald-cut diamond.

Ida's mouth dropped open. *"Mademoiselle!"*

"Isn't it fabulous?"

Despite her usual Swiss formality the housekeeper spontaneously embraced her, muttering something in Swiss German. Then she held Lianne's hands, beaming up at her. "What joy this would have brought Madame Gevers."

"And I spent the day with Tatiana. Just the two of us. It was wonderful, Ida. After all these years of suffering over my baby, now God has given me this."

The housekeeper nodded happily, her eyes suddenly bubbling. "Oh, what a pity Madame Gevers wasn't alive for this day. I know she dreamed of it. She never told me so, but I know she did. Her beloved granddaughter and great-granddaughter together at last!"

Ida's French accent was thick, and occasionally Lianne would miss a word or two, but she'd heard the woman plainly. "Great-granddaughter? Ida, what do you mean?"

The joy on the old woman's face turned to puzzlement. "But Monsieur Julen told you that...I mean, you know that the girl is..." Then Ida's face fell. She clasped both hands to her mouth. *"Mein Gott!"*

"Ida..."

The housekeeper let out a desperate moan, her face filled with anguish. She turned suddenly and shuffled off as fast as she could toward the kitchen, ignoring Lianne's pleas to stop.

Lianne followed her. "Ida, what did you mean? Tell me!"

The woman fell onto a chair at the table and buried her head in her arms. She was weeping. Lianne tried to rouse her from her sudden, bizarre misery. "Why did you refer to Tatiana as Nanna's great-granddaughter?"

After a moment, Ida looked up, her puffy face red, her eyes streaming with tears. "Oh, forgive me, *mademoiselle,* forgive me! I thought he told you. I thought..." And then she buried her head again.

Lianne stood there beside her, numb. What did Ida mean, she thought Max had told her? Told her that Tatiana was...?

A jolt of cold terror went through her. Was Ida saying that Tatiana was Alexandra...her baby? She looked down at the housekeeper, her heart ripping at her insides. "Ida, you must stop crying!" she shrieked. "Stop it, I say!" She took the woman's arm, trying to get her attention.

Ida looked up in absolute misery, sobbing.

"Listen to me," Lianne said emphatically, her voice shaking. "Are you saying that Tatiana is mine? That she was adopted here?"

But Ida couldn't answer. Her head fell back into her arms.

The realization hit Lianne like a car smashing into a wall at seventy miles an hour. She felt faint, her breath wedged in her throat. She pulled out the other chair, almost falling as she sat on it. Her heart was pounding as the notion settled in her brain.

There had to be a mistake. Ida must be confused. Lianne knew it couldn't be true. Her *mother* had made the arrangements for the adoption. It was with a family in New England. Why would her mother lie?

And if it were true, Max would have told her. Long before now. Or Alex! Was he in the dark, as well?

No, Lianne told herself, forcing her brain to think. It couldn't be true. There was some mistake. Ida had it wrong. Surely.

The housekeeper had stopped her sobbing, but her head was still buried in her arms. She seemed unwilling to face Lianne. There was no doubt about her belief. But she could be mistaken.

Lianne rubbed her head, feeling a fine sheen of perspiration on her brow. She heard the clock ticking on the wall. It was as though it were counting off the last minutes of her life. She knew she had to get to the bottom of this.

She stared at Ida's gray head. She tried to imagine Nanna keeping such a thing from her. Surely she wouldn't have. Not Nanna. And would her own mother have done that? Give her baby to Alex's family and not tell her?

There was a certain logic to it, though. If she had known her child was in Geneva with the Julens, Lianne couldn't have stayed away from the girl. Max and Catrina probably wouldn't have wanted her to know. That made sense, too. And there were other bits of evidence. Tatiana was Alexandra's age! A few days apart, but that deception could be fixed easily enough. But could they really have done this to her? Her own mother? Nanna? Alex? Max?

Ida lifted her head at last, looking at her like a dog expecting a beating.

"I don't want you to be upset," Lianne told her, trying her best to sound calm. "If this is true, it's only right that I should know."

"But it's not my place, *mademoiselle*. Madame Gevers didn't even know that I knew. She would die again if she knew I betrayed her."

"Never mind that," Lianne said, her voice quavering. "I want you to tell me how you found out about this."

Ida shook her head.

"I insist!" Lianne said sharply.

The housekeeper took a handkerchief from her apron and wiped her nose. "I overheard *madame* speaking on the telephone to Monsieur Julen. Monsieur Alberte Julen, the father. It was a long time ago, *mademoiselle*, soon after you left the house to return to America."

"What did you hear? Tell me what you heard," she insisted.

"I didn't intend to eavesdrop. I made no effort to do so. I was in the dining room, polishing the silver, and apparently *madame* forgot this. She was in the parlor speaking with *monsieur*. I heard her words very plainly. They spoke of lawyers and bringing the baby from America. They spoke of the child being raised by its own family. They spoke of Madame Catrina Julen's great joy in having a child of her husband's blood."

"Then it was common knowledge Tatiana was adopted?"

"*Madame* was never pregnant, that much was certain. But I'm sure the arrangements were handled discreetly. I wasn't privy to the information, of course. I have no idea whether the girl herself was ever told she wasn't her parents' natural child.''

"I doubt that she was told. I would have heard she was adopted by now—from her at the very least."

Lianne sat in disbelief. She still couldn't fathom that it was really true. Perhaps Ida was mistaken. Hearing one side of a telephone conversation could be misleading.

"Tell me," she said. "Was Nanna aware that you knew about Tatiana?"

"I don't know. I never said anything, of course. And *madame* never spoke of it to me. It wasn't necessary. I know my place, and what is my business and what is not. *Madame* knew this. She never had to worry about me."

It made sense. Everything made sense to Lianne, except why someone hadn't told her. Perhaps her mother and Nanna had wanted to inform her before their deaths, but they'd doubtless given their word, and Tatiana's wellbeing was at stake. But Max, why hadn't he said something? Surely he wasn't going to let her and Tatiana live together in ignorance of the fact?

Lianne took a deep, shaky breath. The shock she felt was perhaps the greatest of her life. What she had learned was at once wonderful and horrible. Her world was turned upside down. Not only for her, but for Tatiana, as well. The poor child…her baby…what would this do to her impressionable young mind? Perhaps that was why Max had kept the secret from her. But, on the other hand, he knew how she had suffered.

She had to talk to him. She had to confirm this report for sure. Until she did she would be a nervous wreck. And poor Ida was beside herself. Reaching out, she patted the woman's arm. "I don't want you to worry about this. The truth is never a bad thing. It is just that I know."

"I thought if you were to marry Monsieur Julen, surely he would have told you. I misunderstood. If I had known..."

"It's all right. I'm sure he planned to tell me." She got up from her chair. "You stay here and rest for a moment. I must telephone Max."

Ida's eyes welled with tears again. Lianne shook her finger like a stern schoolmistress, then left the room.

In the salon she sat down before the telephone, the very same one she'd used that day long ago to hear Nanna inform her mother that she was pregnant. All the anguish that had since transpired, Lianne now saw in a different light. She felt like a child who'd been kept in the dark. And she felt betrayed. Betrayed by everyone.

When she reached for the receiver, her hands trembled, her heart ached. The fact that Max hadn't told her was the most painful aspect of all. The others, in their way, had tried to spare her perhaps. But what was his excuse? Fear?

She dialed the number in San Francisco. When the hotel operator answered, she gave the room number and listened to the phone ringing halfway around the world. It was mid-morning in California. She hoped he was there. But after half a dozen rings it was apparent he wasn't. She waited a bit longer, then hung up the phone, feeling drained and terribly disappointed.

Undoubtedly he was off meeting with officials from the company, the lawyers or someone. It could be hours before he returned. Lianne didn't know if she could wait. It had been nearly fifteen years since her baby had been taken from her, and to wait even an hour more to confirm that she had found her again seemed an eternity.

Her eyes shimmering with emotion, Lianne sat in the mellow light of her grandmother's sitting room. Outside the house the cold Geneva winter had set in. Several minutes away by car a young girl was in her home, ignorant of the fact that she may have spent the day with her natural mother. What would Tatiana think if she knew?

Lianne's hands trembled as she pictured the girl. By sheer force of logic she had looked for Julen blood in the child, but never her own. Seeing Tatiana in her mind's eye, she realized the evidence was there, but it hadn't jumped out at her because she wasn't looking for it. There was no denying it, though. Tatiana could indeed be her long-lost daughter.

She began crying softly then, wanting to rush to Max's house, to take her child into her arms. But then her doubt crept in again. She shouldn't get her hopes up. What if it wasn't true?

She looked at the telephone, cursing Max's business obligations, his absence at this critical time. A well of frustration rose in her. She was desperate to do something. She couldn't sit by, watching the hands of the clock slowly inch around the face. It was then that she decided to turn to Alex. He had to know the truth.

Without bothering to tell Ida she was leaving Lianne got her coat and went out to find her car. She was going to drive to the Hotel Beau Rivage and confront Alex Julen.

# CHAPTER THIRTEEN

LIANNE WAS NEARLY beside herself as she drove across Geneva. A dense fog had settled over the town, making it seem especially cold and forbidding. She was distracted, nervous. And definitely not at her best.

On the Pont du Mont-Blanc an articulated bus suddenly stopped in front of her. She slammed on the brakes, but not in time, bumping into the rear end of the behemoth. It wasn't a hard collision, but it was enough to give her a jolt. The driver of the bus, a heavyset man with a bright red face who wore his uniform jacket unbuttoned, ambled back, looking annoyed. He stood in the cold wind blowing off the lake, examining the back of his vehicle and the front of her car.

The accident caused an instant traffic jam, and cars back along the Quai General Guisan soon began honking. The bus driver, who was muttering expletives under his breath, ignored the tumult.

Lianne, holding her coat tightly at her neck against the cold, got out to see how bad the accident was. There was no damage to the bus that she could see, and not much to the Peugeot. Her front bumper seemed a little bent, that was all.

The driver was shaking his head, looking utterly disgusted. He held up his wrist to look at his watch in the lights of the passing cars, then put his hands on his hips. He hadn't given Lianne much more than a glance.

"Your bus doesn't seem to be damaged," she said, "and I'm in a very great hurry. Let's just forget it, shall we?"

"Not possible, *madame*. Company regulations. When there's an accident, there must be a police report." He threw his hands up in the air. "And me with the best driving record in the division."

"I really don't see why we need bother. At the moment your record is unblemished, so why change that? Your bus is fine, and I don't wish to make an issue of this."

"It was your fault."

"Yes," she said, "it was my fault. So I won't say anything to anyone if you won't."

He gazed back at the line of cars, trying to force their way into the passing lane. "Do I have your word?" the man said. "You won't make something of this later?"

"No. Here," she said, opening her purse and taking a large bill from her wallet. "A hundred francs for your trouble."

The man scratched his head. "All right," he said. "But it wasn't my fault." He stuffed the bill into his pocket. "We'd better leave the area. The authorities will be here in a minute."

They each returned to their vehicles, and when the bus began moving again, Lianne heaved a sigh of relief. Then, after she drove for a way, tears of frustration welled, and her thoughts returned again to Tatiana.

She left the Peugeot at the entrance to the hotel, not even bothering to wait for the valet. She handed the keys to the doorman instead. At the reception desk she confirmed that Alex was in and she got his room number from a reluctant clerk, telling the man to alert Alex that she was coming up. Moments later she was knocking on his door.

Alex opened it. He was in his stocking feet, a charcoal-gray sweater and black corduroy trousers. "What brings my future sister-in-law out on such a wintry—"

Lianne pushed past him, not letting him get out the question. Alex closed the door and turned to face an obviously distraught woman. She was in the middle of the room, looking frightfully determined.

"Alex," she said, mincing no words, "I want the truth. Is Tatiana our child?"

He looked at her, stunned, his lower lip sagging open. "Lianne . . . good Lord . . ."

"*Is* she?"

"Whatever made you—?"

"Don't play games with me. I warn you, Alex. Just tell me. I'm entitled to know." Her resolve faltered at the end and her voice trembled.

"Have you talked to Max?" he asked.

"Just tell me!" she screamed.

He seemed to sag.

"Then it *is* true . . ."

"Who told you?"

"Nobody told me. I found out when Ida let it slip. Not one damn person told me after all this time, including you!" She went and sat on the bed, her entire body shaking.

Alex was motionless. He seemed at a loss, bewildered. Finally he said, "Your mother and my father made the decision, Lianne." His tone was self-justifying.

"*You* knew, Alex. Why not me? Why wasn't *I* told?"

"I don't know. Perhaps they didn't trust your reaction. You were young."

"So were you!"

He went and sat next to her on the bed, his head bowed. "I suppose I deserve a share of the responsibility. But what was I to do? I had no response to the letters I'd written you. I figured you didn't want to communicate with me—or at least that's the way it seemed at the time. My father, my elder brother and sister-in-law, your grandmother, they were all insisting that this was what was to be done."

Lianne shook her head, wiping her nose. "Blame's not the point, I suppose. But I'm shocked. Livid!"

He reached over and put his hand on hers. "I'm sorry. Sorry you had to find out this way. It's not how I would have handled it, but then it hasn't been my decision from the beginning. Don't forget, the first communication you and I have had in fifteen years was just a couple of days ago."

"I don't blame you, Alex." Her voice was low, resigned.

"It's been a terrible situation. I think everybody's suffered with it. You don't know how hard it's been for me whenever I've seen her. I've been her *uncle,* Lianne."

She lowered her head into her hands. "The poor child. The poor, poor child. What will this do to her? What is she to think when she finds out we're her parents and Max is only her uncle?"

"I don't know. Until now I've suffered with things as they've been simply to avoid that eventuality."

Lianne felt like weeping again, but she held herself together. Then she turned to the father of her child. "Alex, I want to see her. I want us to go over there right now."

He shook his head. "No, Max has to be involved. For Tatiana's sake. I've always promised him I wouldn't do anything without his consent."

"Then call him and get his consent!"

Alex got up and paced back and forth. His frustration was evident, but it couldn't have been half of what she felt. She was like a pressure cooker about to burst.

"All right," she said. "If you won't do it, then I will." She went to the phone and gave the operator the number that was on the slip of paper in her purse. In San Francisco the hotel operator connected her with Max's room. She listened to the phone ring. To her surprise he picked up the receiver almost immediately.

"Hello?"

"Max . . ." she said with a low, trembling voice.

"Lianne?"

The emotion in her was so intense that she nearly couldn't speak. Finally she said, "I know Tatiana is my daughter."

He must have been stunned, because he didn't say a word. She waited as the silence hung between then.

Then he said, "Alex told you."

"No, Alex didn't tell me," she shot back. "I found out by accident from Ida. Purely by chance. The question is why *you* didn't tell me!"

"Lianne, I intended to."

"Intended to? How could you have kept something like that from me? You know how I've suffered. You, of all people."

"I was waiting for the right time."

"How can you even say that to me, Max? Supposedly you loved me. All along my daughter was right under my nose, and you didn't even have the decency to tell me!" She had been speaking English because of the depth of her emotion. And so had Max. But he switched to French.

"Listen to me, Lianne. I had more to consider than your feelings and certainly more than my own. This hasn't been easy. Do you have any idea what Tatiana will think, how she'll feel?''

"That's what's worried you—what she'll think of you!" She began crying then. She couldn't help herself.

"Please, Lianne," Max said, "the real tragedy is that you found out the way you did. If this accident hadn't happened, it would have worked out better for all of us."

She was crying so hard that she couldn't answer him. She ignored Max's pleas, shaking as she cried.

Alex, sitting beside her, rubbed her back and her neck. She collected herself again and put the phone to her ear. "I'm going to see my daughter," she announced. "I'll take Alex with me and we'll tell her the truth."

"No," Max snapped. "You can't do that."

"I will, Max."

"No! I absolutely forbid it."

"Forbid it? After all this you're telling me I can't see my own child?"

"Of course you can. But I must be the one to tell her. I insist. For her sake. I beg you."

She knew there was logic in his words, but she was so wrought up, so upset, that she couldn't think straight.

"I'm coming back on the next flight," Max said. "I'll be there as soon as I possibly can."

"And you want me to stay away from Tatiana until then. You want to control her life and my life, just as you have all along. It doesn't matter to you that I need her. It doesn't matter to you that we belong together."

"Of course it does. Don't say that, Lianne. Please don't say that."

"You aren't even her father!" she exclaimed. "You're only the brother of her father. My baby was taken from me. Not just by you, I know, but you're the only one left who was responsible, and you're still trying to keep me from her. How can I love you after this, Max? How can I love you?"

She began sobbing again and dropped the receiver into her lap. There were no more plaintive cries from across the Atlantic. The only sound in the room was her own weeping.

Alex took the receiver and slipped it into the cradle. Then he put his arm around her shoulders.

"Oh, Alex," she said, "how could we have deserved this? We were young and our only sin was to be in love."

He stroked her head. "The main thing is you mustn't torture yourself. And it won't accomplish anything by getting Tatiana upset. It will all be resolved in good time."

Her head snapped up, and when she spoke, her voice was sharp. "And so I'm to sit and wait?"

"No, I think you should get away for a few days. Calm yourself. Get everything into perspective."

She shook her head. "I have no place to go."

"You can come with me. I was planning on going to England for Christmas, anyway. I'm leaving in the morning, as a matter of fact. Things were a little too tense for me around here. I've a dear friend with a lovely country estate. A chap called Stanley Goodson. He's having some people out. It'll be lively and fun. You should come with me, Lianne. It's the best sort of distraction. Exactly what you need."

She looked into his chocolate-brown eyes. Tatiana's father. A parent on the outside looking in, just like she.

"I don't know, Alex...."

"Come with me, Lianne. It'll be better for everyone. Tatiana will need time to adjust to this. And Max is right. He may only be an uncle in fact, but to Tatiana he's always been a father. It's for the best, darling. Come with me.''

LIANNE SAT NUMBLY in the terminal waiting area as Alex negotiated with the airline representatives. His flight was fully booked and he was trying to find a way to get her on board with him. She felt indifferent about the outcome, though she did want to leave town. It would be too hard staying in Geneva, knowing Tatiana was her daughter and being able to do absolutely nothing about it.

Alex had driven her home the night before. He had stayed for a while with her, to make sure she was all right, before taking a taxi back to his hotel.

The evening was a blur. She'd been alternately weepy and angry. But mostly she was sick with longing for her daughter. Alex had gotten her some vodka to settle her nerves, and she'd succeeded in numbing herself, but the anguish wouldn't go away.

The phone had rung a number of times, but she'd refused to answer it, and wouldn't let Alex answer it, either. She'd known it was Max, and she hadn't wanted to talk to him. The seething anger had turned to a dull pain, but there was no point in hashing through everything again. She understood his position, even if she didn't like it. Max had his obligations, but in the end she would see her daughter. Nothing on earth would prevent that.

Alex turned from the ticket counter and gave her a smile. He'd been earnest and supportive throughout the ordeal. She hadn't thought about him much, except for the general awareness that they were somewhat in the same boat. He'd seen their daughter over the years, but emotionally he'd been cut off, the same as she. Neither of them had been parents to the child who was theirs.

When Alex came for her that morning, he'd told her that Max had called him. Alex had explained that they both needed to get away, and that they were going to England for a few days while he tended to Tatiana. Lianne hadn't even asked how Max had reacted. She'd felt too numb to care. She was still in shock, especially after a near sleepless night of thinking incessantly about Tatiana.

Even the future, so important to them all, was too much to deal with. She couldn't bring herself to think beyond the next few days. When Alex packed her into the taxi for the ride to the airport, all she'd asked was when they would be coming back, when she would be able to see Tatiana.

"I'll call Max and discuss the situation with him," Alex had told her. "We'll see how things are going here, then we'll know what to do."

She'd accepted that, putting herself into his hands. Alex was the other parent of her child. He, at least, understood.

And so now she sat amid the tumult of holiday travelers—anesthetized, at the edge of shock. She looked down at the ring on her finger, feeling surprisingly indifferent about it. Her future with Max—something that had been so important only a day earlier—seemed strangely meaningless now. Tatiana had become all-important.

Lianne wasn't sure how she would have felt if her child had turned up suddenly somewhere else—say, after an unexpected call from Boston, bringing word that Alexandra had been found and wanted to see her. Max wouldn't have dropped from the face of the earth, as he had now. She would have been terribly excited and probably would have wanted him with her. Instead, he seemed almost a hindrance to her happiness.

Alex left the ticket counter and came walking over to where she was waiting. He sat beside her, slipping his arm onto the back of her seat. "Well, I've gotten them to try to buy off another passenger at my expense. You're wait-listed first, in any case."

"Oh, it hardly matters. I can drive into France and stay in a country inn somewhere for a few days. What difference does it make where I am?"

"It matters to me, if no one else."

There was a timbre in his voice that made her notice. And his soft brown eyes seemed to confirm what she heard. Poor Alex, she thought. She'd taken him pretty much for granted through all this. But he had his feelings, too. "You've been really sweet," she said, touching his hand. "I'm hardly your problem, though."

"But you are, Lianne. I've only just come to understand that."

THE VAUXHALL he had rented at Heathrow purred steadily through the rolling hills of Wiltshire. Lianne looked over at him in his gray sweater, his hair a bit ruffled from the wind. He looked rather English. She smiled at the notion—the Alex of her youth as British as he was Swiss.

His arm casually rested on the back of her seat and, though he was relaxed, he seemed rather intent on getting to Devon as quickly as possible. The reality of what she was doing hadn't really hit until now. She was with Alex Julen again and going off on some adventure of his making.

Of course, she hadn't really thought of it as going off with him. She was simply getting away from Geneva, and he was connected with her problem. He understood. Alex was as much a victim as she, though perhaps not equally innocent.

During the flight from the Continent, they'd talked. Alex had recounted many of his adventures in life. Lianne had listened to him, thinking at the time he was trying to distract her from all they'd left behind. But as the hours had passed, and she had begun to put developments into perspective, she had started to see that he intended her to be more than just a convenient leaning post.

That didn't please her—not if his intentions were serious. But she had doubts that they were. Alex was struggling, too, it seemed.

Strangely, he was quite different from her memories of him, and different, too, from the way she'd imagined he'd become. Under the urbane veneer was a man with vulnerabilities and sensitivities. He was lonely. That, perhaps, struck her above all.

Of course, he had mellowed. He was less idealistic, less naive. And seeing her again seemed to have affected him. He was going through an ordeal, the same as she. That made her feel closer to him. Lianne realized that, for the first time since his return, she was seeing him as a human being.

Swindon lay off to the north of the motorway as they passed by, moving into a stretch of rolling hills. The fields were fallow, the trees barren, making the English countryside appear somewhat bleak.

It was a blustery day, but the sun peeked out regularly from between the nubby clouds. As they drove, she watched the cattle and sheep on the hillsides and the farmhouses squatting under clusters of naked trees. She would sometimes spy signs of life in the houses they passed—a ribbon of smoke from a chimney bent over a rooftop, a line of wash flapping in the gusty wind.

She glanced over at Alex, tracing the lines of his profile with her eyes, finding it familiar, though it was the familiarity of remembrance. How often she had seen that face, awakening of a morning in Storrs or in her apartment in New York, knowing she had been with him in her dreams.

She had said goodbye to Alex forever that day she'd gone back to their mountaintop. But now here he was again, risen from the dead, just like her daughter.

"Alex," she asked him, "what's going to happen with Tatiana?"

"I don't know. We'll cross that bridge when we get there." He gave her a compassionate look, then gazed up the motorway, falling mute.

She watched the countryside for a while, then said, "My life won't be the same after this. I thought I would die with that piece of me missing. At least that's no longer true."

"It'll work out," he assured her.

She gazed off at the sky, finding solace in the feel of the road under them. She was glad they had left Switzerland, because she needed time to get ready to face Tatiana, and she needed time to sort out her relationship with Max.

Lianne really didn't know where things stood between them now. Whenever she thought of him she felt terribly angry with him for keeping the truth from her.

"Don't think too much," Alex had advised her when the subject of Max had come up on the plane. "Take a few days to clear your head."

But how could she possibly keep herself from thinking about what had happened? Her entire life was up in the air. And she was afraid that the dream of a wonderful life with Max had been destroyed forever.

HOURS LATER they were on the M5 headed south into Somerset, toward Devon and Cornwall. For a while they were very near the coast where the River Severn emptied into the Bristol Channel. Alex told her that Cardiff and the coast of Wales were only about ten miles away, but there was a cloud bank low on the horizon, and they couldn't see anything except glimpses of the gray-green water.

When they passed Burnham-on-Sea, the coastline jutted abruptly off to the right and the motorway continued south, taking them inland again. The cloud cover began breaking up into pink balls of cotton as they exited in the direction of Tiverton and headed west through the rolling terrain.

Soon they left the road and took a country lane, a narrow ribbon of asphalt running between hedgerows and stone walls. Houses abutted the road in the villages they passed through, the doors and shutters hardly more than an arm's length from the car. Large old farmhouses occupied picturesque spots in the landscape, their chimneys rising like sentinels against the afternoon sky.

Just outside the village of Stroxton was the estate of Alex's friend—Stroxton Court, a monolithic heap of drab gray stone, gabled roofs, turrets and chimneys, sitting at the crest of a low rise. A long, twisting drive led up the hill from the road. In the fading twilight the house looked cold, forbidding and Gothic. Inside the gate, in a copse of trees fronting the road, was the village church. It wasn't very large, but it appeared more hospitable than the great house.

There were sheep grazing quietly behind a rusty iron fence surrounding the close. In spite of the animals, the grass and vegetation seemed overgrown and unkempt. Alex put the Vauxhall in gear, and they started up the hill. He was forced to weave from side to side to avoid potholes in the drive.

Alex had telephoned from Heathrow to alert Stanley that there would be another guest. While they were waiting for their rental car, he'd told Lianne a little about his friend, but she had only half listened.

They entered the courtyard and found a beehive of activity. A couple of young men were kicking a soccer ball back and forth among the half-dozen or so cars that were parked against the front hedge. A workman was at the top of a tall ladder, hammering away on a drainpipe. A cat scampered away when they drew close. No one gave them much more than a glance.

They'd hardly gotten out of the car when a large, flabby man of about forty came sailing out the front door and down the steps. He wore an argyle sweater that barely covered his stomach, a bow tie and large, heavy-framed glasses. His dark hair was combed back, and a smile full of delight was on his face.

"Alex, my friend, welcome, welcome. A bit late, but you made it, I see." He came up to them and enthusiastically shook hands with his old friend. Then he turned to her. "And this lovely creature must be Lianne." He smiled benevolently, and with a bit more adoration than was warranted, before taking her hand and kissing it. "Stanley Goodson," he said with a slight bow, double chins showing under his receding chin.

Alex had told her that his friend was eccentric, but Lianne hadn't quite expected the theater. When he said

Stanley was in the diplomatic service, her expectation was sedate eccentric, not outré.

"I'm so happy to meet you," she said, bemused.

Stanley beamed, then looked down suddenly at his feet where a tabby was wrapping itself around his ankles. "Goodness, you'd think I was a fish." He laughed, took Lianne's arm and started leading her toward the entrance to the house. "Can you manage the bags, old bean?" he called over his shoulder to Alex. "If not, I'll send someone out. In the meantime I'll show your lady around."

Lianne went along, wondering how Alex had explained their relationship to Stanley. She didn't think he'd disclosed the fact that she was his brother's fiancée.

"The tribe is gathering tonight," Stanley said as they walked. "But the festivities shan't get under way in earnest until tomorrow." They went up the stairs and into the house. "This evening things are informal. The ball begins tomorrow night and may last a day or two. Could be it won't stop till Christmas."

Lianne looked surprised. "There's a ball?"

"A costume party. Let's describe it that way." He stopped just inside the doors. "You don't have a costume, do you?"

She shook her head.

"Pity," he said, rubbing his chin thoughtfully. "Well, never mind. We've got a trunk upstairs somewhere with old costumes, just for this very purpose."

The outer entry contained little more than a coatrack and the staircase, but the inner hall was a virtual sitting room, rising to a height of two of the four stories of the house. The focus of the room was a massive stone fireplace, twenty feet across and rising to the ceiling. The walls were painted a deep rose and the woodwork was dark. The furniture had a worn, well-used look about it.

But the house was hardly tranquil. Big band music spewed at full volume from a portable phonograph. Stanley walked over and nonchalantly lifted the needle, plunging the room into silence. The laughter of women drifted from the back of the house, but Stanley paid no notice.

"Alex tells me you're a poet."

Lianne smiled indulgently, already amused by her host. "Not quite. Actually I taught literature. Nineteenth-century English poetry."

"Ah, delightful. A favorite period of mine, as well. I rather like Keats's sonnets, though some of his stuff is odious rot. The one that begins, 'Cat! Who hast pass'd thy grand climacteric, How many mice and rats hast in thy das Destroy'd?' is a particular favorite. So much better than 'Endymion,' for example, don't you agree?"

She bit her cheek to keep from smiling. "I prefer Shelley myself."

A girl came down the hall, pushing a cart loaded with cakes, cups and saucers, and pots of tea and milk. "Oh, Mary!" he suddenly said, remembering. "Be a good girl and help Mr. Julen with his bags out in the park. He's the handsome chap with the Vauxhall."

"Yes, sir." The girl left the cart against the wall and went out through the double doors.

Stanley led Lianne to one of the overstuffed couches and sat her down. "So glad you and Alex could make it," he said. "Alex is always such good fun."

"He's talked about your parties."

"I do love to party, as you American chaps say. Most of the group coming up this trip are people in my office. This being Christmas week, I gave the lot of them time

off, except for a skeleton crew, of course. Plus it's to celebrate Amanda's twenty-first birthday. Twenty-one." He
sighed. "Imagine. I could be her father."

Lianne smiled at the man's rambling monologue. She
could see what Alex had meant about it being a distraction to come to England.

"Amanda wanted something a little different," Stanley went on, "so we decided on a costume party. In theory you're to come as your favorite person in fiction or
history. Knowing this lot, we should have a Mickey
Mouse or two." He laughed, completely bemused. Then
a frown crept across his face. "Look at me, what a
dreadful host. I haven't offered you a drink. It's only fair
to warn you, Lianne. I make a damn good gin and tonic,
as Alex will attest, if he hasn't already."

"He did say you helped him develop a taste for them."

Stanley laughed. "Amazing what the bloody things
will do to you, especially in a tropical climate. Lord, I
blush to think of some of our evenings at the Imperial in
Lagos."

"What's this, Stanley?" It was Alex coming through
the double doors. "You aren't betraying me, are you?"

"Good heavens, no, old man. I was simply explaining
why I was about to fix us all a gin and tonic. It is tea-
time, after all."

Lianne looked at Alex, who seemed a bit tentative. She
wondered if he was having second thoughts about bringing her to Stroxton Court. At any rate, she was certainly
beginning to think it might have been a mistake to come.

## CHAPTER FOURTEEN

LIANNE'S ROOM WAS on the third floor at a corner of the house, affording a view of the church and the dark, rolling hills beyond. In the last rays of twilight she could see two or three rooftops in the village of Stroxton, but Stanley had told her it wasn't much of a place and hardly worth a visit.

"Do go down to the church, though," he'd said. "It's rather nice."

As she watched the deep shadows turn to darkness, the bells in the Norman tower of the church began to chime. It made her think of the bells of Saint Pierre in Geneva, though these were far less august, just the carillon of a small country church. But it reminded her of Tatiana and Max, and she felt homesick for them both, the revelations of the past few days notwithstanding.

Lianne knew it wasn't a profitable line of thought. She had to take her mind off of them. Alex was right. She had to give her emotions a rest.

She was feeling a touch woozy from the gin and tonic she'd had with the men. More than anything, it had made her tired. The fatigue of the long day, the lack of sleep from the night before, had gotten to her. But Stanley was eager to be the gracious host, so, while Alex had had another drink, she'd had a tour of Stroxton Court.

They'd gone through the billiard room and library with its black carved wooden mantel, the great dining hall with its single thirty-foot table, and finally the rose garden and croquet lawns. They'd encountered some of the other guests, and Stanley had made the introductions, but she was so fatigued that she had barely managed pleasantries.

In the end Stanley had taken pity on her and had the maid show her to her room. Lianne had lain for a while on the bed, considering whether she ought bother to go downstairs and eat. Her host had told her there would be food set out on the dining room table and she should help herself.

Considering her condition, though, she decided to go to bed instead. She undressed, putting on a flannel nightgown that, like so many before it, was the product of thirty-some New England winters. She got into bed but left the bedside lamp on for a time, not yet feeling ready for the darkness of a strange house.

A terrible sadness gripped her, just as it had the night before when she lay in her bed at Nanna's. The tentative joy she felt at finding her child was masked by the uncertain future and her rupture with Max. Now that her immediate emotions over Tatiana were past, she had a desire to talk to Max, to clarify what he was thinking. She even considered trying to call him, but she had no idea if he was back in Geneva yet, or if he might have changed his mind and stayed in California to finish his business.

Lianne was confused, uncertain of her feelings, even a bit disoriented. Had she really gone away with Alex, leaving the home she'd made behind?

There was a knock at the door then.

"Who is it?" she asked.

"It's me, Alex. I saw your light was still on. May I come in?"

She wasn't in a mood to talk, but she knew she shouldn't be antisocial. Alex had been so very kind to her. She considered getting up and putting on her robe, but there were no locks on the door and she could invite him in without getting up. Seeing her in bed, he might not stay so long.

"Yes, come in," she called through the door.

It creaked open and Alex stuck his head in. "Ah, you *are* in bed. Would you rather I go away?"

"No, I wasn't sleeping. Come in, Alex."

He did, not needing further invitation. He had a glass in his hand, and by the way he walked and the expression on his face, she could see he'd had quite a bit to drink. "I thought I'd see if I could bring you some supper," he said.

"That's thoughtful of you, but I'm not hungry. Mainly I'm tired."

Alex walked to the side of the bed, almost weaving as he stood there. "Sure?"

"Yes."

"Don't suppose you'd like a drink?"

She shook her head. "No, thank you."

"Shall I sit down, then?" He didn't wait for an answer. He sat on the bed next to her, smiling a rakish smile. He took her hand. "So how are you doing? Bearing up?"

"I'm okay."

"I've been thinking about you, even sitting talking to Stanley's crazy friends. How do you like old Stanley, by the way?"

"He's certainly eccentric. But very nice."

"Stanley and I have been through the bachelor wars together."

The comment evoked a definite image of ribaldry and decadence, of women and drink. But there was a vague sadness in Alex's voice, too. Maybe, underneath, he realized how alien it all was to her.

"How is it there isn't someone in your life, Alex?"

An almost wistful expression passed over his face. "You mean a woman."

"Yes."

He shrugged. "I have a friend in Lagos, a lady friend, but we both know nothing will come of it."

"That's too bad."

"Why is that?"

She contemplated him. "I suppose I would like to see you happy."

"And what makes you think I'm not?"

"I don't know that you're unhappy. But..."

He smiled knowingly and took a long drink from his glass.

"It's really none of my business," she said, feeling embarrassed.

Alex leaned over unexpectedly and kissed her on the mouth. He grinned and looked into her eyes. "You're the same lovely, innocent person you were when I met you."

She was shocked but managed to say, "I don't think so."

"Yes, you are. You've lived, of course, but you're still innocent about life." He sipped his drink. "I find it endearing."

Lianne wasn't sure if he was teasing her or not. Alex rubbed her hand with his fingers.

"I find that attractive, just as I did the last time I knew you."

She heard something unequivocal in his voice, a message intended to be heard. She looked down at her hands, anything but his eyes.

"Maybe it's terrible of me to say this, but you still do something to me, Lianne. When I saw you at the park the other day, on that bench, I felt it again. Did you?"

"Naturally I remember my feelings for you," she replied, choosing her words carefully. "I've thought of you often over the years. But our lives have gone on. I'm engaged now. You have your life." She didn't sound as convincing as she had hoped she would.

Looking into his eyes, she understood what was happening. They were alone—off in England in a crazy house with a bunch of crazy people. Alex was drunk and was saying things he wouldn't say normally. And yet she knew he was telling the truth.

He nodded, looking off. "I have my life, sure. But it's a lot emptier than I care to admit." Then he engaged her eyes again. "You may not like to hear this, Lianne, but I've often wondered what would have happened if I'd been braver. What if I hadn't let them push us around."

"I don't suppose there's much point in speculating," she said, hoping to cut off this line of thought.

"We'd have married," he insisted, ignoring what she'd just said. "And we'd have had our family. You and me and Tatiana."

Alex was rambling on in a half-drunken babble. Still, what he said affected her. How could it not? She hadn't fully recovered from the shock of finding her daughter. Now, to hear him talking like this . . .

"Don't, Alex. Please." She lowered her head, and her eyes filled with moisture.

When a tear overflowed, he wiped it away with his thumb. And then he tried to kiss her on the mouth again, but she quickly turned her face away.

"No," she said again, shaking her head. "Please don't do this."

He squeezed her hand. "It's terrible of me to kiss you. I know. I'm sorry. I couldn't help myself."

She looked up at him through her tears. She was speechless.

"You're probably the only person I've ever loved," he said. "I've been marking time ever since."

"Alex…" She didn't want to hear his words. It would be too difficult to forget he'd said them later on, and they would both be embarrassed.

"It's my own fault," he went on. "I've gone into exile of my own free will. I left you behind. And Tatiana. I've paid for it." He drank again, finishing the last of the cocktail. He put the glass down on the table beside the bed. "I hope it doesn't upset you that I say that."

She looked directly into his eyes. "It does, actually."

"I guess I have no right."

"You have a right to your feelings, Alex. But it's too late for us."

"Is it really?"

She wasn't sure if he was being drunk and maudlin or if these were his true feelings. "We're going through a difficult time," she said. "You can't judge things by this."

He smiled with amusement. "I'm not so naive."

Lianne closed her eyes. Two months ago this would have been a dream come true. But now, hearing him say these things to her, she felt nothing but sadness. She lay staring off at the opposite wall, aware of his proximity, feeling dreadful.

"Tatiana loves us both," Alex said.

The words were pregnant with implication, but he didn't take the next step. "Yes, and she loves Max, as well."

"It can't help but affect her when she finds out we're her parents," he said.

"What are you saying, Alex?"

He picked up his glass, but it was empty, and so he put it down again. "That we shouldn't jump to any conclusions. I'm saying we have to take our time and think this thing through. Maybe time is what we need."

"It's the gin talking," she said. "You don't mean what you're saying. I'm going to forget it. And so should you."

"Why?"

"Because I love Max, that's why."

"Do you? Do you really?"

It was hard to tell if Alex was being scathing or merely provocative. "I've been really upset that he kept the truth about Tatiana from me, but that doesn't mean I've stopped loving him."

"Would you love him without Tatiana?"

She looked at him, uncertain what he was getting at. "If anything, she was a problem between us. At least at first."

"But things are different now," Alex returned. "You and I are her parents."

The frustration of the past few days welled up again, overwhelming her. "Please, Alex, don't do this. I'm upset enough as it is." Her eyes flooded again. "I need to be alone."

He looked contrite. "I didn't mean to hurt you. I've had too much to drink. I'm sorry." He took her hand and kissed her fingers. "Will you forgive me?"

"Of course. I think you should leave now. Tomorrow's another day."

Out in the hall they heard a couple laughing on their way to their room, the woman sounding giddy. It occurred to her that Alex had brought her to a bacchanalian orgy, though she wasn't sure whether it was to seduce her or simply to distract her, as he'd said.

"Whatever else I am," Alex said, "I am a gentleman." With that he rose. Then, smiling faintly, he turned and went to the door, where he stopped. "Everything I said tonight I meant, Lianne. Every word." He went out then, quietly closing the door behind him.

LIANNE WAS UP in the morning before the rest of the house. When she went downstairs, the young maid, Mary, was putting cereal and bowls and fruit out on the dining room table.

"I'll be bringin' the tea directly, ma'am," she said. "Would you be wantin' some eggs perhaps? A proper breakfast? The cook will do a mixed grill if you like."

Lianne was hungry, having hardly eaten the day before. "That sounds good. Maybe I will."

The maid set her a place at the table and went off to get the food. While she was gone Lianne fixed herself a bowl of cereal. The tea came, and she sat looking out the great windows of Stanley Goodson's dining room.

It was a sunny day, but it looked cold. Perhaps it was the barren trees. Still, she had a desire to get outside. When Mary brought her eggs, grilled tomatoes and ham, Lianne asked if there was a good place to walk.

The girl recommended a country lane that was particularly pleasant, describing the route in detail. Then she said, "When you get back, ma'am, perhaps you'd like to have a look at the costumes. Mr. Goodson asked me to help you select one.''

''He's really serious, then.''

''Oh, yes, ma'am. He loves costume parties. Says it's his Celtic blood. Something about the winter solstice. Leastwise, they say he has it every Christmas he's not abroad.''

''Has Mr. Julen been before?''

''I don't rightly know, ma'am. I've only been in the house six months now.''

''I see.''

''He does seem an awfully nice gentleman, Mr. Julen. Is he your fiancé, if you don't mind me askin', ma'am?''

''No, he isn't.''

''Didn't mean to pry. I noticed your ring. It's lovely.''

Lianne looked down at her finger and thought of Max. When she awoke that morning, she'd thought of his proposal in Montreux, the plans they had for a life together. But she'd also thought of Alex. And, of course, Tatiana. The situation was complicated, and she certainly wasn't going to explain it to Mary.

When she finished eating, Lianne got her coat and went out the front door of the great house. She strolled across the park and down the drive, retracing the route they'd taken the evening before.

At the foot of the hill she glanced over at the church, but decided not to stop to look around. Instead she followed the path toward the village. At a fork in the road, she took the branch that led off into the countryside.

There was a brisk wind blowing over the fallow fields. It chilled her, making her nose run and her eyes water, but the air was exhilarating and it cleared her head. Alex's visit to her room the night before had sobered her. It had been unexpected, though perhaps it shouldn't have been. There had been some signs, but she'd ignored them.

She was still unsure what to make of Alex. The gin might have loosened his tongue, but it hadn't put all those thoughts in his head. What was she to think? In the midst of her confusion the man who had haunted her memories for years had all but told her he loved her and wanted her again. The reality of that sent an icy chill through her, changing things completely.

The situation was a lot more complicated now. Max knew Alex far better than she did. What would he think? The fact that she and Alex had been lovers once could only amplify his suspicions.

She agonized at the thought, wondering if events may have destroyed their plans for a future. It seemed certain things would never be quite the same between them. The fact that Tatiana was her daughter, and not his, would affect them all. Alex aside, how would they survive that?

She must have walked for five miles by the time she returned to the village. During the course of her walk, she had decided that she couldn't sit idly by and let events carry her along. She had to talk to Max, but she didn't want to telephone him from Stanley Goodson's.

In the village she found a red telephone box next to the bus stop. But it was rather old-fashioned, and it took her a minute to figure out how to operate it, but she was soon listening to the telephone ringing at Max's home in Geneva. Tatiana answered, giving her a start.

"Is your father there?" she asked, trembling at the sound of her daughter's voice.

"Lianne, he's in America. Did you forget?" Her laughter sounded so innocent, so lighthearted, it was all Lianne could do not to weep.

She fought to keep control of herself. "No, I was under the impression he'd decided to come home early."

"Who said so?"

"Your... Uncle Alex."

"Uncle Alex?"

"Never mind, Tatiana. It doesn't matter. I'll talk to your father later. Forget I called."

"You sound a little strange," the girl said. "I mean, the telephone. Are you at home?"

"No. I'm away. But never mind. I'll talk to you later, darling." Her lip trembled. She wanted to tell Tatiana that she loved her, but she couldn't.

She hung up the telephone and stood in the call box, her body shaking. The cold wind whistled about her. For several long moments she was paralyzed. Then she pulled herself together and got the international operator again. This time she called San Francisco.

"I'm sorry," the desk clerk at the hotel said, "but Mr. Julen checked out last evening."

"Did he say where he was going?"

"I don't know. I wasn't on duty. Were you expecting a message?"

"Is there one for Lianne Halliday?" she asked.

"Just a minute, I'll check." After a short while, he came back on the line. "Sorry, no message."

Lianne thanked him and hung up. She turned, leaning wearily against the side of the booth. A small broken-down lorry driven by a farmer passed by. He craned his neck, looking at her. She didn't move. When he was out of sight, she stared at the empty road and the mute houses farther up the lane. It was very quiet except for the wind.

Lianne shivered and began walking back toward Stroxton Court. She didn't know what to do. There was really nothing she could do, not until Max returned to Geneva.

THE TAXI STOPPED in front of the house. Max paid the driver and got out, looking up at the facade of the building, finding it formidable and forbidding, even though it was his. He took his leather suitcase and quickly climbed the steps, unsure what situation he would discover inside. He had been anxious the past two days, and the long flight from San Francisco had seemed endless.

During his brief conversation with Alex, he'd gotten the impression that nothing would be said to Tatiana, and he could only hope that his brother was good to his word. But he'd mainly worried about Lianne, her state of mind, their future.

Those brief moments he'd spoken with her on the phone had been among the most traumatic of his life. He was trapped between two loves, two obligations. Fate had done him a dirty trick, but not without his own complicity. Obviously he'd bungled the situation badly.

Opening the door with his key, Max went inside, only to find Maria passing through the hall.

*"Monsieur!"* she said with her thick Spanish accent. "We weren't expecting you home so soon."

"I had to shorten the trip," he replied, putting down his suitcase and taking off his coat. He handed it to her. "Is Tatiana in her room?"

"Of course."

He nodded and went off through the house, feeling the crisis looming over him, despite the familiar surroundings that would ordinarily have given comfort. He knocked on Tatiana's door.

*"Pase usted,"* she said, thinking it was Maria. But when she saw him, she jumped up from her bed and ran to him. "Papa! What are you doing home?"

Max held her in his arms, tears forming in his eyes at her youthful exuberance, her innocence. He was afraid of what was to come, the blow he'd have to deal.

Tatiana looked up at him, her expression turning to perplexity at seeing his face. "Are you all right, Papa?"

"Yes," he said, smiling. "But I'm very tired."

"You haven't said yet why you came home early. Wasn't the new company to your liking?"

"It was fine. I came home because of something else."

"What?" There was a touch of alarm in her voice as she'd begun to sense something ominous in the offing.

"Come sit down," he said, leading her to the bed.

They sat side by side.

"Is something wrong?" she asked.

"Not wrong exactly, darling. But it's time you learned something very important."

Tatiana looked at him uncertainly, but said nothing. Max sighed deeply, feeling weary and drained. He was determined to get it over with so that they could get into the healing phase as quickly as possible.

"What is it, Papa?"

"Tatiana," he said, taking her hand, "you know I love you as much as anyone in the world. Nothing could ever change that. Ever."

"Oh, Papa, I understand that you love Lianne, too, now. That's not a problem for me."

"Yes, I know. That's not what I'm getting at."

"Then what?"

"Your mother loved you, too. She was devoted to you completely. You may have been the most important thing in her life."

# BIG SUMMER READ

## Summer Reading At Its Best

In July, Harlequin and Silhouette bring readers the Big Summer Read Program. Heat up your summer with these four exciting new novels by top Harlequin and Silhouette authors.

**SOMEWHERE IN TIME by Barbara Bretton**
**YESTERDAY COMES TOMORROW by Rebecca Flanders**
**A DAY IN APRIL by Mary Lynn Baxter**
**LOVE CHILD by Patricia Coughlin**

From time travel to fame and fortune, this program offers something for everyone.

Available at your favorite retail outlet.

# FREE GIFT OFFER

With Free Gift Promotion proofs-of-purchase from Harlequin or Silhouette, you can receive this beautiful jewelry collection. Each item is perfect by itself, or collect all three for a complete jewelry ensemble.

For a classic look that is always in style, this beautiful gold tone jewelry will complement any outfit. Items include:

Gold tone clip earrings (approx. retail value $9.95), a 7½" gold tone bracelet (approx. retail value $15.95) and a 18" gold tone necklace (approx. retail value $29.95).

## FREE GIFT OFFER TERMS

To receive your free gift, complete the certificate according to directions. Be certain to enclose the required number of Free Gift proofs-of-purchase, which are found on the last page of every specially marked Free Gift Harlequin or Silhouette romance novel. Requests must be received no later than July 31, 1992. Items depicted are for illustrative purposes only and may not be exactly as shown. Please allow 6 to 8 weeks for receipt of order. Offer good while quantities of gifts last. In the event an ordered gift is no longer available, you will receive a free, previously unpublished Harlequin or Silhouette book for every proof-of-purchase you have submitted with your request, plus a refund of the postage-and-handling charge you have included. Offer good in the U.S. and Canada only.

## MILLIONAIRE Sweepstakes!

As an added value every time you send in a completed certificate with the correct number of proofs-of-purchase, your name will automatically be entered in our Million Dollar Sweepstakes. The more completed offer certificates you send in, the more often your name will be entered in our sweepstakes and the better your chances of winning.

PROI

"I know this, Papa. That can't be what you're trying to tell me."

"No, darling. What I want you to know is that Catrina and I loved you as much as any two parents have loved their child. We loved you as though you were our natural daughter. But you weren't, Tatiana darling. We adopted you as a tiny baby."

Her eyes opened wide. She tried to smile. "Papa, this is a joke. You're trying to make a joke."

He put his arm around her and held her close against him. "No, Tatiana. It's not a joke. It's the truth. And it's time you know."

"I'm adopted?"

"Yes."

"I don't believe it." She shook her head disapprovingly. "You really shouldn't do this, Papa. It's not funny at all."

"I'm not being funny. I know this is a shock, but it's important that you know the truth. And it's terribly important that you know it never has and never will have any effect on my feelings for you, ever. I can only hope that it won't affect your feelings for me."

Tatiana sat stunned. It was taking her time to assimilate what she'd heard. "I still don't believe you."

"It's true."

She shook her head, her face screwed up. "Why haven't you told me this before if it's so? Why now?"

Max took a deep breath. "Because some things have happened lately, some things that make it essential that you know you're adopted."

"What things?"

He took her hands, holding them firmly in his. Her long, narrow fingers, so much like Lianne's, were warm to his touch. He looked into her eyes, feeling a terrible stab of pain in his heart. This, without doubt, was the most difficult moment of his life.

"You know the baby that Lianne gave up when she was young? The child she had with Alex?"

She waited.

"You are that little girl, Tatiana. You are Lianne's child."

Her mouth dropped open, but for a moment no sound came out. She searched his eyes, almost desperately now. The pain inside him grew more intense. Her lip trembled before she spoke. "That can't be," she mumbled. "I am Mummy's daughter. And yours!"

He shook his head, the tears in his eyes boiling so that her image blurred.

"Papa, you're saying that so I'll love Lianne and want her for a mother. But I already have a mother. This is all very stupid."

"It's not that, darling. Believe me. Lianne herself didn't know. Not until a few days ago. She was as shocked by this as you."

"Then it's true? Lianne *is* my mother?"

"Yes."

"And Uncle Alex is my father?"

Max nodded.

"Uncle Alex . . . my *father?*" Her eyes were filled with horror. Then her face broke, and she was on the verge of tears. "I can't believe this." Tears overran her lids and began streaming down her face. Max clutched her to him, holding her tightly. She sobbed. "Papa, tell me this isn't so."

He couldn't answer her. His own tears were overflowing now.

"Did Uncle Alex know?"

"Yes."

"But he pretended to be my uncle. And you pretended to be my father?" There was horror in her voice—a horror that tore at him.

"As far as your mother and I were concerned, you were our daughter, Tatiana. And as far as Alex was concerned, you were his niece. None of this would have come to light except for the fact that Lianne returned. And I fell in love with her. I couldn't keep it a secret from the two of you, not with you living in the same house together."

Tatiana sat dumbfounded. She wiped away her tears and stared at the floor. "What did Lianne say about this when you told her?"

"She was very upset that she wasn't told sooner. Actually, she found out by accident from Madame Gevers's housekeeper. I intended to tell her later—to tell both of you—when I returned from America, but she found out first."

"Papa, this is all so bizarre. How can I have new parents? I love the ones I have. How can Uncle Alex ever be my father?"

"He needn't be, Tatiana. He's only your father in a biological sense. You'll always be mine."

"And Mummy," she said, her eyes welling again. "I never want to give up Mummy."

"And you won't. That's not the point of me telling you now."

Tatiana was silent again.

Max kissed her temple, and she put her arms around him. "I love you," he told her.

"And I shall always love you, Papa. You shall always be my father. Nothing will change that, ever."

"No, darling," he said, his heart lighter, his spirit soaring for the first time in days. "It shall always be so."

"What about Lianne?" Tatiana asked after a minute or two. "How does she feel about this?"

"I'm sure she's very eager to see you. But I haven't talked to her again. She's gone away for a few days."

"No, Papa, she called here this morning, asking for you."

"She did? This morning?"

"Yes. I thought at first she was at home. And it seemed strange that she should think you'd come back from America. I didn't understand."

"I told her I would be returning right away."

"Then where is she?"

"In England. With Alex."

"She's with Uncle Alex? But why?"

"Because this was all very shocking to her, just as it was shocking to you, and she wanted to go away for a little while."

"Is she unhappy?"

"I suspect she's feeling very confused, just as you must be."

"It's like a very strange dream, Papa. I still don't know if I believe it."

"Eventually you will, Tatiana," he said, stroking her head. "And we'll adjust. All of us. But now it's very important that I go see Lianne. I have to talk to her."

"When is she coming back?"

"I don't know. I must talk to her about that. It seems I must go to England."

Tatiana waited.

"Will you be all right if I leave you for a day or so to find Lianne?"

She looked at him wistfully.

"I know you've received a big shock, and it's come very suddenly. I didn't want it to happen this way, but I had little choice. Lianne wanted to see you as soon as she heard, but I asked her to wait until I spoke with you first.''

''I'm glad you did, Papa. I never would have believed her. Or Uncle Alex, either.''

''Well, it's done now. You'll think about it a great deal for a while, I know. And it may upset you for a time, but in the end everything will be all right.''

Tatiana put her head on his shoulder. He kissed her hair.

''I couldn't confirm a reservation to London,'' he told her. ''But I'm on the list for a number of flights. I have to return to the airport. Will you be okay here with Maria?''

She nodded. ''Will you bring Lianne back with you?''

''I hope so, darling. I hope so.''

# CHAPTER FIFTEEN

STANLEY GOODSON jogged up the front steps of the house with uncharacteristic energy. He paused at the door and looked back at Alex, who followed much more sedately.

"There's nothing like riding on a crisp winter day," Stanley said, seeming almost giddy. The vapors from his breath dissipated in the cold air.

"It's a change from Lagos," Alex admitted.

When Alex got to the top of the steps, Stanley put his arm around his friend's shoulders. "Why so glum, old bean? I hear it in your voice."

"My life is at a crossroads, Stan, and I don't know what to do."

"This sounds like something best discussed over a glass of sherry. What say we repair to the library and have a chat?"

They went inside. Stanley asked Mary to bring them a bottle of dry sherry and some glasses. Then they went into the library where Stanley said, "I take it the crossroads has to do with the lovely Miss Halliday."

"Yes, Stan. I'm coming to think I may be in love with her."

He grinned. "Is that bad?"

"She's my brother's fiancée."

"Oh, dear, you hadn't mentioned that, old bean."

"My life is not without its complications."

Stanley poured them each some sherry. "No, it doesn't appear that it is." They exchanged a silent toast. Then Alex recounted the saga of his relationship with Lianne, going back fifteen years, and bringing the story up to the events of the past few days.

"Well, I must say I'm surprised by the revelations. Sure you aren't a victim of nostalgia? Old loves have a way of getting to a bloke if his guard's down."

"I don't know. I may be as confused as she." He lowered his head and rubbed his eyes.

"What are you going to do?"

Alex looked up at his friend. "I think now the ball is in Max's court. If there's any hope for me, it's to keep her away from him a while."

"Give the old charm some time to work, eh?"

Alex fingered his glass and took a sip. "I don't know. Naturally I feel some loyalty to my brother. But at the same time I don't want her marrying him if she should be marrying me."

Stanley's eyebrows rose. "Has it come to that, then? Marriage."

Alex nodded. "It could."

"How does Lianne feel about that?"

"Max's ring is still on her finger, and the business with Tatiana has her upset. Beyond that, I think she's trying to sort things out."

Stanley tapped his sherry glass thoughtfully with his finger. "If I were in your shoes, I believe I'd talk to my brother and tell him what my intentions were."

"You're probably right. And I did promise Lianne I'd ring Max up." Alex got to his feet. "Well, if you'll excuse me, I might as well get it over with."

The telephone was in a small booth just off the entry. Alex stepped inside and closed the door.

He took the receiver in his hand, surprised at how hard his heart was beating. For a moment he paused, asking himself if he was doing what he really wanted.

He closed his eyes and pictured Lianne, remembering the kiss he'd given her the night before and trying to remember how it had felt to make love to her all those years ago. But the feel of her body, the image of her naked, were lost to him, blurred into the memory of sex with dozens of other women. Lianne stood out in his mind only because of her fresh innocence, her virginal fear.

Alex realized that he was in the same situation he had been in fifteen years before. The seduction he desired was different now, though, as were the emotional stakes. There were others to consider this time—Max and Tatiana. Perhaps the honorable thing for him to do was to leave them all to their happiness and return to Nigeria.

But what of his own needs? Hadn't he paid for the past over the years? Wasn't he entitled to his happiness, too?

Alex knew the choice wasn't his alone. In that sense he was at Lianne's mercy. And Max's. Perhaps that was as it should be. Fate would decide.

Either way he had to deal with his brother. Lianne would want to see Tatiana, no matter what. So he might as well be done with it. He called Max's home in Geneva. The Spanish maid answered.

Alex said, *"Monsieur Julen, s'il vous plaît."*

*"Monsieur* isn't here. May I help you?"

"This is his brother, Alex. Hasn't *monsieur* returned from America yet?"

"Yes, *monsieur.* He's come home and he's gone again. To England."

"To England?"

"Yes, he left earlier today."

"Do you know where?"

"I have no idea. He made some calls and left very suddenly. But Tatiana may know. Do you wish to speak to her, *monsieur?*"

"No, that's all right. *Merci, madame.*"

Alex hung up the phone. The chill of fear came over him. Guilt perhaps. Was Max coming to Stroxton Court, or did he have other business in England? Alex hadn't left the address and telephone number with anyone but his office, and he'd only told them so that he could be contacted in case of an emergency.

He had to know what Max was up to, so he telephoned the Red Cross headquarters in Geneva. Monique Genoud, the little brunette in personnel who kept track of field officers, was leaving for the day when the phone rang in her office.

"Ah, Monsieur Julen," she said sweetly, "you just caught me. And how ironic you called."

Monique had flirted outrageously with him whenever he was in the office and made her admiration plain. But he had no time for flirtation now.

"Ironic?"

"Yes, I spoke with your brother only this morning. He called, saying it was urgent that he find you. Hasn't he telephoned?"

"No. I take it you gave him the number, though."

"Yes. And the address, as well. Stroxton Court in Stroxton, Devon. It's all right that I told him, isn't it? I thought, since he was your brother..."

"It's no problem, Monique. Don't worry."

"Whew! I was worried I might have done the wrong thing."

Alex was thinking.

"Will we be seeing you soon, Monsieur Julen?"

"I don't know. But I'll keep you informed, Monique. Thank you." He replaced the receiver in the cradle, muttering under his breath. *"Merde."*

Alex considered the situation. In all likelihood Max wouldn't be arriving until the next morning. That gave him some time. But then it occurred to him that his brother might have called Lianne. The only way to find out for certain was to ask. He hadn't seen her that day, anyway, between her long morning walk and his ride with Stanley. It was time he talked to her. Besides, her state of mind was the most critical factor of all.

Alex ducked into the library to tell Stanley the wheels of fate were in motion. He didn't go into detail, but said he would meet with him later for a gin and tonic. Other guests who had been out for the day were returning to the house as Alex made his way upstairs to Lianne's room. He knocked on her door and was surprised when the maid, Mary, opened it.

"Oh, Mr. Julen, Miss Halliday is picking out a costume for the ball. Perhaps you can help her decide." She stepped back to admit him to the room.

Lianne was standing by the bed, several garments spread out before her. She smiled at him. "Catch any foxes, Alex? Mary said you and Stanley went riding."

He was pleased at her cheerfulness, and he was sure now that Max hadn't called. Otherwise she would have said something. "About all I got today was a bruised derriere." He grimaced playfully and went over to Lianne, kissing her on the cheek. "They say you covered the breadth of Devon this morning."

"I had a very nice walk."

Mary came over. "Miss Halliday thought she'd be a princess for the ball," she said.

Lianne picked up the pale blue taffeta gown and held it up in front of her. "What do you think, Alex?"

"Very lovely," he said, looking into her eyes.

He noticed a flicker of awareness. Perhaps she was remembering the night before when he kissed her and said some things he probably shouldn't have. But any discomfort was quickly brushed aside.

"It's probably the best choice," she said, glancing at the bed. "It's much too cold to be a Roman slave girl, and I'm sure the tutu is too small, not to mention more appropriate for an eighteen-year-old than someone my age."

"Lianne, you don't look a day over twenty-three," he said, pinching her cheek teasingly.

"Perhaps I should go then, miss," Mary said. "Will there be anything else?"

"No. Thank you very much for your help."

The girl glanced at each of them in turn and silently exited the room. Alex turned to Lianne. For a moment he looked for clues to her state of mind, her feelings toward him.

"I'm not in the doghouse, am I?"

She went and sat in one of the two upholstered chairs that made up the sitting area. "No, not really."

"Well, I have a tendency to get a bit sentimental when I've had too much to drink. Whatever I said, what I really intended was for you to relax and have a good time. I don't want you worrying about Tatiana. The truth is, I really care about your happiness, Lianne." He went over and sat in the other chair.

"I've thought about it a great deal, Alex. I've decided there's not a thing to be done until we get back to Geneva. And you're right, I did need to clear my mind."

"And have some fun?"

A smile played at the corner of her mouth. "Well, I have tried to get into the spirit of this party tonight. Mary told me there's a wonderful dinner planned, then dancing. The distraction is probably good for me. For both of us."

Alex contemplated her, acutely aware of her beauty. He felt a sense of urgency about her, regretting more strongly than ever that he hadn't returned to Geneva earlier when he first learned that she was back. But he still wasn't sure whether he dared hope.

"You know, I was worried that it might have been a mistake to bring you here. Stanley and his friends can be a little strange. I'm used to it, but I hadn't really looked at it through your eyes. I just told myself you needed to get away, forget, have some fun."

"Don't worry about it, Alex."

"You aren't put off, then?" His voice sounded anxious, though he appeared calm.

"I'm hardly in a state of mind to be judging people."

He looked at her carefully. "Not even me?"

She looked at him, really looked at him, for the first time since he'd entered her room. "Is that what you want, for me to judge you?"

"I care what you think."

Lianne wasn't sure what to say. "I have noticed a sadness. It's difficult to put my finger on it, but that's what I believe it is."

He looked surprised. "Funny, I've never thought of myself as sad."

"It's pretty obvious what's troubling both of us," Lianne replied, not wanting to go any further.

He shook his finger in an admonishing fashion. "We've come here to forget all that. At least for a while."

Lianne nodded. "Yes, you're right. We must both try not to think about it. I don't know if I'll succeed, but I'll do my best."

"That's the spirit." Alex reached over and patted her hand. He would have liked to kiss her, but he knew he had to proceed cautiously. A wary look briefly passed over Lianne's face, and he knew it was time to go. He got up, but he couldn't resist touching her cheek, running his finger along its soft, smooth surface.

"I'm sure you'll be beautiful in that dress, a real princess."

"What will you be, Alex?" she asked, looking up at him.

He gave her his best devilish grin. "I'm afraid, my little cabbage, that it's a secret."

LIANNE DID HER BEST to get into the spirit of the ball. With Mary's help she fixed her hair in corkscrew curls. The tiara the girl found in one of Stanley's trunks seemed a bit much, but Mary insisted it was the perfect touch.

Once she had finished dressing, Lianne went to the window of her room and looked out at the moonlit night. The steeple of the church was plainly visible, as were the rooftops in the village. She was able to hear the music from downstairs. It sounded like the party was already in full swing.

Alex had asked if she wished to go down early with him for a drink with Stanley, but she declined, saying she would join him shortly before dinner. As it turned out, she was about the last one downstairs. Making her way along the lower hall, she encountered strange personages from history, some masked, all in high spirits. The noise and gaiety reminded her of fraternity parties she'd attended in college.

She found Alex in the bar with Stanley. Alex was dressed as an eighteenth-century dandy, complete with powdered wig, lace collar, breeches, justaucorps and buckle shoes. Stanley was done up as a Cheshire cat, with great spiked whiskers glued to his upper lip.

"Ah," Stanley said, seeing her at the door, "the princess has arrived!" He introduced her to everyone present who she hadn't already met, then took her over to where Alex waited.

"You look stunning," Alex said.

Lianne touched the beauty mark that had been painted on his cheek. "And aren't you the Casanova this evening."

"Surprised?"

"No."

Everybody laughed.

Before very long the party moved to the dining room. They all found their places. Lianne was seated next to Stanley. Alex was across from her. Their host called first for the wine. A couple of girls who had been brought in to serve went around the table, filling the glasses.

Judging by the laughter and flushed faces, most of Stanley's guests had imbibed a considerable amount during the cocktail hour.

Lianne managed to get through the meal of stuffed sole and roast beef in better shape than anyone else at the table. The merriment stayed at a fever pitch. When the dishes were finally cleared from the banquet table, the lights went down, bringing a hush over the spirited group.

Everyone turned toward the door to the kitchen. The girl, Mary, appeared, carrying an enormous cake afire with candles. She set it down in front of the birthday girl, Amanda, who was dressed as Raggedy Ann, complete with a red mop wig. Stanley, with a glass of burgundy clutched in his fist, led them through a drunken chorus of "Happy Birthday."

Everyone sang as off-key as possible. Lianne leaned back in her chair, numb, but not tipsy. She had tried very hard not to be sullen, and she laughed as best she could, but pretending was becoming a struggle.

Lianne turned to her host. "I'm sorry, Stanley, but I've had too much wine. I'm going to step out for some air."

"Shall I have someone go with you, love?"

"No, I'll be all right." And with a glance at Alex, she lifted her skirts and hurried from the room and into the relative cool of the great hall.

The noise of the party followed her into the outer hall. It was cold outside, so she took a mackintosh from the coatrack, draped it around her shoulders and went out. She stood for a moment at the top of the steps, breathing in the fresh air.

In the sky above the church a full moon was shining so brightly that there was color in the scene, the hills gray-green and the red tile rooftops pale mauve. It was all very beautiful, but she wanted to be back in Geneva where she could see Max and Tatiana.

Suddenly the door behind her opened and she spun around. Alex stepped from the shadows onto the porch. The moonlight exaggerated the theatrical appearance of his wig and costume.

"Are you all right?" he asked.

"Yes. I just needed a breath of air. The closeness and the noise in there got to me. I tried, Alex, but I'm afraid I'm not really in the mood to party."

He brushed her cheek with the back of his fingers. "That's all right."

"I don't want to spoil your evening, too."

"My only disappointment would be not dancing with you. I was looking forward to holding you in my arms."

His eyes glimmered in the moonlight, and she felt terrible. "Oh, Alex..."

He reached out for her then. Lianne shrank away, but he embraced her, taking her into his arms.

"Please don't," she said.

But Alex was undeterred. He tried to kiss her. She turned her face away.

"What's the matter?"

"I don't want this, Alex."

He stood frozen until the reality of her words seemed finally to sink in. Then he relaxed his grip on her. A dark look came over his face. "It's this place...Stanley and his stupid party. I never should have brought you here."

"This isn't me, it's true," she said. "But that's not the point. I've run away from a problem and I shouldn't have. I don't belong here. I belong at home."

Alex shook his head. "Don't judge me by this, Lianne. I was simply trying to get you away from Geneva, someplace where we could be alone."

She looked at him sadly, knowing what was coming.

"Perhaps I should have come right out and said what was on my mind," Alex said, his voice almost pleading. "The fact is, I still love you. When I saw you at Madame Gevers's, it was as though you'd never gone from my life."

She shook her head, feeling misery at his words. Alex didn't understand. He'd romanticized things. What a terrible mistake it had been to come away with him.

He reached out to touch her face, but Lianne stepped back. "No, Alex, there's no point. I don't feel the same way about you. I really don't."

His eyes dropped sullenly. "What do you plan to do then?"

"Right now I just want to be alone. I think I'll go for a walk. Why don't you go back inside and enjoy the party?"

"The party's not important to me. You are."

She looked into his eyes, desperately wishing this weren't happening to them. But she could say no more. She simply shook her head and turned and hurried down the steps.

"Lianne!" he called after her. "Lianne!"

She heard him following, so she began to move faster, picking up her skirts and sailing across the graveled surface of the driveway as fast as she could go.

"Lianne!" he shouted.

Then she heard him fall, tumbling in the gravel. But she didn't stop; she didn't even look back. When she came to the opening in the hedge where the drive entered the park, she was suddenly flooded with light. A vehicle was coming up the drive, its beams piercing the night. It seemed bizarre for a guest to be arriving so late, but Stanley's party was the least of her worries. She jumped back behind the hedge, not wanting to be seen. Then she looked toward the house. Alex was standing dazed in the middle of the gravel park. He clearly had had too much to drink.

Meanwhile, she could hear the car steadily mounting the drive. It was quite near. The headlights were illuminating the opening of the hedge and the side of the house beyond. She heard the crunch of the tires in the gravel as it moved past her. Clutching the coat, she hurried through the hedge and down the drive, running for a way, then slowing to a walk. She looked back and saw that

Alex wasn't in sight. He had apparently thought better of following her.

Relieved, she wondered for a moment where to go, settling eventually on the church. It would be a quiet place where she could take some time to collect herself and think. Lifting her skirts as high as she could, she made her way across the field.

Ahead lay the low wrought-iron fence that surrounded the churchyard. Beyond it were the first of the headstones, thin gray slabs illuminated by moonbeams, tipped and cocked by time. She stepped over the fence and wove her way to the entrance of the church. The door was unlocked, so she pulled it open. The sanctuary was dark, but the moonlight revealed a shelf of matches and candles just inside the door. She lit one of the candles and went inside.

The air in the church was dank, smelling of stone and wood and dust. Holding the candle above her head, she was able to see the vague outlines of the pews. As her eyes adjusted, she saw the stained glass windows above the transepts and chancel.

Lianne crossed the stone floor to the first pew, where she sat down, able at last to collect herself. Max and Tatiana were in her thoughts immediately. If her misadventure with Alex had served a purpose, it was to make clear to her what was really important. The man she loved and the child she'd longed for were in Geneva. And that was where she belonged, as well.

It no longer mattered that Max had kept his secret from her or that Alex had used it for his selfish purposes. All that mattered was the truth. And the truth was that she belonged with Max and Tatiana.

Suddenly the quiet of the church was rent by the creak of the heavy wooden door. Lianne jumped at the sound, her head turning toward the shadowed entry. She felt her stomach clench, fearing that Alex had followed her. The last thing she wanted was another scene, a continuation of her last.

"Lianne?"

The voice in the darkness didn't sound like Alex, but who...?

"Lianne," he said, "it's me."

Max!

Her heart soared as she got to her feet. The candle shook in her hand. "Max..."

"My darling, I had to come for you. I simply had to."

She scooted from the pew and made her way back across the stone floor, her mackintosh falling from her shoulders. Max took her into his arms as she fell against him. He held her then, his hands rubbing her bare shoulders, his lips finding hers.

Her hand with the candle was shaking so badly that he had to take it from her. He continued to hold her against him, kissing her hair. "I'm so sorry for what happened, the way you found out about Tatiana. Believe me, my dearest, I didn't plan for it to happen this way."

"It doesn't matter now, Max. Nothing matters. I feel so stupid for leaving Geneva the way I did. But it was all so overwhelming."

Tears had filled her eyes, and Max wiped them away with his thumb. "Don't worry about a thing. We're together. And Tatiana wants very badly to see you."

She looked up into his eyes. "Does she?"

"I'm sure of it. Come on, we'll go to her together. Right now, this instant."

## CHAPTER SIXTEEN

THE PLANE BANKED on its final approach into the Geneva airport. Lianne could see snowcapped Mont Blanc rising majestically off to the south. Below them Lac Léman glistened in the sunlight. The day was crystalline, sparkling, but she was anxious, afraid, eager, euphoric, uncertain, all at the same time.

When they left the churchyard, they had walked back up the gravel path to Stroxton Court in the moonlight. On the way Max had recounted all the details of his conversation with Tatiana. Lianne had been desperate to know how the girl had taken the news of her true parentage. She was so relieved to find out that her child was all right that she was happy to the point of tears.

But there had been the more immediate concern about Alex, as well. Max had told her that he couldn't leave England without talking to his brother. He had asked her to indulge him to that degree, and she had agreed. She was so happy that Max was with her and that once again things were all right between them that it didn't matter.

Max told her he had booked them on a flight early in the morning and had a hotel room reserved at the airport. They would drive through the night, back to London, leaving little time for sleep, but Lianne didn't care. Max was entitled to time with his brother.

While she was in her room changing and packing, he went to Alex's room. The better part of an hour passed before Max finally returned, looking exhausted, emotionally drained. He wanted to get going right away and so, taking her cases, they went downstairs.

Alex stayed in his room, but Stanley Goodson was at the door to say goodbye to her. Lianne embraced him briefly, making him promise to look after Alex. He assured her that he would, and she and Max went to their limousine. During the drive to London, Max recounted his conversation with Alex.

"We had a talk we probably should have had long ago," he said. "Sometimes we Swiss are a little too cautious and staid for our own good."

"What do you mean?"

"Alex was carrying a lot of resentment toward me that perhaps even he wasn't aware of. And I've been insensitive about it. We both spoke very frankly and for a long time, each of us saying some things that needed saying."

She reached over and squeezed his arm. "I'm so glad, darling. I wouldn't have been able to bear it if I'd ruined your relationship with him. It was foolish of us to go off together."

Max kissed her hand, sighing wearily as they sped through the dark Devon countryside. "No, my love, I'm convinced it was for the best. You both needed this time to settle things, and he and I needed to have our talk. Without the past few days going as they have, things might have been uncomfortable between all of us for years."

"But how will they be now? Did Alex tell you all the things he said to me?"

"If you mean his profession of love for you, yes, he did."

"If he felt desperate, I can understand why he said it," she said, "and I can forgive him. Perhaps I'm to blame, but what I worry about is that it will keep him from our home. Do you think we can have a normal relationship now . . . whatever normal might be?''

"Alex will always be Alex. That won't change. But I think he learned some things about himself. He told me that if you can forgive him, he'll be all right. We talked about Tatiana, too, what he ought to do and how he ought to treat her in the future.''

"And?''

"We agreed that he must be honest about his feelings. The important thing is that he let her set the tone. If she wants to regard him as a father, then that's the way it will be. But Alex realizes he shouldn't try to offer more than he is capable of giving. The worst thing would be to create expectations and then disappoint her.''

"You've been so wonderful about this," she told him. "What would we all have done without you?''

"I've also been the cause of the problem," he said. "I should have told you about Tatiana sooner.''

"I've thought about that, Max. I put myself in your shoes. You weren't in an easy position.''

"I wanted to make sure you loved me for myself alone," he said. "I thought so often of telling you. From the very beginning. But then I didn't want Tatiana to be the reason you chose to be my wife. It was cowardly perhaps, but I needed to be sure you loved me for myself.''

She put her head on his shoulder and sighed. "I can't fault you for that.''

"Ironically I'd planned to tell you when I got back from America, though to this day I don't know how I'd have put it.''

She sat up so that she could look into his eyes. "Don't worry about that, darling. It's behind us now. What concerns me most is how Tatiana will accept me, how we'll manage to be a mother and daughter.''

''Knowing Tatiana, I suspect it'll be easier than you think.''

But Lianne wasn't convinced. She brooded over it during the rest of the flight. Later, when the plane lurched a little as the flaps were being lowered, she looked over at Max. He was asleep. The poor darling. It had been the better part of two days since he'd had a proper night's rest. They'd gotten to Gatwick at dawn and checked into their hotel. They had each showered, then gone to bed for an hour. Max had managed to drift off, his arms around her, but Lianne had lain awake, worrying about Tatiana.

At least now the truth had come out. And Tatiana had had a few days for the reality to sink in. According to Max, the girl had been shocked, but not horrified. Discovering Alex was her natural father was apparently the most distressing part of the revelation. Catrina had passed from the scene long enough ago that Tatiana's emotions about her weren't nearly so immediate. Lianne was filling a vacuum in her daughter's life; Alex wasn't.

But the thought of looking into Tatiana's eyes and seeing her as a daughter was still formidable and overwhelming. Every time Lianne thought about it, tears came to her eyes and her heart ached a little.

Now she looked out the window and saw that they were very near the ground. Max began stirring, and she told him they were nearly home. He sat up and squinted out at the lake, now low on the horizon.

''Well,'' he said, ''sunshine. A good omen.''

Lianne squeezed his arm, holding him until the plane touched down.

They went through customs quickly. In no time they were exiting the terminal building and Max was opening the door to a cab. He gave the driver instructions and they headed off.

Before long the spires of Saint Pierre were in sight. The last time she'd seen that view she was returning to the scene of her heartache. This time she was coming home to her child.

"Max," she said, taking his hand. "If Tatiana's willing, can the three of us take a trip to Connecticut and Boston? I'd like for her to see where she was born. I'd like her to see the house I grew up in, where I went to school, where I worked."

"Of course, darling."

"Perhaps she's too fully Swiss ever to feel her American ancestry, but I'd like for her to see my country firsthand, so she'll know where she came from, where I came from."

"She's still young, Lianne, and a lot more flexible than you might think. And I have tried to give her a cosmopolitan outlook."

"It would be nice if we all spent time in the States, kept a place there maybe."

"Yes, I agree."

Lianne sighed deeply. It was all working out so well. But the big moment still was to come. She looked out the window at the bustling streets of Geneva. It was midmorning. Their taxi was passing the station and turning onto the boulevard James Fazy. Moments later they crossed the Rhône at the Pont de la Coulouvreniere and wound their way through the Plainpalais, pulling up eventually in front of Max's house on the avenue Dumas.

Lianne took a deep breath, her body trembling. She looked at Max. She smiled, but felt more like crying. He pressed her hands to his lips and got out of the taxi.

She stood on the walk, looking up at the house as Max paid the driver and got their bags. Then they went up the steps. Max opened the door with his key, and Lianne stepped into the entryway.

The house smelled of evergreen, like a Christmas tree. Faintly, from the back of the house, came the sound of music. After Max helped her off with her coat, she listened. It was Christmas music—in English.

"I brought Tatiana some tapes from California," he explained. He gestured toward the salon. "Make yourself at home, darling. I'll go get her."

Lianne stepped into the sitting room. In the corner was a Christmas tree, decorated very much as she and Tatiana had done the one at Nanna's. She wondered if it had been her daughter's doing, a conscious gesture.

Lianne walked over to the tree to look at it more closely. The ornaments were practically the same ones they'd bought together. It brought a smile to her face. She leaned over and inhaled the fragrance of the evergreen. A million memories, a million snowy scenes from her Connecticut childhood flashed through her mind, remembrances of the holiday seasons she'd spent with her own mother.

Then she heard someone enter the room. She turned around. Tatiana, in a red jumper and tights, was standing in the doorway. Her light brown hair was pulled back at the sides and hanging down in back. Her cheeks were glowing as though she'd just come in from playing in the snow.

Lianne stood motionless, staring at her. Tatiana didn't move, either. They both waited, Lianne's eyes filling, making Tatiana's face blur so that she couldn't see her expression plainly.

Then the girl, her daughter, started moving slowly toward her. She walked hesitantly, her stocking feet making no sound on the carpet. And she moved with the grace of a ballerina.

Lianne trembled as Tatiana stopped just before her. The girl held out both hands, looking up at her with shimmering eyes. Lianne took the girl's hands, clutching them to her.

Tatiana smiled, her lips opening slowly as she carefully formed a word. "Mother," she said, and nothing more, just that single word in English. "Mother."

# *Harlequin Superromance*®

This May, Harlequin celebrates the
publication of its 500th Superromance with
a very special book . . .

## THE SILENCE OF MIDNIGHT
## by Karen Young

### "A story you'll treasure forever."

Jake and Rachel McAdam have been married for
eighteen years when suddenly their whole world
comes crashing down around them. As sheriff of
Kinard County, Florida, Jake is sworn to serve and
protect its citizens, yet his small son Scotty had been
snatched from under his nose. And just when Rachel's
faith in Jake is at its lowest ebb, fourteen-year-old
Michael arrives on their doorstep, claiming to be her
husband's illegitimate son.

"A novel of love, betrayal and
triumph, *The Silence of Midnight* will
touch you deeply."

Look for . . .
Harlequin Superromance #500
**THE SILENCE OF MIDNIGHT**
**by Karen Young**

Available wherever Harlequin novels are sold

## ♦ *Harlequin*®

# JANELLE TAYLOR

# *Valley of Fire*

**HARLEQUIN IS PROUD TO PRESENT *VALLEY
OF FIRE* BY JANELLE TAYLOR—AUTHOR OF
TWENTY-TWO BOOKS, INCLUDING SIX *NEW
YORK TIMES* BESTSELLERS**

VALLEY OF FIRE—the warm and passionate story of
Kathy Alexander, a famous romance author, and
Steven Winngate, entrepreneur and owner of the
magazine that intended to expose the real Kathy
"Brandy" Alexander to her fans.

Don't miss VALLEY OF FIRE, available in May.

## HARLEQUIN PROUDLY PRESENTS A
## DAZZLING CONCEPT IN ROMANCE FICTION

One small town,
twelve terrific love stories.

### TYLER—GREAT READING...GREAT SAVINGS...
### AND A FABULOUS FREE GIFT

Each book set in Tyler is a self-contained love story;
together, the twelve novels stitch the fabric of
the community.

By collecting proofs-of-purchase found in each Tyler
book, you can receive a fabulous gift, ABSOLUTELY
FREE! And use our special Tyler coupons to save on
your next Tyler book purchase.

Join us for the third Tyler book, WISCONSIN
WEDDING by Carla Neggers, available in May.

---

Following the success of WITH THIS RING, Harlequin cordially invites you to enjoy the romance of the wedding season with

**BARBARA BRETTON**
**RITA CLAY ESTRADA**
**SANDRA JAMES**
**DEBBIE MACOMBER**

A collection of romantic stories that celebrate the joy, excitement, and mishaps of planning that special day by these four award-winning Harlequin authors.

**Available in April at your favorite Harlequin retail outlets.**

# FREE GIFT OFFER

To receive your free gift, send us the specified number of proofs-of-purchase from any specially marked Free Gift Offer Harlequin or Silhouette book with the Free Gift Certificate properly completed, plus a check or money order (do not send cash) to cover postage and handling payable to Harlequin/Silhouette Free Gift Promotion Offer. We will send you the specified gift.

## FREE GIFT CERTIFICATE

| ITEM | A. GOLD TONE EARRINGS | B. GOLD TONE BRACELET | C. GOLD TONE NECKLACE |
|---|---|---|---|
| # of proofs-of-purchase required | 3 | 6 | 9 |
| Postage and Handling | $1.75 | $2.25 | $2.75 |
| Check one | ☐ | ☐ | ☐ |

Name: _____

Address: _____

City: _____ State: _____ Zip Code: _____

Mail this certificate, specified number of proofs-of-purchase and a check or money order for postage and handling to: HARLEQUIN/SILHOUETTE FREE GIFT OFFER 1992, P.O. Box 9057, Buffalo, NY 14269-9057. Requests must be received by July 31, 1992.

PLUS—Every time you submit a completed certificate with the correct number of proofs-of-purchase, you are automatically entered in our MILLION DOLLAR SWEEPSTAKES! No purchase or obligation necessary to enter. See below for alternate means of entry and how to obtain complete sweepstakes rules.

### MILLION DOLLAR SWEEPSTAKES
### NO PURCHASE OR OBLIGATION NECESSARY TO ENTER

To enter, hand-print (mechanical reproductions are not acceptable) your name and address on a 3" ×5" card and mail to Million Dollar Sweepstakes 6097, c/o either P.O. Box 9056, Buffalo, NY 14269-9056 or P.O. Box 621, Fort Erie, Ontario L2A 5X3. Limit: one entry per envelope. Entries must be sent via 1st-class mail. For eligibility, entries must be received no later than March 31, 1994. No liability is assumed for printing errors, lost, late or misdirected entries.

Sweepstakes is open to persons 18 years of age or older. All applicable laws and regulations apply. Sweepstakes offer void wherever prohibited by law. Prizewinners will be determined no later than May 1994. Chances of winning are determined by the number of entries distributed and received. For a copy of the Official Rules governing this sweepstakes offer, send a self-addressed, stamped envelope (WA residents need not affix return postage) to: Million Dollar Sweepstakes Rules, P.O. Box 4733, Blair, NE 68009.

HS1U

# ONE PROOF-OF-PURCHASE

To collect your fabulous FREE GIFT you must include the necessary FREE GIFT proofs-of-purchase with a properly completed offer certificate.

(See center insert for details)